SÉANCE FOR A VAMPIRE

Tor books by Fred Saberhagen

The Berserker Series
The Berserker Wars
Berserker Base (with Poul Anderson, Ed Bryant, Stephen Donaldson, Larry Niven, Connie Willis, and Roger Zelazny)
Berserker: Blue Death
The Berserker Throne
Berserker's Planet
Berserker Kill

The Dracula Series
The Dracula Tapes
The Holmes-Dracula Files
An Old Friend of the Family
Thorn
Dominion
A Matter of Taste
A Question of Time
Séance for a Vampire

The Swords Series
The First Book of Swords
The Second Book of Swords
The Third Book of Swords
The First Book of Lost Swords: Woundhealer's Story
The Second Book of Lost Swords: Sightblinder's Story
The Third Book of Lost Swords: Stonecutter's Story
The Fourth Book of Lost Swords: Farslayer's Story
The Fifth Book of Lost Swords: Coinspinner's Story
The Sixth Book of Lost Swords: Mindsword's Story
The Seventh Book of Lost Swords: Wayfinder's Story
The Last Book of Swords: Shieldbreaker's Story

Other Books
A Century of Progress
Coils (with Roger Zelazny)
Earth Descended
The Mask of the Sun
The Veils of Azlaroc
The Water of Thought

SÉANCE FOR A VAMPIRE

Fred Saberhagen

A TOM DOHERTY ASSOCIATES BOOK
NEW YORK

This is a work of fiction. All the characters and events portrayed in this book are fictitious, and any resemblance to real people or events is purely coincidental.

SÉANCE FOR A VAMPIRE

This book is printed on acid-free paper.

A Tor Book
Published by Tom Doherty Associates, Inc.
175 Fifth Avenue
New York, N.Y. 10010

Tor ® is a registered trademark of Tom Doherty Associates, Inc.

Library of Congress Cataloging-in-Publication Data

Saberhagen, Fred.
Séance for a vampire / Fred Saberhagen.
p. cm.
"A Tom Doherty Associates book."
ISBN 0-312-85562-1
1. Dracula, Count (Fictitious character)—Fiction. 2. Holmes, Sherlock (Fictitious character)—Fiction. 3. Vampires—Fiction. I. Title.
PS3569.A215S37 1994
813′.54—dc20 94-2353
CIP

First edition: June 1994

Printed in the United States of America

0 9 8 7 6 5 4 3 2 1

c.1

Séance for a Vampire

~ Prologue ~

Of course I can tell you the tale. But you should understand at the start that there are points where the telling may cause me to become rather emotional. Because I—even I, Prince Dracula—find the whole matter disturbing, even at this late date. It brought me as near to the true death as I have ever been, before or since—and in such an unexpected way! No, this affair you wish to hear about, the one involving the séances and the vampires, was not the commonplace stuff of day-to-day life. Hardly routine even in the terms of my existence, which for more than five hundred years has been—how shall I say it?—has not been dull.

It is difficult to find the words with which to characterize this chain of events. It was more than grotesque, it was fantastic. Parts of it almost unbelievable. You'll see. Pirates, mesmerism, executions by hanging. Stolen treasure, murder, kidnapping, revenge and seduction. Women taken by force, attempts to materialize the spirits of the dead . . .

I know what you are going to say. Everything in the above list is a bit out of the ordinary, but still the daily newspapers, those of any century you like, abound in examples. But in this case, the combination was unique. And soon you will see that I am not exaggerating about the fantasy.

Some of my hearers may not even believe in the existence of vampires, may find that elementary starting point quite beyond credibility.

Never mind. Let those who have such difficulty turn back here, before we really start; they have no imagination and no soul.

Still with me? Very good. Actually, no one besides myself can tell the tale now, but I can relate it vividly—because with your indulgence, I will allow myself a little creative latitude as regards details, and also the luxury of some help in the form of several chapters written decades ago by another eyewitness. He, this other witness, who is now in effect becoming my co-author, was your archetypical Englishman, a somewhat stolid and unimaginative chap, but also a gentleman with great respect for truth and honor.

As it happens, I was nowhere near London's Execution Dock on the June morning in 1765 when the whole fantastic business may fairly be said to have begun. However, somewhere past the halfway point between that date and this, less than a single century ago in the warm summer of 1903, I lived through the startling conclusion. In that latter post-Victorian year, I happened to be on hand when the whole affair was pieced together logically by—will you begin to doubt me if I name him?—by a certain breathing man blessed with unequaled skills in the unraveling of the grotesque and the bizarre, a friend of the above eyewitness and also a distant relative of mine. And this adventure involving vampires and séances was enough, I think, to drive the logician to retirement.

But let me start at what I will call the beginning, in 1765. . . .

There had been laughter inside the crumbling walls of Newgate during the night; at a little past midnight, a guard in a certain hellish corridor was ready to swear that he had just heard the soft giggle of a woman, coming from one of the condemned cells, a place where no woman could possibly have been. Naturally, at that hour all was dark inside the cages, and there was nothing that could have been called a disturbance; so the guard made no attempt to look inside.

Some hours later, when the first daylight, discouraged and rendered lifeless by these surroundings, filtered through to show the prison's stinking, grim interior, there was of course no woman to be seen. There had been no realistic possibility of anyone's passing in or out. The cell in question contained only the prisoner, the tall, red-bearded pirate captain, still breathing, just as he was supposed to be—for a few hours yet. Breathing but otherwise silent, not giggling like a woman; no, he was still sane—poor chap. And the guard, as little anxious as any of us ever are to seem a fool, was privately glad that he had said nothing, raised no ridiculous alarm.

No one in the prison had anything to say about impossibilities that might have been heard or seen before the dawn.

An hour or so after that same dawn, upon one of those raw, June British mornings suggestive of the month of March, a solemn procession left London's Newgate Prison. At the heart of the grim train emerging from those iron gates there rolled a tall, heavy, open cart in which rode three doomed men, all standing erect with arms chained behind them. Their three sets of leg irons had been struck off only an hour ago by the prison blacksmith. Once out of the prison gate, the cart, departing sharply from its customary route, turned east. These prisoners had been convicted by the Admiralty Court, and as such did not at that time "go west" with the ordinary felons to hang on Tyburn Tree. Instead, a special fate awaited them.

Astride his horse at the very head of the procession was the deputy marshal of the Admiralty. Red-faced and grave, this functionary bore in prominent display the Silver Oar, almost big enough to row with, symbol of that court's authority over human activity on the high seas, even to the most distant portions of the globe. Next came the elegant coach carrying the marshal himself, resplendent in his traditional uniform, surrounded by his coachmen wearing their distinctive livery. After these, on horseback, rode a number of City officials, one or two of considerable prominence. But whatever their station, few amid the steadily growing throng of onlookers had eyes for them, or for anyone but the central figures in the morning's drama.

The high ceremonial cart in the middle of the parade came lumbering along deliberately upon great wooden wheels, which, though freshly greased, squeaked mildly. The three prisoners, standing more or less erect in the middle of the cart, had their backs to one another, and with their arms still in irons, had little choice but to lean on one another for mutual support. The executioner—Thomas Turlis in that year—and his assistant rode standing in the cart beside the prisoners, and a Newgate guard walked beside each of the great slow-turning wheels.

The cart was followed immediately by a substantial force of marshal's men and sheriff's officers, mostly afoot. These walking men had no trouble keeping up; those who calculated the time of departure from the prison had assumed that only a modest pace would be possible. The narrow, cobbled streets made progress for a large vehicle slow at best, and today, as usual, the throng of onlookers grew great enough to stop the death-cart altogether several times before the place of execution could be reached.

All three of the men who were riding to be hanged today had been convicted of the same act of piracy. The tallest of the condemned, the only one with anything exceptional in his nature or his appearance, was Alexander Ilyich Kulakov, red-haired and green-eyed, rawboned but broad-shouldered and powerful, his red beard straggling over his scarred cheeks and jaw. Kulakov was Russian, but at the moment, nationality did not matter. His Britannic Majesty's justice was about to claim all three lives impartially—none of them had any influential friends in London; quite the opposite.

The morning's procession carried its victims east, as I have said. A little over two miles east of Newgate Prison, passing just north of the great dome of St. Paul's, through Cornhill and Whitechapel, past Tower Hill and close past the pale, gloomy bulk of the squat Tower itself, the procession would come to Wapping, a district largely composed of docks and taverns, nestled into a broad curve formed by the north bank of the Thames.

And with every rod of progress achieved by the doomed men and their escort, it seemed that the crowds increased. Last night and this morning, word had spread, as it always did, of a scheduled hanging. Hundreds went to London's various scaffolds every year, but despite the relatively commonplace nature of the event, the route of the procession was thickly lined with spectators. As often as not, when the high cart stalled in traffic, folk leaned from windows or trees to offer the condemned jugs or bottles or broken cups of liquor.

Kulakov's usual craving for strong drink seemed to have deserted him. He stared past the reaching arms and what they offered, and ignored the excited faces; but his two fellow prisoners did their best, even with their arms bound, to take advantage of the gifts. The executioners, with a practical eye to making their own job easier, assisted the pair to drink, now and again fortifying themselves from the same jug or bottle.

One of the Russian captain's former shipmates was well-nigh insensible with drink before the ride was over.

It was the other of the two English prisoners who, in

that age when death was so often a social function, had a small handful of relatives present; these—weeping, expostulating, or stony-faced, according to their several temperaments—tagged after the cart and were jostled to the rear by the sheriff's men.

The authorities had long practice with such processions from Newgate; and this enabled them to time the arrival of the cart at Execution Dock to coincide almost precisely with the hour of low water in the tidal Thames, this being the only time when the gallows was readily accessible.

For hundreds of years, pirates and mutineers had been executed on this spot, while for occasional variety, a captain or mate would be dispatched for murderous brutality toward his own crew. On this morning, several of the fruits of last week's executions were still to be seen, each hanging in chains on its own post. Gulls and weather had already reduced the dead faces to eyeless, discolored leather and protruding bone, raking the passing ships with empty stares. Their continued presence was intended to impress the thousands of seamen on those ships as examples of the Admiralty's long arm and exact justice.

The posts displaying these veteran corpses had been erected along the riverbank at various distances from the now ominously empty gallows. The latter was no more than two posts and a cross-beam, the horizontal member being not much higher than ten feet above the strip of muddy ground and gravel exposed now at low tide.

Somewhat closer to the gallows itself than were last week's bodies, another set of three stakes, also ominously empty, waited for today's victims.

Crowding nearby land and water were spectators even more numerous than those along the route. Folk of high station and low were out this morning, their numbers not much diminished by the weather, which so far had not improved. Every comfortable vantage point, and some perches fit only for the stoic or the acrobatic, had been occupied. The windows and terraces of taverns and other riverside buildings, as well as docks and jetties, were thick with onlookers. Scores of small boats passed to and fro, or had cast anchor in the river. The current was very slow just now, with the tide about to turn. A barge moored no more than forty yards offshore afforded rows of seats for those willing and able to pay. At a somewhat greater distance over the broad face of the Thames, the crews and passengers of a couple of anchored ships presented on decks and rigging rows of pale faces. Well beyond these larger craft, the shadowy shapes of docks and buildings on the south shore loomed out of cold mist and drizzle.

One of the watchers, ensconced in a high-priced seat in the window of a tavern built upon a nearby promontory, was a dark-haired, smooth-skinned woman of somewhat exotic dress and remarkable appearance. Despite the sunless pallor of her skin, her countenance was undoubtedly Asiatic. Today she was keeping to a position where she herself remained inconspicuous, her pallid face shaded from even this clouded daylight. She was sharing a table—though she was not eating or drinking—with a well-dressed, well-fed, stoutish man of middle age, named Ambrose Altamont, a commoner very recently come into startling wealth. The weathered condition of Altamont's face suggested that he was no stranger to the sea and tropic suns.

The table was bare before the woman—she had assured her new patron that she was not hungry—but the man had dishes and bottles aplenty in front of him. He was dining early today, by way of celebration, on lamprey pie—then considered a rare treat—and sampling good wine.

As nearly as I can discover, Altamont at this point did not, strictly speaking, know that the woman with him was a vampire. That fact and all its implications still lay over his horizon. He certainly understood that she was strange—for several nights now he had reveled in her exotic antics in his bed. Whatever the limits of her strangeness, whatever disadvantages were yet to be discovered, here was an attractive female who gave delight and satisfaction beyond anything he had previously encountered in almost fifty years of a thoroughly unsheltered life. Altamont might well have betrayed a business partner for her favors alone—even had there been no jewels.

The creaking high wheels of the tall cart fell silent as the vehicle eased to a halt on Execution Dock. While the massed guards cleared a space of spectators, the prisoners—their bodies stiff with confinement, two of them reeling with drink, all three chain-laden—were helped down. The severely drunken man had to be lifted bodily. Then, one at a time, the sober Kulakov first, the three men were led—or carried—down through mud and gravel to the rude platform, which consisted of only a few boards laid in mud beneath the gallows.

Waiting for them at that threshold of eternity was the chaplain, Mr. Ford, Ordinary of Newgate, ready to lead repentant sinners in prayer or persuade them that they should seek divine forgiveness. No one today had thought to provide a Russian Orthodox clergyman; but if one had been present, the Russian doubtless would have snarled at him, as he did at Mr. Ford.

Under the circumstances, whatever prayers were possible for Kulakov, the first victim, were soon said. Then a ready noose was placed around his neck and he was blindfolded.

Meanwhile, at the tavern table, the pale and sheltered but vivacious lady had allowed herself to be distracted from the show by a sudden impulse to admire yet again a gift she had very recently received: a wonderful bracelet, fine gold-and-silver filigree sparkling with red rubies and clear diamonds. This masterpiece of the jeweler's art came into view upon her white and slender left wrist when she deliberately drew back her full sleeve to reveal it.

"It fits you loosely," her companion commented, his voice rich with wine and satisfaction.

"I'll not lose it. Where are the other things?" she inquired softly. "Your brother has them, perhaps?" Her voice was small but determined, her English marked with a strong accent, hard to define, but certainly as Eastern as her face.

Altamont winked at her and smiled. "They're where they'll be safe for the time being—and you may lay to that." Turning away again, he squinted, in the practiced manner of a ship's captain, through his sailor's brass-tubed glass at the proceedings on shore.

Confident as Altamont was that no one could overhear their talk, he lowered his voice when he added: "My own suspicion—I've no proof of it, mind—is that they were meant as a gift for the Empress Catherine of Muscovy, from one of those nabobs in the East. Or they might have belonged to the Russian church, some of their clergy smuggling them abroad to keep them out of Her Imperial Majesty's hands. I hear Catherine's developed a taste for churchly property, as did our own dear Henry long ago." He shot his companion a sharp glance. "The Russian might have given you a better answer than I can give, as to who the first owner of your bangle was. Not that it much matters now."

The dark-haired woman did not seem to care. Indeed, her fascination with the beauty of the ornament was as apparent as her lack of interest in its origins. "Then the other things must be just as rich as this?"

The man almost sneered in his pride and his amusement. "Richer, by God! Half a dozen pieces in all, rings and necklaces, in the same style, but even more extravagant—a king's ransom. I am surprised you had no chance to see them on the voyage. You must have shared the Russian's cabin, sailing back to London."

The woman let her long sleeve drop, concealing jewels and precious metal. "Cap-tain Kulakov kept all well hidden."

"No doubt. I think he meant to keep such great treasure all to himself, and maybe to some of his men who knew of it. But to cheat his English partner—"* Altamont smiled and shook his head. "Well, greed, like pride, goeth before a fall. And now the Russian hath lost all; his treasure, his woman, life itself. Almost I could feel sorry for him—why are they taking so long about his stepping off?" He squinted through his glass again.

A prosperous man, Mr. Altamont, even before his recent dramatic accession of new wealth. He felt himself capable of handling even greater prosperity without undue difficulty. At the moment, his countenance was alternating between frowns at the delay and a faint expression of abstract pleasure as he shifted from wine to hot buttered rum while watching from his comfortable chair.

The pallid woman remained patiently seated with him. Though the air on this June morning had turned quite mild, she was glad to shelter here indoors; in her case, it was in fact neither chill nor damp but the mild English sun that threatened.

On shore the experienced Thomas Turlis, and his assistant who was hardly less qualified, were proceeding about their business with deliberate speed. The junior member of the official team had already climbed to straddle the cross-

*The details of the efforts of the pirate partners to cheat each other have never become perfectly clear, nor are they essential to our story. A perusal of Admiralty records of the time indicates that alliances between pirates and politicians were by no means as uncommon as all right-minded people would like to think.—D.

beam, where he sat waiting until Turlis had guided his first victim halfway up the ladder, Kulakov's feet on the rungs awkward with the weight of chains and terror. Then, receiving from his senior's hand the loose end of the short rope already snug around the victim's neck, the assistant quickly and efficiently secured it tightly to the heavy cross-beam.

The red-haired man cried out, loudly and articulately, in the last moments while he waited for the noose to choke off his breath.

"Al-ta-mont!" There followed a string of violent un-English words, sounds carrying well across the water between the two points on the curving shore.

"I understand very little Russian, really," the man at the table remarked comfortably. "Which no doubt is just as well."

"I un-der-stand a little, as with Ain-glish," the watching woman remarked abstractedly. "I spoke to him last night," she added after a pause. "He think he have give the jewels to you only for safekeeping, not?"

"You saw him last night?" Briefly her companion turned a puzzled but fascinated frown in her direction. "Really, I think that you did not, for you were pretty steadily with me. As I have good cause to remember, having got but little sleep." Lecherously Altamont displayed bad teeth. "But you know, I would wager my new fortune that it would not be beyond you to gain entry to a condemned cell—not when the guards are men."

"I spoke to him," the woman repeated. Not with an air of insistence, but as if she had not heard her companion's denial. "But he would not believe that I was real. I think these Russian must be very—what is word?—su-per-stitious." Pulling her dreamy gaze back from the shore, she fastened it upon the man beside her. "Will you believe me, Al-tamont, when I try to tell you *what* I am?"

He made a small noise compounded of amusement and

satisfaction. "I think I understand well enough what you are. So, you visited the condemned cell, did you, and had a chat? And what do you want me to think that you told dear Alexei? That we have both betrayed him? That the jewels are all mine now, while he is come to dine today on hearty-choke and caper sauce?"

The woman very slightly shook her head. "He did not need me to tell him that you keep the jewels." Perhaps she intended to offer some explanation about her activities last night, or drop more teasing hints; but at the moment, her full attention, like that of all other watchers, had become focused on the shore.

For the space of a held breath, the raucous cries of even the least reverent onlookers were silenced. Turlis, the older and paunchier of the hangman pair, with his feet planted solidly in mud—the planks had been disarranged in Kulakov's last awkward stumbling—took hold of the ladder and with a strong, twisting wrench, deprived the bound man of all physical support . . . except for that now afforded him by taut hemp, the smoothly clasping noose.

The drop was a short one, no more than three feet at the most, in this case not nearly enough to break the neck bones, to tear and quickly crush out life and consciousness from the vulnerable soft tissue of the spine and brain stem. There was only the steady, brutal pressure of the rope to squeeze the windpipe, veins, and arteries. Kulakov's powerful frame convulsed. His bound arms strained, his legs and feet moved in a spasmodic aerial ballet.

Hearty-choke and caper sauce.

The fact that Kulakov had been first to be hanged meant that comparatively few among the audience were paying his prolonged death struggle as much attention as it must otherwise have received; rather, the fascinated scrutiny of the mob now rested in turn upon each of his colleagues.

Altamont commented knowingly to his companion that the knot of the rope had very likely slipped from the favored location behind the Russian's ear to behind his neck—but how could Altamont have known that, at the distance, unless he had made some private arrangement to have the knot deliberately adjusted in that wise? Trying to get the better of Altamont, as the man himself would have assured you, was likely to result in truly frightful punishment.

As for Kulakov, he had been denied his broken neck, so that he hung for a quarter of an hour, intermittently twitching and tensing in agony, all breathing not quite cut off.

"Are they not going to finish him?" Altamont's comment, coming after five minutes or so, was dryly lacking in surprise. "It would seem not."

It was common in such cases for one or both hangmen, when not entirely lacking in pity, to seize their client by the legs and drag down with their full weight upon the poor wretch's body to assist his soul on its way out of it. But at the moment, the executioners were busy. If any friends or relatives of the condemned were in attendance, that office might fall to them. But in Kulakov's case, no one had come forward with any such merciful intention.

One after the other, the two remaining pirates followed their captain to the scaffold. The executioners gave no thought to taking down the body of the first man to be hanged, until the third was dangling, and they had paused to fortify themselves with rum. The two Englishmen went quickly, so there was no need for relatives to intervene.

When, in the chief executioner's professional judgment, the third man had been well and truly hanged, he gave curt directions to his assistant. Between them, the two men loosened the knot holding the first body to the crossbar—there would be no wasteful cutting of the rope—and lowered their grim burden to the muddy shore. Already the feet of the hangmen splashed in water; at this hour the lower Thames was entering that part of its unending tidal cycle in which the rising weight of ocean a few miles distant forced the river swiftly back toward its source, as if it would convey the brackish tide up into the middle of the great island.

Now Kulakov's body, hands still chained behind its back, had been dragged some twenty-five or thirty yards from the gallows, to its next temporary resting place. There, with some difficulty, it was being chained upright, feet at ground level, to one of the three tall, empty stakes that had been driven deep into the muddy sands. By tradition, the freshly hanged at Execution Dock remained so mounted until their already lifeless lungs had been drowned thrice by the high tides.

One after the other, the Russian's now-unbreathing comrades joined him, were fastened to the trees that stood one on either side of his, forming a ghastly Golgotha. Surely, in some of the onlookers' minds, the tableau evoked thoughts of a certain antique and much more famous triple execution. But no one commented aloud upon the fact.

By the time the dead body of the third pirate was thus displayed, and the day's task of the hangmen essentially concluded, many of those watching had gone on about their business.

But perhaps they had missed something of importance. Did a murmur of morbid excitement pass through the remaining crowd when the central one of the newly chained corpses was seen to move? Could it be that the captain and ringleader of this pirate band was still not dead after having been hanged for a quarter of an hour?

Such an event would not have been without precedent.

We will assume that Altamont, in his dry way, even commented to his companion upon the most famous such case, which some of those watching Kulakov might have seen with their own eyes—that of William Duell, executed at Tyburn a quarter of a century earlier, in 1740. Duell, though only sixteen years of age when hanged, had been widely noted for his sadism. Convicted of rape as well as murder, his body was turned over to medical anatomists . . . but when finally placed on the dissecting table, it displayed certain faint signs of life. The surgeons, ready to try a different experiment than that originally scheduled, applied their skills at healing and soon had the patient sitting up, drawing deep breaths and drinking warm wine.

Duell had cheated the hangman after all. Returned to Newgate, he was eventually ordered to be transported to America.

Hangings here at Execution Dock, with tide-drowning added as a flourish under Admiralty auspices, were somewhat more thorough. No one put up on one of these stakes for show had ever tasted wine again. Certainly the sharp-eyed Altamont did not find the signs of life so stubbornly displayed by today's first hanged man at all perturbing; rather amusing.

Altamont, alternately smirking and frowning over his latest glass of hot buttered rum, made a few remarks on the case of young Duell to his fair companion, who took a somewhat different view of such phenomena.

The woman said in her abstracted way: "I think we will not have to worry about Kulakov—he will die to-day. I spent but little time with him last night."

"Oh, he'll die today, and no mistake." The man stared at her for the space of several rummy breaths before adding: "Up to your mystification, are you, Doll? I've noticed you have a taste for riddles. But do go on with it—I like it well."

Altamont and the very un-English woman he called Doll—he had tried her real name once and found it unpronounceable—remained in their snug tavern window for an hour longer, until he had made sure with his own eyes that the swiftly running tide had raised the surface of the Thames well above that pale dot of a distant, red-bearded face. Then, humming a sea song to himself and more than content with the day's events so far, the prosperous observer called for his waiting carriage, offered his arm to his woman, and leisurely took his way to the Angel Inn on the south bank, where snug, warm rooms awaited them.

Early next morning, Turlis and his helper returned to the scene to check on their most recent handiwork. June at that latitude brought full sunlight well before many folk of any class or inclination were up and about. Both men expressed mild surprise on observing that the central stake of three was now unoccupied, the chains in which they had hanged the Russian's body for display lying in the mud below, still looped and locked together but quite empty. Surely mere tide and current could not have done this—yesterday these experts had secured their trophy well. But there were obvious explanations. Either relatives had shown up belatedly to spirit his corpse away—or someone, even in this enlightened seventh decade of the eighteenth century, had coveted morsels of hanged man's flesh as an aid to practicing the black arts of magic.

The hangmen, discussing these possibilities, were momentarily distracted by the sound of shrill feminine screaming. The sound was repeated several times, carrying readily over the water, through the bright incongruous early morning sun, all the way from the south shore. They were only momentarily distracted; at the river's edge in Wapping, such racket was common enough. Actually, what Turlis and his comrade heard were the screams of horror uttered by some innocent female servant who had just opened the door of a certain room in the dockside Angel Inn.

More than a hundred years would pass before any rational investigator connected that hanged man's disappearance during the night with the shocking sight that met the maid's eyes a few hours later. Not that the maid was startled by the walking undead form of Alexander Ilyich Kulakov—she was perhaps an hour too late for that. No, she had unsuspectingly come upon a corpse much more severely mangled.

Shortly after the midnight immediately following the execution, Altamont had been awakened by something in his room. It was a supreme despair, more than terror, that choked off his first scream in his throat when he beheld what had roused him and now stood beside his bed. It was the figure of Kulakov, still wearing the prison clothes in which he had been hanged. The Russian's red beard was dripping water, his dead face a ghastly livid hue; his strangled throat, though no longer required to breathe, made croaking noises. But his limbs were free of chains, and his white hands were half-raised and twitching, groping toward the bed. The pirate's eyes, the only feature appearing to be fully alive in that corpse countenance, were fixed on Altamont.

Doll in turn was awakened by Altamont's hoarse abandoned cry. On seeing Kulakov, she registered mild surprise—so, she had been wrong about Kulakov's dying a true death yesterday! It was obvious to her that the Russian, stimulated by her repeated attentions on the voyage and in his Newgate cell, had, after all, become a vampire instead.

The woman immediately slid her compact, dark-nippled, quite un-English body naked from the bed. She smiled, and before her bedmate's uncomprehending eyes melted into mist-form and disappeared—pausing only long enough to pick up her jeweled bracelet from the bedside table, and slip it on her wrist. The bangle went with her when she vanished—we who are wont to travel in that fashion generally carry with us a few small items, most commonly our clothing, when we go changing forms.

Kulakov paid little attention to either the woman's

presence or her departure. The red rage filling his mind concentrated his attention elsewhere. In the next moment, the hands of the undead man had fastened their icy, awkward grip on Altamont. Then the vampire—new to the powers he had been given, almost as bewildered as his victim by his own seemingly miraculous transformation, and still unsure of how to handle it—the neovampire plucked the treacherous, nightshirted Englishman like a louse out of his bedclothes, and cast him aside with stunning force. In the next moment Kulakov, moving in a kind of somnambulistic fury, groaning and grunting foul Russian expletives, began ransacking the room in search of his stolen treasure. Drawers, bags, and boxes were hurled about and emptied, furniture shifted in a grip of giant's strength. All in vain.

A moment later the searcher grunted in befuddled triumph, on discovering some small, hard objects sewn into a quilt or featherbed. Carrying his find to the moonlit window, smashing the dim, smoky glass in a reflexive move to gain more light (not that his newly empowered eyes really needed any more, but Kulakov did not yet understand this fact) he ripped the cloth to shreds. Inside, to his great disappointment, the searcher discovered only sand and gravel, what was to him mere ordinary dirt. In anger he hurled the torn cloth from him, letting its worthless contents scatter into the Thames below.

It flashed across Kulakov's mind that Altamont, rather than risk carrying the treasure about with him in London, had very likely given it to his brother for safekeeping.

And he turned to complete his vengeance upon Altamont.

The doomed Englishman had turned back to the bed and now had both hands under his pillow. In a moment they were out again, not holding gems and precious metal, but newly armed with a loaded pistol and a dagger. A tough, resourceful man, old Ambrose Altamont; but both weapons very quickly proved completely useless.

There was really not much more noise—the pistol was never fired—and those among the others breathing at the Angel Inn who were awakened by muffled screams and thumps only grumbled and went back to sleep. Soon enough—well before Kulakov really thought of trying to force him to tell where the jewels were hidden—Altamont had ceased to breathe.

Kulakov, having thus achieved a kind of victory, was suddenly, overwhelmingly, weary. Once more he returned to his search for the jewels that he still thought might be here somewhere. Struck by what seemed to him a good idea, he went to search in the connecting room.

Only a minute or two after the hanged pirate had stumbled out the door, the woman called Doll, a much more experienced vampire than he, reappeared in the room of carnage. Doll was as naked as when she left—more so, for she no longer wore her bracelet—and entered as she had left, in mist-form through the window. Around her in the predawn light, as she resumed a solid human shape, the other denizens of the Angel Inn still slept.

Picking her way fastidiously among great spatterings and gouts of gore, she stopped for an opportunistic snack, bending to bestow a sort of prolonged kiss upon the now-faceless body on the floor. There was, she thought, no use letting so much of the good fresh red stuff go to waste.

Only when she straightened up, neatly licking her lips clean, did she happen to glance out the window and notice to her horror that the cloth bag which had contained her earth, her only earth, lay torn open and emptied, caught on a spiky paling a few feet outside the window, just above the energetic river.

Kulakov was no longer in the room to hear her, but she

screamed at him in her own language that he had slain her, scattering her home-earth thus.

Perhaps it will be helpful to some readers if I choose this point for a brief digression: To each vampire, certain earth is magic. The soil of his or her homeland is as essential as air is to breathing human lungs. For a day, for several days in the case of the toughened elders of the race, the nosferatu *can survive without the native earth. After that, a twitching, unslakeable restlessness begins to dominate and a great weariness soon overtakes the victim, culminating in true death. It is not an easy dying; the sharp stake through the heart, or even the scorching sun, are comparatively merciful.*

Kulakov in his confused state, still having no success in his monomaniacal quest to repossess his treasure, heard the woman's despairing cries and came back from the adjoining room.

Doll had put on her clothes again. Gibbering and pleading in her terror, she tried to bargain with him. She spoke now in her native language, which Kulakov had learned to understand. She told the Russian that she knew with certainty where the stolen ornaments were hidden, and that she would give them all to him in exchange for only a few pounds of her native earth.

Somewhere in the great port, among the hundreds of ships that had brought in by accident soil, plants, and vermin from the farthest reaches of the globe—somewhere among all those far-traveled hulls, surely, surely there must be one whose cargo or bilge or windswept planking contained a few pounds, a few handfuls even, of that stuff more precious now to her than any gems or lustrous metal.

The Russian, his understanding still clouded by strangulation and rebirth, heard her out. Then he had a question of his own. He whispered it in fluent English: "Where are the jewels? They are not here."

Doll switched back to her imperfect English. "Are you not listen to me? I tell you where the treasure is, I swear, when you have help me find the soil I need. The jewels are not here. But they are all safe, in place you know, where you can get them!"

"I know." The pirate looked down at the red ruin on the floor. *"He* gave them to his brother, who has them at his country estate, somewhere out of town. His brother who helped him to betray me."

In near despair the woman clutched his arm, her long nails digging in, a grip that might well have crushed the bones of any breathing man. Once more she spoke in her own language. "Will you not listen to me, Kulakov? *I need my earth!* By all the gods of my homeland—by whatever gods you pray to in your Muscovy—I swear that if you help me find the earth that I must have, the treasure shall all be yours!"

The Russian mumbled something; perhaps he meant it for agreement. But he was almost stupefied. His need for rest had suddenly grown insupportable. Overwhelmed like an infant with the necessity for sleep, he abandoned his solid form and drifted away, sliding out again in shifting mist-form through the window.

The woman, unable to obtain his help, began her own search in desperation, and in deadly, growing daylight. But alas for poor Doll's hopes of immortality! Upon the whole long winding Thames on that June day there floated not a single vessel containing any of the special soil her life required.

But Russian ships, carelessly bearing with them some of the soil of Muscovy, though rare in this port were still discoverable. Kulakov by some instinct managed to locate the hidden, earthy niche he needed in one of their dark holds.

New vampires, like new babies, will often require long periods of sleep. Three weeks later when he awakened, out of a long vampirish nightmare of being hanged, he was back in St. Petersburg, the capital of his native land.

~ 1 ~

(Being the first chapter of an untitled manuscript in the handwriting of the late John H. Watson, M.D.)

For many years, as my readers may know, it has been my good fortune to chronicle the illustrious career of my friend Sherlock Holmes, and even on occasion to play some small active part in the solution of problems that have come before him. Of all the cases I can remember, in an association that lasted more than twenty years, perhaps the most mysterious—in the true meaning of the word—as well as the most truly terrifying, was one in which the final solution seemed to come literally from beyond the grave. Only now, some fourteen years later, have circumstances at last set me at liberty to describe the matter of the séances and the vampires. And even now, what I write on the subject must be only for posterity. By Holmes's own instructions, it must go, with a small number of other manuscripts similar in subject matter, into the most secure repository of the Oxford Street branch of the Capital and Counties Bank. And there these pages must remain for years or decades, for centuries perhaps, until a certain extraordinary password is presented for their removal.

The case, like many another of peculiar interest, began for us in a routine way. It was an oppressive day in early July of 1903. My wife had been called out of town by family necessity and was paying relatives an extended visit. In her absence, I had returned for a time to my old lodgings.

Holmes, in a restless and energetic mood, had begun that morning's activities before dawn with an unusually evil-smelling chemistry experiment; he had followed that, as if to make amends, by an interlude of sweet violin music. When I came down to breakfast, he had scissors, paste, and notebooks arranged upon a table, together with a sheaf of loose newspaper clippings and other documents, and was cross-indexing his collection of criminal information. My friend looked up to inform me that a Mr. Ambrose Altamont, of Norberton House, Amberley, Buckinghamshire, had made an appointment for a professional consultation and was soon due to arrive.

"Altamont—surely the name is familiar."

"The family has been very recently in the newspapers—the drowning tragedy of last month."

"Of course." Before the client appeared, I had found the relevant clippings in Holmes's files and by reading them aloud, refreshed both our memories with regard to the affair, which had taken place on the twentieth of June. Holmes had already noted several points about the case that struck him as peculiar.

By all reports, Louisa Altamont had been an attractive and lively young lady, engaged to be married later in the summer to an American journalist. She had perished tragically when the small boat bearing her, her fiancé, and her sister had inexplicably capsized upon a tranquil river.

Their outing had seemed, up to its disastrous conclusion, to have been a routine boating excursion upon a long June evening. Her fiancé, being a good swimmer, had survived without difficulty, and had readily enough rescued Rebecca Altamont, the younger sister.

"Does the girl's father suspect foul play?"

Holmes shook his head. "I doubt that, Watson. If he did, he would not have waited two weeks to consult me."

Ambrose Altamont arrived punctually and was shown up to our sitting room. He was a well-to-do gentleman of forty-five or thereabouts, of average size and unremarkable appearance, save for the black armband of mourning that he wore. At first glance, he gave the impression of being both energetic and worried.

As soon as the introductions had been completed, Holmes and I naturally expressed our sympathy in our client's recent bereavement. I received a strong impression that our visitor's natural grief had been compounded by some fresh worry.

He acknowledged our condolences in a perfunctory way, delaying no longer than was necessary before getting down to business.

"Gentlemen, my daughter has now been dead for approximately two weeks. Already there have appeared swindlers, vultures seeking to prey on the grief-stricken. I refer to the Kirkaldys, the well-known brother-and-sister spiritualist mediums." The speaker's tone was one of utter contempt.

"I have heard something of the pair." Holmes was now leaning far back in his chair, loading his pipe while he regarded our visitor through half-closed eyes.

"Then perhaps you will understand. These cheats have managed to convince my wife that Louisa is not really gone. I mean they would have Madeline believe that conversation with our dear, dead girl—even a face-to-face encounter, even physical contact—is still a possibility."

"Indeed," Holmes commented quietly. Something in his tone caused me to glance in his direction, but he did not look at me.

Altamont continued. "Despite the fact that I have often expressed to Madeline my unalterable opposition to any such ghostly carryings-on, my wife has not only invited these charlatans, these fortune-tellers, into our house, but has allowed them to establish a most pernicious influence over her. They have convinced Madeline, who is all too ready to be persuaded, that our sweet girl, whom we have buried, survives in spirit-land and that she is still within our reach. Only last night, while I was absent, they overwhelmed her with some trickery." Altamont paused; his voice had fallen to no more than a whisper filled with loathing.

"Pray give us the details."

Our visitor regained control of his emotions and resumed. "As I have mentioned, Abraham and Sarah Kirkaldy are a brother-and-sister team. You will know, if you know anything of society, that they have established a considerable reputation in their field. Both are quite young. The name sounds Scottish, but I know almost nothing of their past."

"That may be discovered, if it becomes necessary. Continue, if you will."

"Business kept me in London until late last night. When I returned home, my wife met me, in a state of terrible excitement, and I heard the story from her. The Kirkaldys had prudently taken themselves away before I returned."

"Then you have never actually met the couple?"

"That is correct."

"Continue, if you will."

Holmes and I listened with close attention as our client repeated his wife's story of the séance, which, according to the usual method of such affairs, had been conducted in a darkened room, ostensibly with all doors and windows locked. The sitting had culminated in the apparition which had so affected her.

According to her husband, Mrs. Altamont described the phenomenon as a solid materialization of the dead girl. In the darkness of the séance room, the mother had not only exchanged a few words of conversation with this barely visible figure, but had actually kissed and embraced it, in the perfect conviction that her own Louisa had come back across the border of death to visit her.

"I can only think," Altamont concluded bitterly, "that this apparition must have been actually some partner, or hireling, of the mediums, whom they had brought stealthily into the house. There may have been some connivance on the part of one or more of our servants—though I had believed them all to be loyal."

"Perhaps," Holmes mused, "it was young Sarah Kirkaldy herself who played the role of your late daughter?"

Our visitor shook his head. "Madeline assured me that she was holding one hand of each of the mediums when the apparition entered the room."

"Thus allowing one hand of each to remain free?" My friend shook his head and smiled with grim amusement. "I fear it is often difficult for the lay person to believe what amazing feats a skilled conjuror may achieve in a darkened room, even when both hands are supposedly secured—especially when the audience is eager to believe."

Our visitor had been much affected by his own story. While he paused to recover himself, Holmes added: "It is apparent, Mr. Altamont, that you yourself have not the least doubt that the manifestations which so moved your wife were sheer trickery."

"What else?" When neither of us replied, the man in his agitation rose from his chair and began to pace the floor. But he soon paused. "Mr. Holmes, I am an agnostic. There are moments, I admit, when I almost wish that I could accept last night's events as genuine; but if the church of my fathers cannot convince me that the spirit of my girl survives in heaven, how can I credit for a moment this damnable imposture upon an earthly plane?"

I observed that the strain was telling seriously on Altamont. The act of pouring out his troubles had only increased his excitement rather than relieving it. I suggested loosening his collar, and my offer of brandy was accepted.

He wiped his brow. "Gentlemen, you must excuse my emotion. The fact is that my beautiful daughter is dead, and nothing can change that. I must—I will—take some action against these scoundrels. I have thought of the horsewhip, but I fear that such action on my part might turn Madeline, not to mention the law, utterly against me."

"In that you are correct." Holmes had obviously been moved by our visitor's story, and his voice was sympathetic as he asked: "You have gone to the police?"

Altamont shook his head. "I am convinced that it would be useless. So far, this pair of villains have been too clever to ask directly for money. But last night—through this unidentified young woman, this confederate they have enlisted to play my daughter's part—they hinted broadly about missing treasure."

"Indeed? That seems a new approach."

"I am determined that it must not be successful."

"Of course. What exactly was the message conveyed by the young woman—whoever she may have been?"

Altamont seemed to be making an effort to remember. But then he shook his head. "Madeline did not give me the exact words. Some kind of a complaint regarding stolen property which must be restored—God help us!—so that Louisa's spirit may obtain eternal rest. I am mortally certain that if my wife does not spontaneously offer to enrich these scoundrels, this supposed treasure will loom larger and larger in their succeeding performances, until eventually it is made to seem our duty to produce it and hand it over. Meanwhile, there is no law against conducting séances. If there were, I fear that half the people my wife and I know socially would be in gaol." Our visitor gave the ghost of a smile.

Holmes was wearing that abstracted expression which generally betokened a keen and growing interest. "And you really have no idea of what treasure, or property, was meant?"

Altamont shook his head emphatically. "None whatever. The family estate in Buckinghamshire is, of course, quite substantial."

Holmes nodded, and was silent for a time. Once or twice I thought him on the verge of speaking, but he did not. "How can I help you?" he asked at last.

Altamont smote his fist upon the table. "Expose these wretches for the swindlers they are! I am sure that events will sooner or later make their true nature plain, even to my wife, but it would be intolerable for this tragic farce to be prolonged. Spare no expense, Mr. Holmes. I want the scales lifted from Madeline's eyes; it will be hard on her, but the longer the discovery is postponed, the worst it must be. Better to face the harsh facts now than to spend years as the slave to a delusion."

Holmes considered the problem quietly for a minute, then asked: "I suppose your wife wishes to repeat the séance?"

"Indeed, she is very eager to do so, even against my opposition, and this morning she talked of little else. In fact, she has pleaded with me to be present at the next sitting. Madeline has tried also to enlist the sympathy of our surviving daughter, Rebecca, and of young Martin Armstrong, the man to whom Louisa was to have been married next month. But I am sure that Martin, being a sensible young man, entirely agrees with me."

"And supposing such a repeat performance does take place, when and where will it be held?"

Our client made a gesture signifying resignation. "No

doubt Madeline will want to have it in our house, as before. As far as I know, she has not settled on a time. Perhaps my absolute and solemn prohibition would delay the affair by as much as a day or two." Altamont smiled grimly. "If either of you gentlemen is married, you will understand. I believe that my wife still hopes to convince me to attend."

"She is really eager for you to do so?"

"Oh, not if I remain hostile to the idea. She is eager, as she puts it, for me to demonstrate an open mind. I have the impression that the Kirkaldys, knowing me to be a hardened skeptic, are not quite so anxious for my presence at their next performance. Of course I have not spoken with them on the point."

It was decided among the three of us that a date for the next séance should be set, and that Holmes and I would attend, probably incognito, playing the roles of amateurs in psychic research, business acquaintances of Altamont who had convinced him to be open-minded about the possibility of communication with those who had gone beyond the veil.

Before our visitor departed, we obtained from him some detailed information relevant to the case, including the address of Martin Armstrong. The young man, we learned, was employed as a correspondent for an American newspaper, and was now working out of an office in Fleet Street.

When our client had departed, my companion turned to me with an expression half-serious and half-quizzical. "Well, Watson?"

"Mr. Altamont has a just grievance, in my view."

"So it would seem, at least on present evidence. But we must, I think, move carefully. The most obvious, worldly, down-to-earth explanation in matters involving supposed occult activity is not always the correct one."

Something in my companion's voice as he uttered those last words again made me look at him closely. I frowned. "Holmes—"

"Yes, old fellow, I have in mind a subject on which we have not spoken for a long time. Six years ago we shared a certain experience—one which led us rather deeply into what many would call the world of the supernatural. Those events have not been a frequent subject of conversation between us since then—"

"No," I said. "No, they have not."

He smiled faintly. "—but I think I may safely assume that you have not forgotten the affair?"

"I have not forgotten, Holmes. I never shall."

"Nor have I. It would be impossible to forget any detail of the incontrovertible evidence we both observed then, of human life beyond . . . if not beyond death, at least beyond burial and the grave."

"Then it is your belief . . ." Still the words were hard for me to say. I am sure that I unconsciously lowered my voice. "Your belief that the Altamont girl may have become . . . a vampire?"

He sighed and began to reload his pipe. "I say only that on the basis of the evidence so far, we must keep our minds open to that possibility. Are you with me, Watson?"

"Of course!" And I endeavored to put into my voice a heartiness I was far from feeling.

For the next hour or so Holmes and I discussed mediums and their methods; he proved to be well versed in the more common methods of fraud, and outlined some of them.

I objected: "But if the events in the Altamont household took place just as our visitor described them, it is hard to see how any of these methods of deception could have been employed."

"Not at all. Remember that our report of the incident comes only at third hand. And, as I cautioned our client, it is astonishing how easily someone willing to believe, as Mrs. Altamont so obviously is, may be deceived."

Holmes also outlined a plan to look into the background of the mediums—he proposed to begin by consulting Langdale Pike—I believe I have mentioned the man before, in other accounts of Holmes's achievements, as his human book of reference upon all matters of social scandal.

Louisa's fiancé, the young American Martin Armstrong, proved to be an intense, energetic man obviously still grieved by his loss. He had met Louisa in his native country while she was visiting there with friends, and had then followed her back across the Atlantic. For some months before coming to London, Armstrong had served as the St. Petersburg correspondent for his American newspaper, one that proudly continued the tradition of the brash *New York Herald,* founded some decades earlier by James Gordon Bennett.

Armstrong had been much pleased to be reassigned to London, where he would be near Louisa Altamont. Shortly after his arrival, around the middle of May, he had proposed and had been accepted.

Holmes was now eager to seek him out, and with a little judicious use of the telephone it was soon arranged that Mr. Martin Armstrong should lunch with us at Simpson's in the Strand. To judge by the eagerness of the voice on the other end of the line, the American journalist was very well pleased at the prospect of obtaining an exclusive interview with the famous Sherlock Holmes.

My friend and I arrived at the restaurant a little before the appointed time of one o'clock. I observed as we entered certain ominous, cryptic symbols that had been drawn in white paint on the pavement just outside the door; these puzzled me until I remembered hearing that the street was soon to be widened, and the building containing our favorite restaurant was to be rebuilt.

When I commented sadly on this fact to Holmes, he replied, in a rare nostalgic mood: "I suppose it is inevitable,

Watson, that eventually all of our old haunts will be transformed. Only yesterday I learned that Newgate Prison is scheduled to be demolished—the work may already have begun—and replaced by a new Central Criminal Court to be constructed along Old Bailey Street."

"That will be a welcome change indeed," I ventured.

"Nothing remains the same. It is even possible, Watson, that neither of us is as young as he once was."

I could not very well dispute that observation. But neither could I see how the passing of our youth was relevant to my objection. While no one would regret the removal of the infamous pesthole of Newgate, an operation decades—if not a century—overdue, the transformation of our restaurant of choice was quite another matter. A lengthy period of closure would be inevitable, and the reopening when it came would surely see a new, and very likely less competent, staff on the premises.

Holmes had a favorite table at Simpson's, from which he was able to watch the busy street, while at the same time any private conversation he might wish to conduct was relatively secure from eavesdroppers. Martin Armstrong soon joined us at that table.

The man who came to introduce himself was about twenty-five years of age, middle-sized, fair-haired and strong-featured, well dressed in the modern style that might be expected of a successful journalist. He greeted us with what must have been only a shadow of his usual breezy American manner, naturally subdued by the recent tragedy. He, like Altamont, was wearing a black armband, and plainly the loss of his fiancée had hit him hard.

In response to my companion's first questions, Armstrong immediately confirmed his agreement with Mr. Altamont's assessment of the situation at Norberton House.

"Yes, I've already heard all about last night's séance, gentlemen. Louisa's mother phoned me this morning and gave me the whole story. She's very excited, and seemed upset when I couldn't share her enthusiasm.

"After that, I talked with Rebecca—that's Louisa's younger sister. She wasn't at the house last night, but she knew of the performance and is concerned about her mother."

As our conversation continued over lunch, it became clear that the young American was perhaps a less determined—or more diplomatic—agnostic than Louisa's father. But the fiancé was just as strongly convinced that the Kirkaldys—though he had never met them—were scoundrels whose ultimate goal must be the extraction of money from the bereaved family.

Armstrong was also in hearty agreement with Altamont that professional investigative help now seemed to be in order to prevent any fraud and to save the family from further grief.

The young man mentioned that his New York newspaper had in the past carried out an exposé of fraudulent psychic practitioners in America, and he offered his cooperation.

This led to a discussion of investigative techniques, and so to the promised exclusive interview with Holmes, and also—a development which rather took me by surprise—to a conversation between myself and the journalist, in which my views were sought for publication. These talks occupied us through most of our luncheon.

Some minutes had passed in congenial discussion, when Holmes interrupted to ask whether Armstrong had recently noticed anyone following him.

Our companion put his notebook down on the table and blinked at him. "Following me? Here in London? Certainly not. Why do you ask?"

"Because there is a rather unsavory fellow out on the pavement, a foreigner I am sure, who appears to be taking a definite though furtive interest in our table." Holmes nodded slightly toward the plate-glass window giving on the street, which was in front of him as he occupied his customary seat. "No, don't look round just yet. A Russian, I would wager—there is a certain style of dress affected by the political refugees from Moscow and St. Petersburg. He is a small man, wearing a black coat and dark cloth cap, clean-shaven, with something of the Slav about his cheekbones; he has come and gone three times in the past two minutes—no, don't turn around! He is there again."

Armstrong indeed looked as if he wanted to turn around, but he did not. "No, I have no idea why anyone would be following me. Of course, I have spent almost eight months in Russia, on two separate tours of duty. I can assure you that there, between the revolutionaries and the secret police, and the countless intrigues involving both, one almost expects to be followed."

Holmes shrugged slightly. "Perhaps the attentions of the gentleman outside are really directed toward myself. That would not be unheard of. But at the moment I know of no reason for anyone of his type to take such an interest in my activities."

Meanwhile, I had been attempting to observe the object of Holmes's scrutiny from the corner of my eye, and thought that I had had some success. Without turning my face directly toward the window, I suggested, in a low voice, going out into the street and collaring the spy.

Holmes shook his head minimally. "No, old fellow, I think not. If the man is still there when we leave—perhaps. But for the time being our admirer has taken himself away again."

The mysterious observer did not return again, and our luncheon was concluded without incident.

~ 2 ~

On the appointed day, exactly a week after our first meeting with Ambrose Altamont, Holmes and I, in response to our client's invitation, journeyed to his country house. At Victoria Station we boarded a train to the sizable village of Amberley in Buckinghamshire.

We arrived in midafternoon. Martin Armstrong, who had come down from London a day earlier, had promised to meet us at the local station with his motorcar. For some reason, I had rather expected an American machine—perhaps one of the new Oldsmobiles—but in fact, the journalist was driving one of the Mercedes-Simplex models of 1902, a two-seater capable of carrying five or six passengers easily. Armstrong had so far recovered from his tragic loss as to take a proud interest in his new automobile and to discuss some of its finer points with us. According to some notes that I jotted down at the time, this vehicle was rated at forty horsepower and equipped with the patented scroll clutch and four gears forward.

Only now, confronted by this evidence of material prosperity, did I fully realize how successful Armstrong must be in his chosen profession. Later I was to discover that he had successfully published one book in America and was at work upon a second.

Norberton House, as Armstrong informed us, was about three miles from the village, set in fine farming and hunting country. The day was still sunny and warm; recent rains had left the countryside fresh and green, and as we rode, we enjoyed the sight of summer fields and hedgerows.

Along the way, we queried our companion as to whether there had been any new developments relating to our business; as far as Armstrong knew, there had not.

Holmes also asked whether Armstrong had observed any new indication that he was being followed, either here or in London, and the American replied in the negative.

We learned too that neither Mr. nor Mrs. Altamont had changed their respective, and diametrically opposite, positions with regard to the mediums; but Mr. Altamont had managed to convince his wife that he was now ready to approach the subject with an open mind. One result of this announced change in attitude was that the Kirkaldys were now established in the house as guests.

We were about halfway to our destination, approaching a bridge spanning a small river, when our driver slowed the motor. "This is the Shade," he informed us tersely. "One of the tributaries of the Thames. If we were to follow it downstream from here, we should come, within a quarter of a mile, to the place where the thing happened last month. Follow the stream a mile or so farther and we'd be at the boundary of the grounds of Norberton House."

In response to a request from Holmes, Armstrong stopped his automobile just past the bridge. My friend was obviously interested, and dismounted from the car. In a moment we had joined him at the stone balustrade overlooking the river, which was here fifteen or twenty yards in width. Pointing downstream, Armstrong informed us in a low voice: "The exact spot where our boat capsized cannot be seen from anywhere along the road. But it lies only a few hundred yards from here."

Sherlock Holmes gazed thoughtfully in the indicated direction. "It is almost impossible that there should be any real clues discoverable after such a lapse of time. Still, I should like to see the place."

"Easily managed. We can reach it by this footpath."

Leaving the automobile standing clear of the bridge at the edge of the road, we walked along a grassy, lightly worn riparian path that curved in accordance with the river's bends. Presently a noise of violent splashing reached us from ahead, along with a cheerful outcry in childish voices. Moments later, I caught a glimpse of white bodies through the greenery, and we came upon a small pile of discarded clothing. Two young lads were engaged in diving and swimming from the bank. Holmes hailed a pair of wet heads bobbing in the water, put them at ease with some remarks about the hot weather and their sport, then asked several questions. Wide-eyed, the boys protested that they had been nowhere near the river on the day when the lady had been drowned.

"Is it deep here, then?" Holmes inquired.

"Not at all, sir. I can touch bottom anywhere, 'cept right here in the channel." Raising both hands above his head, the speaker, who was near the center of the stream, disappeared from view by way of demonstration.

We waved farewell and moved along. When we had gone another forty yards or so, to a position halfway around another bend, and the sounds of childish innocence had resumed behind us, Armstrong informed us that we were now looking at the exact place where the boat had tipped.

Here both green banks were lined with trees, willows in particular, among which our path followed a twisting course. Insects droned among the leaves and branches, many of which closely overhung the water. There were no natural hazards visible, and certainly no turbulence in the placid flow beyond that caused by a small fish jumping.

Thoughtfully, my friend surveyed the opaque surface of the stream, brown with the soil it carried, then scooped up a little of the water, which looked clear in his palm.

"Was the level much different three weeks ago?" he asked.

"No." Armstrong, standing with arms folded and head down, was naturally subdued.

"The water at this point cannot be much deeper, I suppose, than it is upstream where the lads are bathing?"

"Perhaps a little, not enough to matter. The channel all along this part of the river is certainly deep enough to drown in—eight or ten feet, I'd say—and it lies everywhere near the center of the stream. But for most of its width, the stream can be waded."

"You have been boating on it frequently?"

"Even swimming in it several times. And boating, with Louisa, on two earlier occasions, before . . ."

Holmes nodded sympathetically. He looked upstream and down. "Nowhere does the current seem particularly swift."

Armstrong shook his head. "It's not, of course. Not anyplace within miles of here. I've made a rough measurement, pacing beside it with my watch; no more than two miles an hour. A man can walk a great deal faster than that. That's one reason the whole business is still—" he gestured awkwardly "—still so hard to understand. And wait till you see the boat we were in! Not a punt or a canoe, but a regular, solid, broad-beamed craft of the dinghy type. Quite difficult to tip. There was some talk at the inquest of a possible collision with a submerged log, which I thought made little sense."

"Was that the coroner's conclusion?"

Armstrong shrugged. "No one was able to produce a log, either sunken or afloat. The verdict was just 'death by misadventure'—the officially accepted theory seemed to be one of jolly horseplay among the boaters getting out of hand, that we'd all crowded to one side and turned her over. That might easily explain what happened, except it isn't true."

"You did not publicly dispute the accepted theory?"

"I tried, at first, but gave up. What was the use? In any case, the ruling was essentially that Louisa died by accidental drowning—what else could it have been?"

"But when her body was eventually discovered, it lay far downstream from here."

"Yes, very far. Almost a mile."

Holmes's attitude and voice remained sympathetic. "As I understand it, there were only the three of you aboard the boat?"

"Yes. Louisa and myself—I was manning the single pair of oars, at least during most of the outing—and Louisa's younger sister, Rebecca."

My friend looked at our companion keenly. "How do you explain the boat's capsizing, Mr. Armstrong?"

The young man uttered a small, bitter sound, not quite a laugh. "Do you know, Mr. Holmes, I believe you're the first one to come straight out and ask me that question. Many people . . . *look* at me as though they are certain I must be somehow at fault, that someone aboard must have been doing something foolish at the time, to tip the boat. But very few have said so. And not even the coroner has put that question to me in so many words. To hear it actually comes as something of a relief." With a swift movement, he bent, picked up a pebble from the muddy margin of the stream, and hurled it violently into the water.

"Well?"

Armstrong faced us and spoke calmly. "The only answer I can give you is that I am as puzzled as everyone else. I was rowing—quite gently, I assure you—sitting in the middle of the center seat and facing the girls, who were both sitting in the stern. None of us were trying, either playfully or in earnest, to capsize our vessel. No one was leaning over the side. One moment we were cruising along as smooth as you please—and the next, we were tipping violently, and a moment after that, we were all three in the water."

" 'Tipping violently,' you say?"

"Very much so. The only way I can describe it, gentlemen, is that it was as if something—something on the order of a giant sea monster perhaps—had seized the boat and shaken it. Rebecca agrees. But of course that makes no sense at all." The young man shrugged. It was as if, with the passage of time, his attitude had become hardened and fatalistic.

"Had you been out in the rowboat long?"

"Something less than an hour." Armstrong paused to sigh, then proceeded, in the tone of a witness repeating a story already told a hundred times. "It was getting late, and soon it would be dusk, and we decided to go back. We had come upstream some distance, between half a mile and a mile I'd say, from the little dock at Norberton House.

"I had just turned the boat around and had rowed a few more strokes—gently, as I say, because we were now starting to go downstream. I was preparing to ship one oar and let the current carry us back—keeping one oar in the water as a paddle, to steer with and fend off the bank as necessary, you understand?"

"Of course. Go on."

Armstrong hesitated momentarily. "Then there was . . ."

Holmes waited a moment before prodding. "There was what?"

"Nothing, nothing at all. I mean there was only the violent shaking, from some invisible cause, and we capsized. For which I have no explanation, reasonable or otherwise."

My friend shot me a glance. "Could Louisa swim?"

"Not at all."

"How can you be certain?"

"Well, that's not a skill possessed by many women, particularly in this country, or so I'm told. But I'm certain in her case, because when we were setting out in the boat she even joked a little about it. She said something, in a light-hearted way, about having to rely on me to . . . rescue her if there was trouble. And then when it actually happened . . ."

The young man's mask of near-indifference cracked, and he found it necessary to pause for a moment.

Presently he continued: "When the thing happened, the idea even passed through my mind—while I was diving, again and again, trying to find her—it even occurred to me that there ought to have been some chance that the big skirts and petticoats, you know, the things women wear, that those garments might have trapped air and could keep a girl afloat for a time. But nothing . . ." Again our witness was compelled to halt.

"But nothing of the kind happened," I concluded for him.

Armstrong nodded, his face once more downcast.

"I take it," Holmes remarked after a moment, "that the boat was not visibly damaged in the accident? And that it was later returned to the family dock? Just so. I should like to see it."

Armstrong blinked at him. "I'm sure there will be no difficulty about that."

"When you first swam or waded ashore, did you come to this bank or to the opposite?"

"This one."

"And in helping Rebecca ashore?"

"This one again. That needed only a moment or two. Then I went back into the water, looking for Louisa. I dove, and dove again . . ."

Holmes raised a hand; for a moment, no more need be said. One look at the muddy shoreline was enough to convince him that no trace could still endure of the events of three weeks ago.

Presently we began in silence to retrace our steps along the path, and soon regained our motor. Armstrong had no difficulty in cranking the machine to life. Only a short drive remained to bring us to our destination.

The manor called Norberton House stood on what Armstrong told us were approximately twenty acres of partially wooded, parklike grounds. Judging from the design of the house, which was constructed of mellow red brick, I thought it had been built in the late eighteenth century, or at least remodeled and enlarged at about that time. Two wings, each two stories high, extended west and east of a central hall.

"The family has a private burial ground?" Holmes inquired, as our machine swung in from the public road to the gravel drive.

"Sir?" Young Armstrong, turning his head, seemed to doubt that he had heard the question accurately above the roar of the motor.

"I am asking about Louisa's interment—was it nearby?"

"Yes—the cemetery is no more than about half a mile away." The driver, both hands momentarily busy with controls, indicated the direction with a nod.

"Below ground, or above? Pray forgive what must sound like great impertinence; I have my reasons."

"In the old family mausoleum," replied young Armstrong wonderingly, and favored my friend with a strange look indeed.

Holmes expressed a wish to see the cemetery as well as the boat. "Before dark this evening would be best, but if that proves inconvenient, the matter can wait until the morning."

"If you wish, I am sure there will be no objection." But the young man was frowning; plainly he did not understand.

Upon our arrival at Norberton House . . .

~ 3 ~

At this point, dear reader, I—Dracula—believe that the proper flow of narrative requires us to interrupt the estimable Watson.

The good doctor would have been much startled had he been able to observe what was happening in the cemetery, even as he and Sherlock Holmes were racketing toward Norberton House in that primordial Mercedes driven by Martin Armstrong.

Even as those three men were about to alight on the Altamonts' doorstep, a certain young woman of whom Holmes and Watson had heard, but who had not yet confronted them, a pretender to psychic power named Sarah Kirkaldy, accompanied by her even younger brother, Abraham, was paying a visit to the Altamont family burial ground. The living members of that family had no more idea than the dead ones that the Kirkaldys were there, and it appeared to the brother and sister on entering the small cemetery that except for themselves, the place was utterly deserted.

Sarah, who had prospered greatly in the last couple of years, was well-dressed, dark-haired and attractive, lately well-fed and almost plump, normally busy and bustling in her manner. Her object this afternoon in calling upon her clients' dear departed relatives had nothing at all to do with establishing communication links between this world and the next—in Sarah's view, only gulls and fools believed such visiting possible. Instead, her purpose was eminently mundane and practical: to note down as many as possible of the names and dates engraved upon this library of tombstones that extended back in time for several centuries. With this material, in conjunction with stories and traditions acquired locally, it should be possible to construct a useful family history.

Experience had convinced Sarah that such a history (nowadays we might call it a data base) could be an asset of inestimable value in the séance room, able to provide identities as well as credible subjects for conversation that might be introduced by talking spirits just arrived from the Great Beyond.

Originally, Sarah had wanted to conclude this graveyard reconnaissance before the first séance with Mrs. Altamont. But various circumstances had postponed the expedition until now. And in fact even now the attempt to note down names and dates had not got beyond the first page of the small notebook—because in the past week Sarah had been forced to the conclusion that another matter was far more urgent. That was the real reason she had made the effort this afternoon to get her brother out of the house, well away from eavesdropping servants and distractions, out here in the open where she could bully him freely, argue with him fiercely if necessary—at all costs, settle something between them that had to be put right.

Abraham, a rather tall, thin youth with mouse-colored hair and an irregular face (in fact he would have made a good stand-in for Poe's Roderick Usher) stood at the moment staring—though not as if he were actively looking for anything in particular—at the walls of the Altamont mausoleum. This was a rather elaborate construction the size of a two-room cabin or bungalow, mostly marble, decorated with some early Victorian angels and allegorical figures, statues and bas-reliefs carved in soft stone and already weathering away. There were no real windows. The massive single door, itself securely locked, was also defended by an extra, outer guard of barred iron gates placed at the entry to the small porch. By now, approximately three weeks after Louisa's funeral, the flowers which had then been deposited both inside and outside her tomb had long since faded and died.

At the moment Sarah was holding notebook and pencil together in one hand, both objects for the moment forgotten. Staring intently at her brother, she asked in a low, sympathetic voice: "Do y' feel like talkin' t' me yet, Abe? Having a real talk?"

Abraham did not immediately look at her. It took him a little time to come up with a reply. "About what?" His voice was soft and tentative, as if here in the cemetery he might be afraid of awaking ghosts.

"You know what. About what happened the last time we sat round the table in the dark. When Mrs. Altamont was with us. It's a week and a day now."

No response.

"It's nae guid, Abe, to just keep on putting me off. We've *got* t' talk about it, before tonight." Sarah paused again; a Scottish burr that she usually tried to repress, or modify, had begun to show in her speech. "If we dinna talk about it now, we might as well forget aboot tonight's sitting, because I'm nae gang to do it."

Abraham's mouth opened, but closed again, hopelessly, without having produced an answer. He turned away.

With relentless patience, the girl walked around him to stand again directly in his line of sight. "That's it, see. Either talk about it, solve it somehow, or gi'e up the whole business. Nae more doin' spirit sittin's for the gentry. Gi'e up and change our names again, and maybe go back t' hoosehold service, where we were two years ago . . . if we could get any references now."

Her brother's face was becoming heavily clouded with some deep emotion, but still he had nothing to say.

"Abe, you remember what 'twas like—being in service? *I* remember it—verra weel!"

Turning in a small circle like a bewildered animal, he scraped and scuffed his expensive boots in the tall and unkempt grass. He looked decidedly unhappy.

Sarah was not going to let him turn away from her. "If we dinna talk now, Abe, you'd best make your plans to gae back t' yon. Scrubbin' oot chamber pots and livin' in a closet. Because what happened eight days ago scared me, bad. I ken it scared you, too. But maybe if we talk about it, we can find some way t' go on."

Still no comment. But Sarah, who knew her brother, decided he was really listening now. She dropped her voice to a more confidential tone. "Let's just go over what happened last time, love. Ye'll do that much for me. All right?"

Abe nodded, minimally.

"All right. We sat doon wi' the auld—wi' Mrs. Altamont. Things began proper enough, just aboot the way we always do them. Right?"

Another nod.

"Then you went intae your trance—"

Abraham winced, as at a painful memory. He said, in a voice not much louder than a whisper: "I dinna remember much o' what happened after that. I dinna really want to know."

"It's nae good tryin' to put me off, Abe. I ken you remember more than you let on, because I see you're worried now. I tell ye we maun talk about it afore we try tae dae anither sittin', and we've got one on the docket for tonight.

"Now—you told me it was one o' those times when you really go into a trance. You really went somewhere—inside your own head, I mean. Right?"

Abraham muttered something.

"What's that?"

"I said, I began t' see things."

Moving closer to her brother, Sarah petted him, hugged and comforted him, while she pursued him with more questions.

In effect she started over, discussing some of the preliminary effects—the ghostly rappings from under the table, the table itself moving without apparent physical cause—she had used them during their last sitting—"afore things started to go queer." She also said a few uncomplimentary things about the old woman of the house, Mrs. Altamont.

"Are you listening t' me, Abe?"

"Aye, I'm listenin'."

"We did a' that—and a' went weel eno'—and then *it* happened—right?"

Abraham nodded slowly. Now he was looking at his sister hopefully, as if waiting to be provided with an explanation.

Sarah sighed. "What happened was, there came—from somewhere—another woman, a girl, into the room—aye?"

"Aye."

" 'T'wasna me, movin' aboot the room in white. Ye ken that?"

"Aye."

"A' th' doors t' th' room stayed closed, and so did a' the windows—as far as I could tell. Dark as it was, I saw her plain enough to ken that she was there. And I heard her talk. And you saw her too."

"Aye." It was a whisper barely audible.

"Aye, I thought y'did.

"And the auld bitch saw her too, and she let go both our hands and jumped up and ran and clutched at the one who'd just come in—remember?—a'cryin' and a'screamin' oot *Louisa, Louisa*—she had nae a moment's doot that nicht, an' t' this day, she still thinks 'twas really her daughter. The auld woman's convinced we can bring her dead girl back again."

Abraham muttered: "We brocht up . . ."

"What's that y'say? Coom, lad, speak up now."

"We really brocht up . . . something, last time." Abraham's voice was a defeated whisper. "We really did. Maybe *'twas* that girl—Louisa."

"Dinna gie me none o' that!" Sarah was unshaken. Her contempt was quiet, but implacably firm. "Neither o' *us* are seein' ghosts an' bogles!"

The haunted, pleading eyes of Abraham had turned at last to fasten fully on his sister's eyes, where they remained. His dry lips formed the silent query: *Then who—?*

She patted his arm. "Aye, who? And why was she there? That's what we maun think aboot, and find an answer. *I* dinna ken who she was! Or how she got in an' oot! All I can be certain of is that 'twas a girl, a real girl.

"She came in wearin' a white dress, nightgown, something of the kind."

"Aye." Abraham was still seeking grounds for hope, not really finding any. "Likely 'twas the white gown she was buried in."

"Enough o' that, I say!" Sarah brooded, glowering, tension in her face spoiling her real prettiness. "First I thought it must be someone tryin' to play a prank on *us*. But 'twasn't that. Not the old woman anyhow. She took this girl for her own bairn come back, right enough. No play-acting there. Hugged her and kissed her . . . you listenin' to me?"

"Wot you think?" Abe's voice was suddenly much louder and cruder than it had been until now.

Sarah was relieved at this new tone, taking it as a sign of recovery. "You saw her plain? You'd know her again?"

"Course I saw her plain. First with my eyes shut. Then—"

Abe broke off suddenly, and in the same instant turned

his face away from Sarah, toward the tomb in which Louisa Altamont had been laid to rest with some of her ancestors. A moment later, clutching at his sister's arm, he exclaimed: "Shh! Someone's there . . ."

Biting off whatever words she had been about to utter, Sarah turned, half-expecting to see again the girl in white, up to some new prank. But Sarah was surprised. No more than ten feet away, just at the corner of the Altamont mausoleum, as if he had come up soundlessly along its far side, was standing a tall, red-bearded, pale-faced man, apparently thirty-five or forty years of age. The newcomer was tastefully and elegantly dressed in the style of an Edwardian gentleman—except that he wore a countryman's broad-brimmed hat, as if he sought protection from even today's mild daylight.

The red-bearded man was not so much confronting the Kirkaldys as looking just past and above them—his expression was at the same time remote and forbidding, and he had materialized as quietly as a ghost. There was something remote in his gaze, too. From where he was standing now, close beside the old stones wreathed in their summer vines—or from just a little farther off, around the corner—he might have heard a great deal.

In the silence Sarah became aware of droning summer insects—there was something at once sleepy and vicious in the sound—and of the small noises made by the shallows of the Shade, which was murmuring over a bank of pebbles just behind a wall of streamside greenery.

Fighting back a sensation of faintness, Sarah took it upon herself to start the conversation. Years of training in service threatened to take over; she actually curtsied. "Guid afternoon, sir," she heard herself say humbly.

"Good afternoon." It was a deep voice, speaking clear and excellent English tinged with a foreign accent of some kind she could not immediately identify. "Why are you here?" The greenish eyes still looked past the Kirkaldys rather than at them; the demand sounded proprietary, brusque and unconditional. This was evidently some relative of whom she had not yet been informed.

Stumbling and stuttering, Sarah tried to come up with a reasonable explanation for her presence, and her brother's, in the family plot. Fighting free of her old servile manners, she remarked how interesting were the intricate designs in the stonework on some of the tombs, and the abandoned, two-thirds-ruined chapel that looked down upon the graves from a small rise of ground. She waved her little notebook in which she had already written down some names and dates.

Then she introduced herself and Abraham.

Their names seemed to mean nothing to the tall red-haired man, nor was there any way to tell, just yet, whether he had accepted Sarah's lame explanation for their presence. "You may call me Mr. Gregory," he said, then paused, seemingly waiting for her to do so.

Sarah wondered, but was not about to inquire, whether Gregory was a last name or a first. She made a gesture somewhere between a bow and a curtsy. "Mr. Gregory, then," she murmured. Meanwhile Abraham still stood silent, like one stunned—Sarah felt her own chill of fear when she realized how terrified her brother had become.

Gregory, in no hurry about anything, stood with hands behind his back, looking at the Kirkaldys quite directly now, surveying them as he would two servants of dubious character, menials who were somehow necessary to him, and whom he therefore might be forced to engage against his better judgment. Then Sarah began to get the impression that whatever this man was thinking about so privately was steadily, inwardly, enraging him; and she found herself saying an inward prayer of thanksgiving that this rage did not seem to be directed against her and Abe.

At last the man who stood facing them announced: "You are the two who, a week past, conducted the sitting, the séance, in the house." He gestured minimally, a slight movement of the head, toward the distant Altamont home, invisible from here behind its woods and orchards.

"We had that privilege, Mr. Gregory, yes." Sarah needed a great effort to keep from adding "sir," to keep from groveling. In her mind she repeated the private vow she had made to herself two years ago: She would not be a servant anymore, never again. *Would not!*

Gregory seemed oblivious to whatever the two young people before him might be feeling. "I heard you speaking to your brother just now about the girl in white who appeared at your last sitting. Oh, your visitant was indeed Miss Louisa Altamont, I assure you." He stopped and waited, as if inviting comment.

Sarah had her mouth open, to comment or perhaps to argue but she closed it again in silence.

The red-haired man went on: "But she did not come out of her grave because *you* called her—no." That was a strange idea, even an amusing one, provoking a grin of white, sharp teeth. "No, it was I who bade Miss Altamont walk that night, and I who sent her to you in the house." Again the speaker paused, as if expecting a question or even a challenge. When none came, he resumed:

"She had not far to go, of course, from her new home—" he patted the marble wall beside him "—back to the house in which she lived her breathing life." And the tall man once more pointed in the direction of the house half a mile away. Then he leaned with the same hand against the tomb beside him. "Now do you understand?" He studied the stunned faces of his audience and appeared satisfied by what he saw. "Of course there is no need for you to understand."

In the next moment Gregory pulled a pair of gold sovereigns from his pocket, and tossed them arrogantly into the grass at the feet of his two auditors, as if he might be throwing tuppence to a crossing-sweeper. At the sight of gold, Sarah involuntarily sucked in her breath, but neither she nor Abraham went scrambling to pick up the coin. Not yet.

Now the red-haired one demanded: "When do you sit with the Altamont woman again? Of course she must be clamoring to have another visit with her daughter. There is a plan?"

Abe and Sarah looked at each other.

"Come, come. Surely she is eager to once more see her little girl?" There was a certain tolerant amusement in Gregory's attitude now, coexisting with a great, strained arrogance—and under all, the sense of implacable, relentless anger. "Louisa tells me that her first visit made quite an impression on her dear mother. Dear Mother's great excitement prevented her from successfully discussing business last time, but I suppose I ought to have expected that. Next time, however, Louisa is going to be quite insistent. There is the business of a certain stolen property that must be addressed—an old debt, with interest, to be collected. *When do you sit with the old fool again?*"

"Tonight." The word seemed dragged unwillingly from Sarah's lips. She was trying to resist being bullied, but against this man the struggle had already proved hopeless. Still, one more effort seemed essential. "But see here . . ."

"Yes?"

"Her young lass Louisa's *dead.*"

Gregory stared at her, so long and steadily that Sarah began to fear she would faint. At first the man glaring at her was grim; then for a few moments he had to struggle with an inner amusement so intense it threatened to keep him from coherent speech.

But when he spoke again at last, his voice was still mild. "You need not concern yourselves with the precise degree of death Miss Louisa has experienced. Understand?"

"Aye," whispered Abraham.

"Aye," murmured Sarah—though in truth she was far from understanding.

"You need not worry about where Miss Louisa dwells, in this world or the next—provided she comes to you when you call her. As she will come! You need not worry about where Miss Louisa sleeps, or what she wears, or how she comes and goes. Or what kind of nourishment she now requires"—the green eyes flared at them—"You are to pay heed *only to what she demands from her family.*

"Your task is to help Louisa persuade her dear parents to do a certain thing—you understand?"

"Aye."

"Aye, sir."

"You must convince Mr. and Mrs. Altamont that one thing is absolutely essential—that they must grant whatever wish their returning daughter may express to them during the séance—you understand?"

"Yes sir," said Sarah this time.

Gregory's fierce gaze shifted to Abraham, who quailed visibly before it. "Yes sir," said Abe, the words seemingly dragged out of him by invisible force.

Mr. Gregory nodded slowly. Perhaps, confident that he had established firm control, he allowed himself to relax a little. "And who else," he inquired, "is going to be with you in the dark room tonight, when Louisa calls?"

Sarah drew a deep breath. In for a shilling, she told herself silently, in for a pound. Whatever Mr. Gregory's goal in the game of spirits and séances might be, since she and Abe were in the same game, she wanted to be on Gregory's side and not against him. Also the mention of property, of debts and interest to be collected, spoke to the savage greed that poverty had already kindled in her soul.

She said: "Mr. Altamont is comin' this time. Says he's willin' now tae look at the whole business wi' an open mind."

"Excellent. So, another Ambrose is now head of the house. The keys to all the family wealth will be firmly in his hands." At this point Gregory suddenly fell silent. For a moment or two, Sarah had the eerie impression that while the man's body remained standing before her, his eyes still glaring in her general direction, his mind had abruptly cut itself adrift, his thought entirely departed elsewhere.

The silence stretched on, while insects hummed and the little river murmured around rocks and snags. Absently the red-bearded man raised one hand, to rub the back of his neck beneath the broad hat brim.

Then abruptly he was back from wherever he had temporarily absented himself, back and glaring at the two Kirkaldys as he had upon first confronting them.

As if unaware of any interruption, he said: "No doubt Altamont's wife has given her dear modern Ambrose an interesting report about the visitor she entertained last week. No doubt the head of the family has formed his own ideas on the subject—and who else will be there?"

"See here, sir." Sarah stubbornly cleared her throat. "If Abraham and mysel' are tae sit again tonicht—"

"Indeed you are going to do that very thing, as I have just been telling you. Why not?"

"—why then we ought tae ken, to be told, just what—"

"You have just been told all that you need to know. Conduct your séance. Convince the old folk that they must do what their daughter tells them about the treasure. Do as I say and you will be well paid. But if you cross me, you will die horribly."

The threat was uttered in a clear voice, but without any emphasis at all. Somehow, this very indifference made it starkly convincing.

The green-eyed man broke the silence by demanding: "You have not yet answered my question. I will tolerate no insolence. Who else sits with you tonight?"

"Well, sir, I hear Mr. Martin Armstrong is coomin'. That's the American gentleman as was engaged to be married to Miss Louisa."

This information was received with a curt nod, betokening no surprise. "Anyone else?"

"Mrs. Altamont said today that two more men, very interested gentlemen, friends o' her husband's, were comin' doon frae London."

"You have their names?"

"She didna say. She said they were the ones as made her husband change his mind aboot the sittin'."

"Ah. More spiritualists, I suppose. We could take steps to discourage them—but doubtless it matters very little." And at this Mr. Gregory fell silent, once more staring into space over Sarah's head. He nodded thoughtfully, and again she got the strong impression that this terrible, terrifying man was somehow drifting away mentally. For the moment, his mind, all his bitter plans and hatred, were no longer—thank God!—focused right on her and Abraham.

Again Gregory lifted a pale hand to rub absently at the back of his neck, as if it might be hurting him. He leaned his head on one side, as if to ease a muscle strain. After a moment, he added in a near whisper, as if completing some inward thought: "That will be important for Gregory Efimovich."

"Beg pardon, sir? For who?"

The red-haired man seemed not to have heard the question. Still he continued to stare at nothing.

Abraham suddenly stooped to pick up the two gold pieces from the ground, snatched them up and put them in his pocket.

Gregory did not appear to notice.

And then, abruptly, the commanding figure in front of Sarah was looking directly at her once again. The pale man rasped out orders. "You will proceed with your plan for tonight—just as I have told you. And you will speak to no one of me, or of our meeting here."

First Sarah, then Abraham, mumbled acknowledgment of these commands.

His green eyes once more clear and sharply focused, Gregory dug more gold out of his pocket and threw it to the young couple. This time Sarah, quick and practical, caught one coin right out of the air.

Gregory went on: "I assure you that Louisa will be there tonight. If you promise the mother that her lost daughter will be present, no doubt she will reward you with more gold." He paused expectantly.

His audience, falling easily into old and well-trained habits, again promised to obey.

Crisply, Gregory gave more orders. He wanted another meeting with the two of them, here, at this spot, in exactly twenty-four hours. If he did not appear at the appointed time, he would leave them a message—he showed them exactly where he would place this communication, in a crevice between crumbling stones in the side of the Altamont mausoleum.

The roar of Martin Armstrong's motor, carrying Holmes and Watson from the station to the door of Norberton House, floated faintly into the cemetery from the distant road. But none of the three people in the cemetery at that hour paid it the least attention.

And now, let Watson have a turn again.

~ 4 ~

Upon our arrival at Norberton House, Holmes and I were welcomed—under our own names.

Though our original plan had called for us to appear incognito, Holmes on reflection had decided that he at least was too well known, and very likely to be recognized unless we were both of us thoroughly disguised—and disguise, too, had its disadvantages.

"Upon the whole, Watson," my friend whispered to me when we had a moment to ourselves, "other considerations being equal, the simpler a plan, the better."

"I can readily agree with that."

"Also there is an innate advantage in being truthful whenever possible. Mr. Altamont must simply tell his wife that we, the well-known investigators, are open-minded on the subject of séances and have persuaded him to be the same. Surely that is near enough the truth that it need not trouble our consciences."

On entering the house, we were greeted good-humoredly by Madeline Altamont, a slender, fair-haired lady of about the same age as her husband. The lady's figure was still graceful, and her countenance still retained much of what must have been a truly impressive youthful beauty.

Mrs. Altamont met us wearing a white dress, a spring-like and celebrational garment. Smiling and cheerful, she made a point of telling us that she had abandoned mourning. And indeed, there was no black wreath upon the door of the house, which was decorated with fresh flowers in almost every room.

Altamont himself was in town on business at the time of our arrival, but when our host appeared shortly before dinner, we saw that he had given up wearing his black armband.

The servants wore no tokens of mourning either. The butler, Cooper, showed us to our rooms, which were on the first floor, just down the hall from Martin Armstrong's.

"Your mistress seems very cheerful, Cooper," my friend commented as we followed our guide upstairs. It was a gentle probing, an attempt to sound the dispositions of the servants in the matter at hand.

"Yes sir." Cooper, with our bags in hand, paused on the stair long enough to look at us carefully, one after the other. "We can only hope that she will remain so, sir. That no fresh occasion for grief and disappointment is going to arise."

"Amen," said Holmes softly. And we left the matter at that for the time being.

A question of my own, on a different matter as we were nearing the top of the stairs, evoked from the butler a more cheerful response. This had to do with the history of the family, a subject in which Holmes and I had conducted some intense research over the past week. The Altamonts had lived in this house at least since the early eighteenth century, before the time of our client's ancestor and namesake, a certain Ambrose Altamont who was said to have died in London, murdered under peculiar and violent circumstances in the year 1765.

The estate had then passed into the hands of a brother, named Peter, of that ancestral Ambrose. Our research indicated that a rumor about a family treasure had started at about that time.

There were, as so often is the case in old houses where one family has remained in occupation for centuries, a dozen or more ancestral portraits, mounted in an ascending line along the stairway. Cooper's reply to my question confirmed that one of the portraits near the top was indeed that of the Ambrose Altamont who had died in 1765. Beside that portrait hung another, of the Peter Altamont who had inherited the estate. The resemblance between the brothers was notable.

As soon as the butler had left us, Holmes privately expressed to me his own concern for Mrs. Altamont's welfare: "There is one thing we may be sure of, Watson; whether the mediums are pure charlatans as her husband supposes—or whether the true explanation proves to be more *outré*—her current state of happiness stands on a false basis and cannot last."

In the circumstances I felt vaguely guilty about practicing even a slight deception upon the bereaved lady, by pretending an innocent enthusiasm for the coming séance. But I was able to reassure myself with the thought that I was doing everything for her own benefit.

Holmes was still keenly interested in inspecting the rowboat which had played such an important part in the recent tragedy, and as soon as we were settled into our rooms, Armstrong undertook to be our guide. He led us down through the garden behind the house, along a path which incorporated rude stone steps built into the gentle slope. Soon this winding descent took us out of sight of the house, among shrubbery and tall flowers to the small dock and boat shed beside the river. Here our guide pointed out to us the boat that had been involved in the strange incident. The small craft, painted a dull and undistinguished gray, lay bottom-up on wooden blocks in the shade of some tall elms, where it had been placed the day after the drowning. Our guide informed us that although the boat had been examined several times for damage, none had been discovered.

Holmes whipped out his magnifying glass, and after a quarter of an hour of intense effort, announced that he was able to detect small scratches in the gray-painted wood of the gunwales, near the prow.

"The fine indentations are on both sides, and very nearly symmetrical. Of course there is nothing to prove that they were made at the time of the tragedy."

Armstrong appeared to be strongly affected by Holmes's discovery and announcement. But the young man made no immediate comment.

I thought Holmes meant to question him further, but before he could do so a fair young woman, of perhaps seventeen or eighteen years of age, descended the rude steps and path from the direction of the house. Martin Armstrong stood up and introduced us to Rebecca Altamont, who unlike her mother was still wearing mourning.

Rebecca bore a strong resemblance to her mother, and later we heard from several people that Louisa also had done so, all three women being slender and blonde.

When Holmes in the course of our conversation asked Miss Altamont whether she planned to attend this evening's séance, she responded that she did. Her tone was firm rather than hopeful, that of someone determined to perform a disagreeable duty.

Rebecca, at least at first, kept guarded her own opinion on the subject of séances. Meanwhile she asked several questions, with the evident object of finding out whether Holmes and I were truly enthusiastic spiritualists. She appeared somewhat relieved to learn that we claimed no more than to have open minds.

When asked about her own beliefs, she stated somewhat

defiantly that she was in general agreement with her father and young Martin: The séance must have been a fraud. But I received the strong impression that the young woman's main concern was to shield her mother from further grief rather than to expose the mediums, or even to protect the family fortune.

Rebecca Altamont bestowed on the fatal rowboat a single glance of obvious repugnance, and then turned her back on it. I glanced at Holmes, but he chose not to mention to her his discovery of the peculiar marks.

Holmes wanted to hear Miss Altamont's version of her sister's drowning, and the events surrounding that tragedy.

After protesting that she was weary of discussing the matter, the girl went on to give an account generally confirming Armstrong's. She had been seated in the stern of the rowboat with her sister, both young ladies facing forward, toward the young man, who naturally sat amidships, facing them as he rowed.

"Then, Mr. Holmes, we experienced a violent shock."

"As if the boat perhaps had struck a sunken log?"

"No! Not like that at all." The young woman shook her head decisively. "That suggestion was made more than once at the inquest, but it is wrong. What happened was more like . . . as if some huge creature had reared up under our prow, which rose partially from the water."

"Armstrong," I ventured, "mentioned the idea of a sea monster—fancifully, of course."

"I know," said Rebecca, staring at me somberly from under the brim of her summer hat. "And then, in fact, the boat seemed to be gripped and *twisted* in a way that neither Martin nor I have ever been able to explain. The only suggestions we can make seem fanciful, I know, but I have been able to think of no better way to convey the sensation of what was happening." And Miss Altamont stared at Holmes and myself with earnest hopefulness.

This account, while certainly strange enough, was still consistent with Armstrong's version of events—and with the marks that seemed to indicate some grip of prodigious strength had been fastened upon the boat. Yet my friend did not pursue the point at once.

Shortly after our return to the house, we encountered the mediums—and the Kirkaldys proved to be as curious about us as we were about them.

The attitude of Mrs. Altamont toward the Kirkaldys was almost that of a fond aunt, or even of a doting mother. She insisted that they must be accommodated and treated, by both servants and family, as honored guests. The lady of the house had her way in this, as in much else, though I thought privately that at least some of the servants had other ideas—more in sympathy with those of her husband—regarding exactly what kind of treatment the mediums deserved.

Sarah, bustling and almost plump, dark-haired and in her very early twenties, was plainly the more aggressive of the pair, a shrewd young woman active in a business way. She was simply dressed, but her clothes were not inexpensive. Her brother Abraham, the supposed sensitive, was perhaps four or five years younger, a tall, frail lad of gentle appearance, evidently less concerned about his appearance, with soft brown hair and eyes, and the almost invisible beginning of a mustache. His sister alternated between doting on him tenderly and treating him severely. She seemed to be genuinely convinced that her brother was really sensitive in psychic matters.

In fact, I thought there was a moment at the dinner table when he actually seemed about to go into a trance—staring into space, with soup dripping unnoticed from the spoon he held. I thought he might even be drooling from the corner of his mouth, and it occurred to me to wonder if the youth suffered from some mild form of epilepsy.

Toward the end of dinner, Rebecca Altamont, as if growing apprehensive about the evening's prospects, suggested that the séance might be more likely to succeed if it were postponed by twenty-four hours—or that another sitting held on a certain future date would be even more certain of success.

She added wistfully: "That day would have been Louisa's twentieth birthday."

Sarah looked at the speaker sweetly. "What are birthdays on the other side? It is the death day that is the real birthday."

Mrs. Altamont was thrilled. "My dear, what a beautiful way to look at it! Thank you. Let us go on with it tonight."

Then talk at the dinner table returned to harmless social generalities and remained for a few minutes on that level.

I did my best to maintain a polite standard of conversation while remaining alert for any signs of fraud. But with my experiences of six years earlier never far from my thoughts, I could not be other than open-minded on the subject of supernatural manifestations.

Soon enough, the subject of spirit sittings again engaged the dinner table. The Kirkaldys were willing to talk in general terms about some of their past successes—without revealing names or dates—though they were reticent about any other aspect of their history. They were orphans, they said, and their family was a painful subject; they begged to be excused from any discussion on that topic.

The subject of materializations came up, and Martin Armstrong, adopting the manner of the investigative reporter, asked Miss Sarah Kirkaldy why darkness seemed to be required.

I remember that she smiled sweetly at her questioner as she produced a ready answer. "The necessity for darkness during materialization is in harmony with the creation of all animal and vegetable structures, as the former are built in the darkness of the womb of the animal body, and the latter within the darkness of the soil."

Armstrong did not appear to be impressed. "I suppose that where it is necessary to produce phenomena in this manner, fraud may find a ready entrance."

Her smile did not waver. "I feel confident we can all depend on you, sir, and on these other gentlemen from London, to make sure that nothing of the kind occurs."

Mrs. Altamont was delighted with this answer, and applauded. Obviously, this lady, even prior to Louisa's drowning, had already developed an enthusiasm for séances, for she spoke of having attended several at other people's houses. And when tragedy struck her family, the lady had been ripe to be "helped."

One strong objection to the theory that we were about to witness a simply fraudulent performance was the problem of where, if some accomplice was intended to play the role of Louisa, such an impostor might currently be concealed.

Ambrose Altamont had joined us before dinner. Afterward, to help Holmes and myself find answers to this and other difficulties, our host took an opportunity to conduct the two of us on a short tour of the house and the immediate grounds, under the guise of showing us the gardens.

Proceeding slowly, we three circled the house. There were no dogs to be concerned about, both of the senior Altamonts having a general dislike of the species. Ambrose also claimed to suffer a physical sensitivity to the animals. That, I thought, might make matters easier both for impostors—if any—and for investigators.

Holmes took the opportunity to ask what room or rooms were immediately above the library in which the séance was to be held. Two bedrooms, our host replied, but in that part of the house, there was no direct communication between floors.

During the course of this tour, Ambrose Altamont suggested to us that the house and the grounds could be swiftly searched, without warning, before darkness descended on us entirely, in hopes of exposing any planned trickery before it came about. The master of the house assured us that he had a couple of trusty servants ready to undertake the task.

Holmes expressed his opinion that such a search was unlikely to discover anything useful.

When we returned to the house, Mrs. Altamont remarked worriedly in my presence that today the Kirkaldys did not seem quite their usual selves.

"I thought the young woman gave quite a good account of herself when questioned."

"True enough, Dr. Watson, but to me—and I know her better than you do—Sarah looks quite haggard, as if some new problem had come up just this afternoon. But she says there is nothing."

"I suppose it could be the presence of Mr. Holmes and myself."

"She says not. Oh, I hope devoutly that the strain, whatever it is, will not prove too much for the poor girl."

I commented that I thought that unlikely; still, I thought that both brother and sister did look rather worn.

Sarah spoke rather mechanically of the possibility that no manifestations would occur at tonight's sitting. She said that such a negative result was frequently the case when conditions were not right.

Privately I was quite ready to attribute this seeming reluctance to perform to the presence of investigators—ourselves. But Holmes was not so sure.

So far, at least, tonight's sitting had not been canceled. Still, I could not escape the feeling that if the two mediums had felt themselves perfectly free in the matter, they would have preferred at least to postpone it.

Mrs. Altamont in conversation informed me that the

S.P.R., or Society for Psychical Research, had been founded in England in 1882. Its purpose, she stated, lay in the pursuit of objective research, not worship or the giving of spiritual solace.

Actually, as Holmes himself later pointed out to me, the practitioners and enthusiasts of mesmerism (or "hypnosis," as certain medical men had called it for a generation) were not likely to support the S.P.R., for they generally regarded spirit-rappings and table-turnings as fraudulent or foolish.

I commented that Holmes must have been doing a good bit of private research into these matters since 1897. He replied that he had begun his studies in the subject considerably earlier. "My two years in Tibet were not wasted, Watson."

"You have never spoken to me at length of what happened during that time."

"Your enthusiasm for such matters, old fellow, has been remarkably restrained. Suffice it to say that I thought the time had not been wasted when we had to face our peculiar difficulties of eighteen ninety-seven."

With the onset of the long summer twilight, and the drawing near of the hour for our appointed confrontation with the spirits, the physical atmosphere in and around the house seemed ever to grow more oppressively sultry. The rain that had threatened earlier did not come. Louisa's mother, all eagerness to begin the sitting, beseeched and encouraged her reluctant pair of sensitives to bring her daughter once more before her.

When Mrs. Altamont, reminded of Louisa, wept, one of the mediums told her: "The veil, as we know, is very thin, and you must let yourself be comforted with the certainty that she is not far away."

And suddenly Abraham gave indications of an extreme reluctance to conduct the séance at all. I saw and heard him, looking and sounding rather ill, propose quietly to his sister that they abandon the plan and leave the house at once.

Sarah Kirkaldy needed several minutes to argue and cajole Abraham into going on.

Listening, while trying not to appear to do so, I heard her last remark, which seemed to clinch the case: "Remember a' the chamber pots an' dirty boots!"

~ 5 ~

At five minutes before eleven o'clock, the appointed hour for the sitting, we all heeded the increasingly impatient, though still polite, urging of our hostess and assembled in the library.

This was my first opportunity to inspect the room where the séance was to take place, and once inside I gazed about with considerable interest. I wanted to see whether the mediums intended to use some elaborate wooden cabinet, or framework, as a so-called "spirit cabinet." I had heard such devices described and knew that they were favored by certain of the Kirkaldys' rivals; other psychic practitioners adopted an alternate method and simply curtained off a corner of a room by a suspended sheet or blanket, thereby achieving the same end of concentrating the "spirit force."

When I commented on the absence of any such device, Mrs. Altamont informed me that she had seen them used by others, but added—rather proudly, I thought—that the Kirkaldys could readily open the necessary pathways to the other world without such aid.

Nevertheless I remained alert to the possibility of physical trickery. The old oak wainscoting of the walls, and the extensive built-in bookshelves, formed ideal places, I thought, for concealing a secret door. I considered trying to make a careful examination—but surely Altamont himself would have been aware of any such contrivance had it existed in his own house.

The library was, as in most houses, on the ground floor. It communicated with the rest of the house by two interior doors. It was by one of these doors that we entered the room from the main hall, while the other, in the opposite wall of the library, opened into a narrow passage leading toward the kitchen and the servants' quarters.

Thunder grumbled in the distance as we assembled near the massive round table of dark wood which occupied the center of the room. Meanwhile the servants, following the orders of their mistress, were closing all the room's windows and drawing thick draperies over them. The electric chandelier had been switched on—Norberton House boasted a modified Swan System, dating from the 1880s, for the private generation of electricity—but even so, the corners of the room were dark and I began to find the atmosphere intensely oppressive.

Two large old mirrors, one framed in gilt and one in silver, both of which hung upon the east wall, were now starved for light. The room, being at the southwest corner of the house, would have been bright in ordinary daylight, for it was well supplied with windows. The three in the south wall were really French doors, extending almost from floor to ceiling and giving on a narrow terrace, beyond which I could glimpse the shrubbery forming part of the extensive garden through which Altamont had conducted Holmes and myself.

Thunder sounded again, closer this time.

The room contained comparatively little furniture. In the center of the broad red carpet, as I have already mentioned, had been placed a round table of dark wood, large enough for all of the participants to take their seats around it—and, as I thought, heavy enough that any experiments in psychic table-tipping would be truly impressive if they succeeded. In the center of the table, a single candle of red wax burned in an antique silver candlestick.

Holmes and I had already discussed in private, and later in the company of Altamont and Armstrong, the common varieties of tricks to be expected on such occasions. Our list, by no means complete, included the wind-up music box concealed in a spirit guitar, the musical instrument extended on a black folding pole from the spirit cabinet and seen to hang glowing in midair whilst being played supposedly by some spirit's fingers. Other tools of the trade included luminous paint, loops of dark thread for moving objects, and entire white, gauzy costumes, capable of being folded into incredibly small spaces for concealment. There were also telescopic reaching rods, and specially built shoes, easy to slide off and on again, allowing use of the medium's feet in various manipulations.

All of these preliminary arrangements having been completed to the Kirkaldys' satisfaction, the servants were sent out of the room. I thought I observed Cooper exchange a meaningful glance with the master of the house; I strongly suspected that one or more servants had secret instructions from Altamont, to keep guard, to be prepared to capture and hold any intruder.

The Altamont servants, as I had already begun to realize, were as sharply divided as their employers on the matter of spiritist phenomena, and some of them had no liking for the mediums and were eager to detect fraud.

At the request of Sarah Kirkaldy, Holmes and I made sure that both interior doors leading out of the room were bolted shut. We then moved on to examine the windows, satisfying ourselves that they were tightly closed and locked.

The hour of trial was now at hand, for the eight of us who had gathered in the darkened library. Besides Holmes and myself, our party included both parents and the sister of the recently interred girl, and the two Kirkaldys, as well as Martin Armstrong.

Holmes had already given me (and later Altamont and Armstrong) our final instructions, which in my case included orders not to try to seize any apparition—unless Holmes did so first.

The late twilight had been deepened, the fall of night hastened, by heavy clouds. Following our preparations, the time was a few minutes after eleven.

The Kirkaldys cautioned us against trying to turn on a light during the séance, or trying to touch any figure that might appear. They said they had good spiritualist reasons for these cautions.

I had expected the mediums to specify the seating arrangements, but neither of the Kirkaldys had any specific plan to propose. They deferred the question to the lady of the house, and Madeline Altamont, as a gesture of goodwill, left the decision to her husband. He in turn followed a plan which Sherlock Holmes had earlier suggested we should try, if possible, to follow.

I found myself seated directly facing the south wall with its three French windows. Young Rebecca Altamont had the chair immediately at my right. Beyond her was Martin Armstrong, and after him, Mrs. Altamont. Proceeding counterclockwise around the circle, Ambrose Altamont sat next to his wife. Then the young woman who claimed psychic powers, Sarah Kirkaldy, took the place where her left hand would be held by Louisa's father—secretly still the most determined skeptic. Next was Sherlock Holmes, who sat facing directly west. Abraham Kirkaldy completed the circle, being seated between myself and Holmes.

Sarah, as soon as we were all in our places, signaled to her brother with a small nod.

Before sitting down, Abraham Kirkaldy, suddenly assuming a look of dignity that belied his youth, stood gripping the back of his chair and gave a little speech. His Scottish accent, normally not very noticeable, grew stronger under stress.

"Ladies and gentlemen, I find m'self possessed o' certain powers—" here the youth paused momentarily, casting his gaze from one of us to another, not so much in challenge, I thought, as in a pleading for acceptance "—and these I shall be pleased to demonstrate, if it be possible, tonight. I shall be glad if you can throw any further light upon them. I hae little or nae control o'er them. They use me, but I dinna use them."

I thought this utterance had something of the air of a memorized speech, but it was delivered with real solemnity.

We settled into our chairs. Only one light now remained in the library—the single candle in the middle of the table.

Sarah Kirkaldy turned a pale face toward me. "Dr. Watson, will you blow out the candle, please?"

Without releasing my grip on either of the hands I held, I leaned forward and complied. Instantly, deep darkness engulfed us, moderated only by a faint ghost of illumination that entered the room from the nighttime garden, traces of light creeping in past the edges of the heavy drapes covering the mullioned windows in the west wall and the large glass folding doors in the south.

My last impression of the Kirkaldys, before the candle went out, was that they were both actually frightened, more excited than anyone else in the room, with the exception of Mrs. Altamont. Abraham's hand in mine twitched and trembled slightly.

"Hold the circle tightly . . . the power is here . . ." Again it was Sarah's voice we heard, while I thought that Abraham, just at my left, moaned slightly. Peering as accurately as I could toward him in the heavy darkness, I could see only a white blur of face. I could not tell whether or not his eyes were open, nor indeed could I have relied upon my eyes to determine who sat beside me. His hand now lay limp and dry in mine, as if he had fallen asleep.

I had been expecting something in the way of preliminary effects, and for all I know now, the Kirkaldys had indeed planned some fraudulent demonstration—but nothing of the kind took place. The deep darkness had endured for perhaps five minutes, perhaps longer, before an event occurred which was very strange indeed, though perhaps few or none of our party found it totally unexpected.

Though I was absolutely certain that neither of the hands I held had escaped me for an instant, despite all of our precautions, someone—or something—else, besides we eight who sat at table, had now come into the room.

In the near-perfect darkness, it was naturally impossible to be sure of any but the crudest contours of this figure; but what appeared to be a real, material form, that of a young girl in some kind of loose, flowing white garment, was certainly now standing, motionless, just inside the central pair of French doors. I was facing in that direction, and had been watching alertly, but still, except for the sudden appearance of the figure itself, I had seen no telltale sign that any of those windows might have been opened, or any disturbance of their draperies, which were outlined by a very faint illumination from outside.

In the gloom, I could not clearly see Louisa's mother, seated three spaces to my right, nor could I be certain that she had turned her head toward the visitor. But I could tell from the sharp sound of her indrawn breath that she had immediately become aware of the new presence.

A moment later, Mrs. Altamont began a joyful, almost hysterical though low-voiced, sobbing and keening.

The general reaction around the table was expressed by a louder sound, a rustle of clothing, a sharp tug that came transmitted like a galvanic shock round the circle of clasped hands, and the heavy scrape of chair legs on the carpet. I thought that Mrs. Altamont would have leaped to her feet, but a girl's or woman's voice, one I did not recognize, commanded sharply: "Don't break the circle!"

At the same instant the soft grasp of young Rebecca tightened upon my right hand with convulsive force; and I recall making a mental note of the fact, as a peculiarity to be remembered, that through all this, the right hand of Abraham Kirkaldy remained limp in my left.

"Who are you?" The question was put sharply, in the voice of Sarah Kirkaldy, and the fright in her voice was chilling.

To me, the soft answer, in a clear, new voice, was more frightening still: "I am Louisa—Louisa Altamont."

At that, both of Louisa's parents uttered incoherent sounds. Martin Armstrong also began to speak, but fell silent again before I could be sure of even his first intended word.

The figure in white, supposedly that of the drowned girl, was still standing near the curtained French windows. Now she changed her position slightly. Then, speaking in thin, halting tones like one entranced, like one repeating a lesson learned by rote, she recited: "There is a great wrong that must be righted before I can find rest. A stolen treasure that must be found—and given back—"

Whatever course the recitation might have taken from that point, the speaker was denied the opportunity to complete it. Her words were drowned out by the loud, repeated cries of Madeline Altamont. Despite the urgings of Sarah Kirkaldy, the mother could not or would not be silent, but continued a terrible struggle to force her own questions upon the attention of her daughter.

Ambrose Altamont, seated between his wife and Sarah, was, of all the people round the table, actually nearest to the apparition when it came in, but with his back turned to it.

Now Altamont, straining against the pull of those to right and left who gripped his hands, had twisted halfway around to confront this visitor with whom his wife was pleading. Against the background of the westernmost pair of French doors I could see the man's dim shape rising partially from his chair, and I heard him utter a dreadful, hoarse, incoherent cry.

A moment later the father, wrenching his hands free from the grip of those holding them, stood fully erect and went lurching toward the figure in white. He succeeded—as he reported later—in touching Louisa's hand. At this moment also, he was able to look closely into her face, and to hear her voice, perhaps murmuring words bearing upon some secret that he and his elder daughter alone had shared.

Altamont called her name, hoarsely, again and again. He was obviously overwhelmed by the conviction that after all, against all his beliefs and expectations, this was truly his daughter, restored to him by some miracle of spiritual power.

When the voice of the apparition replied to him, I thought that it had changed, become notably less forced and unnatural. "Father, I'm all right, really . . . except I . . . I can't . . ." She added more, but nothing that I could hear distinctly.

Moments after the circle of clasping hands was broken by Altamont's defection, it had utterly disintegrated. I jumped to my feet, with the final orders given me by Sherlock Holmes still ringing in my ears—we had discussed in advance what ought to be done in the case of some chaotic development like this.

My first effort was simply to turn on the electric chandelier. I had taken careful note of the position of the switch, on the wall to my left, beside the door leading to the hallway. My original intent, however, proved impossible to achieve in the darkness and confusion. Colliding blindly with other people and stumbling over fallen chairs, I found myself somewhat disoriented, groping over a blank wall after a switch that seemed to have perversely moved itself.

The night was full of cries and shouts in both men's and women's voices. Martin Armstrong, who had been sitting between Rebecca and Mrs. Altamont, later recounted that he had found himself stunned, confronted with the staggering fact that the woman he loved was not dead after all, but rather that she stood living, here in the same room with him. Martin had drawn his feet under his chair, in preparation for an all-out leap toward Louisa. He was filled with a mighty determination that he would at all costs not allow her to escape—

In the middle of all this, Abraham Kirkaldy cried out in a changed and terrible voice: "Stop! I see—" His words broke off at that point, his utterance degenerating into a hoarse cry of sheer horror. But a moment later his voice rang out clearly again: "Stop! A thing from hell is here among us!"

This declamation was followed by sounds from other members of the gathering, groans and protests, and a howl that raised the hair on the back of my neck.

Next young Kirkaldy shouted that the visitant should "Go back to your grave!"

I heard Martin Armstrong cry out like a man caught in the grip of a sudden and terrible new emotion, raising a desperate shout that rose clearly above the other confused noises in the room.

And I could distinguish the voice of Sherlock Holmes, masterful and incisive, urging calm, urging those present to let the figure alone. But alas, none of the others who heard him were paying much attention.

Armstrong, as he told me later, actually succeeded in reaching the visitant and attempted to prevent her getting away, meanwhile shouting for lights. But with a strength beyond the human, and a determination that Armstrong found inexplicable, the slender girl twisted and pulled herself free.

By this time, both of Louisa's parents were also clutching at the mysterious intruder, struggling with a terrible earnestness to hold her, as if they would by their own efforts cheat Death of his prize after all.

The girl's voice in the dark was heartrending. "Mother. *Father* . . ."

Listening, I received the impression that the undead girl was striving in agony to accomplish something. It was not a mere physical effort, but an attempt to convey to her parents that there was something that must be done before the recently undead, she herself in particular, could rest. Something that Louisa's parents must do—for *her* benefit.

"There is an ancient wrong which must be righted." And Louisa—increasingly I felt convinced that this was she—as if under some great compulsion, kept repeating a refrain of words to this effect: "What was stolen must be returned . . ."

Then suddenly the voice of the spectral figure broke off. And in another moment, surrounded and beset by the very people who had most loved Louisa Altamont during her breathing life, it abruptly turned and tore itself away.

The object of all tearful outcries and entreaties fled. I saw, in near darkness and yet with a convincing clarity, how her departing form made a ghostly, half-transparent image at the window-doors, white in the delicate illumination which crept in round the edges of the dark drapes. None of the three French doors opened, yet somehow, without so much as stirring one of those heavy folds of cloth, she had in a moment gone past them and was outside the house.

A moment later, the most easterly set of curtains was ripped aside, as Martin Armstrong, floundering in darkness, in desperate pursuit of his beloved, reached the French windows and found himself stopped there by latches and solid glass.

I could hear Armstrong, still calling the name of his beloved in an agony of hope, fumbling with the unfamiliar catch to get the window open, but failing to do so.

For a moment longer, the form that he pursued was clearly visible just outside, where light from other windows in the house cast a partial illumination across the terrace.

Armstrong, frustrated, turned back from the window with a muttered oath. He picked up one of the chairs from near the table, spun round again and swung it hard, smashing the window open. A second blow was necessary to widen the gap sufficiently; a moment later he had plunged out through the gap thus created, with Louisa's father close on his heels.

Sherlock Holmes, now shouting loudly but uselessly in a great effort to prevent some terrible mistake, and perhaps hoping to influence the girl by some means other than main force, followed the other men out. There came an additional crashing and shattering of glass.

Abandoning my effort to find the light switch in the unfamiliar room, I needed another moment or two to reach the broken window, then to stumble out through the enlarged gap and across the terrace after my friend. At the time I did not notice that I had torn my coat sleeve and scratched my arm on a jagged corner of glass.

But having reached the terrace, I could once more clearly see Louisa—I was now convinced that the visitor was indeed she, though vastly (and to my mind sickeningly) transformed. The girl in white stood near the center of the terrace, surrounded by a small group of struggling people, including her father, her fiancé, and Holmes.

The large expanse of one of the French doors, still unbroken and still closed, reflected the scene on the terrace brightly, illuminated as it was by sporadic moonlight as well as by light washing out of the house through the windows of other rooms. In that mirror I clearly saw the struggling group reflected—all save the central figure.

Our blond-haired visitor in white cast no trace of any image in the glass.

I thrust my hand, as if by instinct, into the pocket where I customarily carried my old service revolver, on the occasions when I went armed. But then I remembered that my revolver was still in London and realized that in any case the time had not come for using deadly force.

I had not been appointed judge, much less executioner. But whatever hopeful doubts might have persisted in my mind at the beginning of the séance were now gone. The nature of the horror we faced was clear. Beyond all question, the young girl in white was a vampire.

~ 6 ~

In the next instant I was bumped violently from behind by Abraham Kirkaldy. No doubt the impact, heavy enough to send me staggering across the terrace, was entirely accidental. The young medium had come stumbling out through the broken window after me, and on recovering my balance I turned to see him groping slowly with outstretched arms, as if in a trance, in the general direction of the figure in white.

Again and again the youth, his head thrown back, cried out his warnings about a thing from hell. He gestured wildly, emphasizing his unheeded commands that the intruder should go back to the nether regions whence it had come.

The gaunt lad was still standing close beside me as he shouted, pointing with an outstretched arm, though not at the figure of Louisa Altamont, but rather into the darkness beyond it. Once more he called out sharply, trying to banish from the house and terrace whatever entity it was that he alone, among us breathing folk, could see.

It was plain to me that the young man's fear, his attempt to assert authority, were not directed at the vampire girl. But for a moment I thought that she seemed to hesitate, as if on the verge of trying to obey his orders.

Then something almost invisible sighed softly in the night beside me, and I belatedly became aware—by what senses I am still not sure—of a heavy and forbidding presence. I saw—trying to regain the memory, I can only assert that I thought I saw—the suggestion of a masculine, malignant face, of greenish glaring eyes, their gaze directed not at me but at the young medium.

The air around me sighed again, and sang. I heard a savage impact—I could distinguish no weapon, but perceived only a dim, rushing movement in the air—and in that moment Abraham Kirkaldy collapsed upon the stones of the terrace without a groan, felled by a single blow that had torn his scalp and partially crushed his skull. Of Kirkaldy's attacker, I retained only the vague perception which I have already tried so inadequately to describe.

In the next few moments I beheld a sight which made my brain reel in new horror. Swiftly the figure of the girl in white swirled near the medium's fallen body, and bent low over him as if to bestow a kiss. Then she looked up, and in the moonlight I saw, by the dark stains around her fresh young mouth, that she had tasted his blood before she fled—or before she was pulled away, by the same almost-invisible power that had struck him down.

In the press and urgency of these events, I had momentarily lost sight of Sherlock Holmes, but now I caught a glimpse of my friend again, still endeavoring to keep Altamont and Armstrong away from the figure in white.

And then, in the next moment, Holmes was gone.

Quite distinctly I beheld his lean, strong body, legs kicking helplessly, caught up like a child's by some nearly invisible power, and whisked away in the departing rush of the malignant presence which had by now left my side. Let me repeat that at no time on the terrace had I been able to perceive this intruder as a distinctly human form. Rather I was aware only of a dim inhuman horror, which now vanished quickly into the depths of the nighttime garden, carrying Holmes with it.

Again I wished for my revolver, though even had I been armed I should hardly have dared to fire for fear of hitting Holmes himself. Running as quickly as I could toward the spot where I thought I had seen my friend and his kidnapper vanish, I caught one more glimpse of a shadowy figure—or possibly a pair of figures—darting on, some distance ahead of me.

Doing my best to keep my speeding quarry in sight, I carried on the chase for another forty yards or so, a distance that took me well down the slope and into the lower garden. Running in the darkness, I stumbled through flower beds and at last came crashing to a halt in the middle of some thick shrubbery. At that point, I was forced to admit to myself I had lost the trail.

I had succeeded in extricating myself from the bushes, and had just regained the proper path, when from the direction of the terrace I had so recently left, a woman's voice sounded, giving vent to a loud outcry of grief and desperation. Immediately I decided that I had better return to the house.

At a sound from behind me, I turned my head. My heart rose momentarily at sight of a dim figure walking uphill toward me, its feet crunching with a reassuring, solid hesitancy upon the gravel of the path. But it was only Martin Armstrong, who had left the group gathered just outside the house and followed me in my futile pursuit. Quickly overtaking me on his younger legs, the American had run some distance farther down into the garden, past the point where I had lost the path. But presently he, too, had lost sight of what he pursued and had decided to abandon the chase.

He came up to me now, out of breath but with an obscure triumph in his voice. "They're gone, Watson. They were too fast for me in the darkness. What did you see?"

Vaguely I was now aware that I had somehow torn my sleeve and trouser leg, and that I was seriously out of breath. "No more than a dim figure," I gasped. "But Holmes went with it. It carried him away."

Armstrong's vague outline beside me nodded. "That's very much what it looked like to me. They went in this direction—but there must have been more than one man, wouldn't you say? To abduct Sherlock Holmes in such a fashion?"

I murmured something.

During this brief exchange both of us had been trudging steadily uphill, and within a minute or so of our departure we were back on the terrace, where confusion and excitement reigned. Armstrong and I rejoined an uncertain number of dim figures that were still moving about in almost complete bewilderment, though now in relative quiet. Realizing that under the circumstances, very little could be accomplished without more light, I reentered the library through the broken window and went immediately to switch on the electric chandelier.

Inside the house, the impact of servants' fists could now be heard through both of the library's locked doors, as well as their muffled voices demanding to be answered, pleading for reassurance against the overwhelming evidence that something had gone terribly wrong.

Again, as in my earlier attempt, my progress toward the electric switch was impeded by disarranged furniture, and by collisions with one or more other people who were still moving about at cross-purposes in the darkened room.

When at last my fingers closed on the switch, and the lights in the library chandelier came on again, the sudden glare revealed Louisa's mother, sitting near the library table in one of the few chairs which remained upright, the flowers on her gay dress now sadly crushed and torn. With the impact of the dazzling light, Mrs. Altamont screamed. Her outcry was promptly repeated, became a dirge of renewed loss that went on and on. It was echoed by a fresh scream from out on the terrace, in the voice of young Sarah Kirkaldy.

Meanwhile both the father and the fiancé of Louisa Altamont had followed me back into the house. The older man and the younger alike were joyfully stunned—but the two of them were not, as I was soon to discover, rejoicing for exactly the same reason.

It was Altamont who spoke to me first. "She came back . . . I touched her, Dr. Watson. Twice I touched her hand, her arm." Extending his own trembling fingers, Louisa's father went on to tell me, in a halting, altered voice, of how he had held his daughter's hand and had been able to see her at very close range in the darkness. They had exchanged some words of mutual recognition. "She came back!" he repeated, softly marveling.

We now drew back the draperies from the windows, so that the electric light fell out strongly through the glass upon the terrace just outside. Asking a pale-faced Rebecca Altamont to see that my medical bag was brought down to me at once, I went out on the terrace again. My chief concern was for Abraham Kirkaldy. He was still lying almost exactly where I had seen him fall, although his sister, adding her lamentations to the noise, had lifted the young man's gory head into her lap.

Both of the elder Altamonts, as well as Martin Armstrong, had suffered minor injuries from broken glass and collisions in the dark, but none requiring my immediate attention. Hurrying to the side of the fallen youth, I bent over him and made an examination with the aid of the glaring electric chandelier inside. Immediately it was obvious that young Kirkaldy had suffered a severely torn scalp, and almost certainly serious injury to the skull beneath. The wound had the appearance of having been made by a hard blow with some sharp and heavy weapon. As usual with a serious laceration of the scalp, there was considerable bleeding. But at the moment, the victim still breathed.

While I was examining the young man, someone else, I believe it was Armstrong, at last went to unbolt and open the room's interior doors, admitting the servants who had been pounding on them and demanding to know whether their master and mistress were all right.

Altamont now had a joyous answer for the clamoring servants, who now poured into the library bearing lights and a variety of improvised weapons. "She came to us! To her old parents—and I had doubted, but I shall never doubt again!" He went to try to comfort his wife, who, rather than rejoicing in Louisa's return, was bemoaning her renewed loss. Neither had really taken any notice as yet of the new tragedy on the terrace—or of the kidnapping which had seemingly just occurred.

Looking around in the confusion, the fact struck me again, with even more ominous force than before, that Sherlock Holmes was still nowhere to be seen.

One of the servants had now brought my bag. Having done my best to stanch the bleeding of young Kirkaldy's scalp wound—there was nothing else I could do for him at the moment—I quickly descended once more into the garden a few yards west of the terrace and shouted Holmes's name repeatedly. But there was no reply. It seemed to me that he had been made to vanish into a darkness whose ominous silence swallowed violence and death alike.

Now I had a few moments in which to look about the library. Perhaps Louisa had dropped something, left some actual trace of her presence in the house? But in the general disarrangement and confusion I could discover nothing.

It upset me at the time, but perhaps it is not really to be wondered at that in the circumstances, confronted by marvels and by violent injury, no one else seemed much concerned about the fact that Holmes was missing. I believe it was generally assumed that he had gone in pursuit of some intruder, despite my denials that that had been the case. Even though I was sure that my old friend had been in distress when I last saw him, I was still able to hope that he would soon return.

Despite my attempts to give myself such reassurances my worry grew.

Meanwhile, the various minor injuries suffered in the outbreak of violence kept me busy for a time in my professional capacity. At intervals I went outside again and looked and listened, but neither my borrowed electric torch nor my ears gave me the slightest encouragement regarding the success of any renewed search.

The screams uttered by Louisa's mother had by this time declined into low, exhausted moans. Obviously the woman remained for the moment inconsolable. In a low voice she had begun lamenting, over and over, the fact that her beloved Louisa had been here, within reach, and then had been somehow driven away again.

Mrs. Altamont, evidently in some forlorn hope of tempting her lost daughter back, asked that the electric lights be once more turned off. Of course the request had to be refused, and I invoked my medical authority firmly enough that the servants obeyed me. Meanwhile young Rebecca Altamont was trying, in a broken voice, to comfort her mother, even while struggling to suppress her own sobs.

Louisa's father, obviously shaken to the depths of his being by the experience through which he had just passed, sympathized with his wife's grief, but the main focus of his attention remained elsewhere. The man kept wandering in and out of the house, from the terrace to the library and back again, looking about him hopefully at every step, as if he thought his daughter might appear again. At length he came inside, let himself down in one of the chairs turned sideways from the table, and sat there staring into space, his mouth open, his expression vacant, as if unaware that his hand was still bleeding from a piece of broken glass. A servant who came to help him was ordered absently away, so that the blood continued to drip, unnoticed by the victim, upon the carpet.

On approaching him with my professional manner I had better success, and soon succeeded in getting his hand bandaged. Still Altamont, though yielding to my ministrations, seemed scarcely aware of his injury. Gradually I understood that the man had undergone something approximating a religious conversion, during the last few minutes of darkness following the appearance of his daughter—the image, the figure he had seen, had very probably touched, had been genuinely that of his little girl.

As I tied the knot securing the bandage on his hand, he roused himself from this ecstatic trance to become aware of who I was and what I was doing. His manner turned grim. "I was wrong, Watson, I was terribly wrong. Oh, forgive me, Louisa—the blessed spirits will forgive me, I know they will!"

"The blessed spirits?" I asked hollowly—my thoughts were still full of that shadowed horror which had hung near me in the darkness, and had struck twice at members of our group.

Martin Armstrong, who had now collapsed into another chair nearby, was also overjoyed, but while listening to Louisa's father, kept shaking his head in obvious disagreement. "No," the young man interjected at one point. "No, sir, you don't understand. Oh, she came back, she did indeed! But the blessed spirits had nothing to do with it!"

The father, however, ignored this comment, and springing up suddenly from his chair, began clutching at one person after another, weeping in his growing joy and his continuing amazement.

Repeatedly he told us how Louisa, in the brief interval when she had been present, had spoken to her father of things no one else could possibly have known. Though stunned with astonishment, he was certain of her identity.

"And then . . . and then . . . certain things happened. There was a dreadful interference . . . which drove her away again." Once more a stern expression came into his face, and he looked around the room, as if seeing it for the first time since the lights had been restored. "Where," he demanded, "is Mr. Holmes?"

Armstrong, in the background, was still in smiling disagreement, but made no further argument.

Tersely I explained, as best I could, the situation with regard to Holmes.

As he heard me out, Ambrose Altamont, his clothing disheveled, his hair standing on end, assumed a new expression. Presently he began to speak in a much harder voice. In a few moments I understood—he now blamed Holmes and me for his daughter's untimely flight and the accompanying violence.

"Sir," I protested, "it was neither Holmes nor I who struck down the young man lying on your terrace!"

Energetically he waved off my protests. "No, of course not. Not with your own hands. But it was the interference, you see, that caused the trouble—it must have been."

I would have protested, but fiercely he waved me to silence. "There are dark powers as well as light. I was warned about such things, but I would not listen. I did not believe, because I had not seen." Then Altamont paused, seeming to reconsider. "Not that it is entirely—perhaps not even chiefly—your fault. I must share fully in the blame, Dr. Watson. I must curse the day when I brought you two here to interfere."

Our client—now evidently our former client—went on to express great concern over the fate of Abraham Kirkaldy, which he at last seemed to realize, and to issue me a stern warning that all further harassment—by which he evidently meant all investigation—of the mediums must cease. Obviously the spirits were angry at our hostile intrusion, and with some justification.

Yes, Altamont was saying in effect, it was certainly too bad if something terrible had happened to Holmes, and if something even worse had happened to the poor young man—yes, he, Louisa's father, blamed himself for bringing in the detectives.

He fixed me with the eye of a fanatic, even as he attempted to comfort his wife. "Can you understand now, Doctor, that we are dealing here with powers that must not be mocked? I tell you sir, my worst fear now is that tonight's interference may have driven our little girl away from us for good!" And Madeline Altamont screamed again.

Meanwhile Martin Armstrong and I had begun to insist that the police be called in—some unknown person had committed an act of violence which was almost certain to prove fatal. And—a servant discovered the fact while we were arguing—a robbery had taken place as well. A safe in Ambrose Altamont's study was found open, and some items of jewelry it had contained, all fairly ordinary things of no enormous value, had been taken.

Fortunately, Norberton House was equipped with a telephone.

The local constabulary were on the scene within twenty minutes following my call. A quarter of an hour after their arrival, they were in agreement with me that the help of Scotland Yard would, in this case, be very desirable if not absolutely essential. Holmes was still missing. No trace could be found of the weapon which had struck down Abraham Kirkaldy, while it was obvious that his injury must be due to something more than an accident.

Four more hours passed, and full daylight had broken over the scene before Scotland Yard's help arrived, in the person of Inspector Merivale, whom I was heartily glad to see.

Merivale was a tallish man with keen blue eyes, dark hair, and a small mustache of which he was rather vain, frequently stroking or smoothing it with a finger. He was, I knew, regarded by Holmes as one of the best of the younger detectives at Scotland Yard. On his arrival he justified this opinion, as I thought, by temporarily setting aside the clamor of other witnesses wanting to be heard, to listen very seriously to my testimony regarding the disappearance of Mr. Sherlock Holmes. To my disappointment, it soon became apparent to me that the representative of the Yard more than half-believed that Holmes had vanished of his own volition, and would reappear in the same way when he was ready.

Needless to say, I made no mention to anyone, including Merivale, of Holmes's earlier suspicions regarding vampires, and how they had been confirmed. Whatever help my old friend might need from me, I would be unable to provide it while confined in an asylum.

An energetic search of the immediate vicinity revealed no trace of any skulking strangers—or of Holmes. At the direction of Scotland Yard, plans were made to bring in a dog to follow the trail. Within an hour of Merivale's arrival, the animal and its handler were on the scene, and I provided them with some items of clothing Holmes had brought with him from London and which were now in his room. But after following what seemed to be the right trail through the garden for twenty yards or so, the brute came to a sudden stop, howled pitifully, and absolutely refused to go on.

Despite what had happened to young Kirkaldy, Merivale professed himself doubtful that Holmes faced any immediate peril; fraudulent mediums were not, as a rule, violent. Then he added: "You know, Dr. Watson, better than anyone else, what he's like. The tricks he's played on all of us down through the years."

I shook my head wearily. "Nothing that happened last night was a trick, Inspector. Not on our part, at any rate."

All the police were willing to do whatever they could for Sherlock Holmes; but after the most thorough search possible of the house and grounds, they had no trail to follow.

I thought, but carefully did not say, that a powerful vampire, even when put to the inconvenience of carrying a breathing victim, was unlikely to leave any discernible trail, particularly after dark.

It was at that point that I happened to catch a glimpse of myself in one of the dark old mirrors still hanging on the library wall. Taking note of my eyes red-rimmed and sleepless, my torn sleeve, the blood of Abraham Kirkaldy which had dried upon my hands and clothes, I was forced to admit to myself that I could do nothing more. And that there was only one person in the world to whom it was now possible for me to turn for effective help.

Being forced to the admission made it no easier to accept.

~ 7 ~

Ascending briefly to my room, I changed my clothing and washed my hands. Under the circumstances, sleeping in Norberton House for even an hour was of course out of the question, and I promptly came downstairs again. In the midst of the excitement already prevailing in the household, my announcement that I must return to London as soon as possible created no particular stir.

On my orders, the unconscious form of Abraham Kirkaldy had already been carried into the house and placed on a sofa in the sitting room next to the library. A local physician well known to the Altamonts had been called in, and I was quickly relieved of any further responsibility for the patient. I am sure that the local police would have preferred that I remain in the house along with the other witnesses, but Merivale quietly overruled them. He had a carriage outside, he said, and offered to drive me to the station.

Armstrong immediately spoke up and volunteered to convey me there more speedily, in his motorcar.

I thought that the young American had some particular reason for wanting to speak to me in private, or at least without the inevitable interruptions to which our conversation would be subject in the house, and so I accepted his offer. But just as we were about to leave, Inspector Merivale suddenly announced his intention of accompanying us.

It was perhaps six o'clock in the morning when the forty-horsepower engine of Armstrong's Mercedes allowed itself to be cranked to life and the three of us departed from the sleepless Altamont household. Few people in the other houses we passed appeared to be stirring, though the summer sun had risen hours earlier.

Armstrong's motive for creating an opportunity of serious, uninterrupted conversation with me—I thought he rather welcomed a chance at the inspector also—was soon apparent. While driving, the young man strove earnestly to impress us both with the importance of an unremitting effort, made by all concerned, to find his living bride-to-be.

Armstrong was unshaven and looked haggard, as I daresay we all did following our sleepless night. But the young man was also intensely animated, and his whole bearing and attitude testified to his high elation.

Despite his weariness, the gaze he turned on me was luminous and triumphant. "She's alive, Dr. Watson—you saw her!"

His enthusiasm aroused in me only a mixture of darker emotions. "Is she?" I replied. "I can swear only that I saw someone enter the library while we sat round the table. It was a woman, I believe. A vague shape moving in almost total darkness."

My answer failed to dampen Armstrong's cheeriness. "But you didn't get as close to her as I did. And you had never met Louisa before last night. It was she, I have no doubt of that!"

In fact, it seemed to me that during the confusion on the terrace, I might have, for a moment, approached the apparition almost as closely as had Armstrong. And I was only too certain of what I had seen, in the way of a mouth stained with human gore—and of what I had not seen in the reflecting glass. But there was nothing to be gained by arguing the point with Armstrong.

The young man's state of exaltation persisted. He continued to murmur joyous variations on his central theme: that his beloved Louisa was still alive.

But from time to time, his overpowering joy in the survival of his beloved alternated with fresh concern about the dangers which she might even now be facing.

"There are the two mediums—inspector, you must have the truth out of them!"

My medical experience told me that Abraham Kirkaldy was dying and would almost certainly never be fit to answer questions, even though the Altamonts were determined to provide him with the best care possible. But Sarah Kirkaldy was still on the scene and capable of speech, though presently in a state of shock; and Armstrong expressed his determination to have the full truth from her as soon as possible.

Merivale, looking at the young man with curiosity, assured him grimly that Sarah had already been seriously questioned, that a police matron had been summoned to stay with her, and that further intensive interrogation was planned. Also the background of both Kirkaldys would be thoroughly checked out.

I was firmly convinced that Armstrong's current views regarding his beloved were mistaken, and I was determined not to encourage them.

"I think," I said, "that the investigation from now on must certainly follow a different course."

"You bet it will!" And Armstrong had nothing more meaningful to say until we were inside the station waiting for the train.

We had reached the station in ample time, there being no sign as yet of the early train. At that hour we had the platform to ourselves. For a minute or two we stood waiting, I with my bag beside me, when Armstrong suddenly burst out again, as if with the enthusiasm of some fresh discovery: "She's alive, Watson! Do you realize that?"

Still I could not even pretend to share the young man's passion. In his innocence he meant, of course, that Louisa Altamont was still alive in the normal breathing sense—and I had seen convincing evidence that that could not be so. Again I muttered something noncommittal.

Armstrong sobered, seeing my doubts; but he had misinterpreted them. He added: "Not that she is safe, of course. Yes, I quite see that. They—whoever they are—have kidnapped her. Yes, I think there can be no other explanation. So my darling is still in deadly danger, and therefore I say we must move quickly."

"Kidnapped!"

He blinked at me, and then at the inspector. "Yes. Surely you see it now? Behind it all must be an attempt to get at Louisa's parents, to extort money from them—that must be it. You heard the words she was compelled to say, about seeking the return of some stolen treasure?"

"I daresay we all heard something of the kind." And I exchanged looks with Merivale, who had been listening to us intently and who, from his helpless expression, appeared to be drifting farther and farther out to sea.

"Well, then!" Armstrong paced and gestured expansively. "Naturally the Kirkaldys must be involved in the plot. They would know clever ways, conjurer's tricks, for bringing a person in and out of a locked and sealed room, like the library last night. But they're obviously not the chief villains. You've only to talk to Sarah, and look at what's happened to her brother, to understand that. Someone else must be the brains behind the whole affair. Someone else who was there in the dark last night, and struck down Abraham. Inspector, you agree with me, don't you? You see how things must stand?"

Merivale heaved a sigh. "Can't say I feel confident just

yet, sir, that we have any explanation that'll properly fit all the facts. But it looks like murder now, and you may rest assured that we'll do our best to get to the bottom of the business."

I really believe young Armstrong did not hear this reply, that he was aware only of its soothing tone; for even as the words were spoken, he had gone momentarily rapt again, lost in the exaltation of knowing that his Louisa—as he thought—still breathed. But a few seconds later he had once more turned to me, wearing a puzzled look.

"Watson, excuse me, but did I miss something? I fail to understand why you're so anxious to return to London before Louisa has been located—and while Mr. Holmes is still missing. It seems to me that if he's really been taken captive as you suggest, the same people must be holding both of them."

I gave some excuse regarding my old war wound and murmured something to the effect that I should not be of much help in searching the countryside. In addition, I assured the young man, there were matters in London which demanded my immediate attention. Meanwhile, of course, I was privately sure in which direction lay my only real hope of helping Holmes.

Inspector Merivale had so far made no comment regarding my eagerness to depart, and offered none now. But the Scotland Yard man smiled at me in a knowing and yet irritated way; his expression seemed to say that he was well aware some secret purpose must underlie my removal to London—that the disappearance of Holmes had very likely been a deliberate contrivance, part of some scheme carefully worked out in advance by the great detective, which I was privileged to share to some degree; and that he, the inspector, rather resented being left out of the intrigue.

In the circumstances I could say or do little to assure him that such was not the case.

"Mesmerism, that's it," Armstrong suddenly announced with an air of triumph. Looking at each of us in turn, he nodded decisively. Evidently, during his intervals of abstraction, the young American was working out to his own satisfaction the details of a theory explaining the mystery of Louisa's reappearance.

" 'Mesmerism'?" the inspector inquired wearily.

"Yes. As I said before, it has to be some kind of a gang, very well organized, and they've been holding her captive under a hypnotic influence. Nothing else will quite explain all the details, such as Louisa's being compelled to say exactly what they wanted, when she was among us."

Merivale, whose night must have been very nearly as sleepless as Armstrong's or my own, drew a long, slow breath, and then at last gave vent to his irritation. "See here, sir, we'd better get one or two things straight right now."

"Yes?"

Merivale's voice was blunt. "Did you, or did you not, see Miss Louisa Altamont lying dead less than a month ago? Did you not see her put into the family vault?"

"I . . . had thought I did." The young American looked grim for a moment. Then his face cleared and he burst out: "But now I know better! Inspector, I am certain that the living girl I saw last night—and touched, and spoke with, in that dark room and on the terrace—I *know* she was my Louisa. Great God, don't you suppose I could recognize the one I—" For a moment his feelings overcame him.

Presently, having recovered himself, Armstrong went on in a calmer voice. Evidently it was only now becoming clear in his mind that the great and joyous fact of Louisa's resurrection might not be nearly as obvious to others as it was to him.

"As to the identity of the poor girl we buried last month . . . well, the truth is, I was totally mistaken. It's been said that all dead bodies look alike. It was certainly someone who in life must have strongly resembled Louisa."

Merivale still fixed him with his steady policeman's gaze. "You are asking us to believe that the corpse of some stranger—a body that I suppose was conveniently provided by this gang of which you speak—was put into the Altamont family mausoleum? Under Louisa's name?"

Armstrong only glared back stubbornly.

The inspector persisted. "And their motive?"

"Money."

"Ah? But I am told that neither of the Kirkaldys has ever asked for money. There was the robbery, of course, though certainly not of any treasure. We have yet to see how that's connected with the rest. And in my experience, sir, people attempting a swindle or extortion may begin by kidnapping. But not by faking a death, or committing murder, and then bringing back a ghost."

"Inspector, all I know is that last night—"

Merivale interrupted brutally. "You realize that your theory requires Louisa's parents to have been mistaken, too, at the time of the burial? That they did not know their own daughter?"

There was a brief pause before Armstrong replied, but his answer when it came was serene with quiet triumph: "They knew her last night. And so did I."

Merivale was momentarily taken aback. But then, seemingly determined to settle once and for all this theory of a revived Louisa, the inspector returned relentlessly to the attack. "Forgive me, sir, I know these are painful matters, but if we are to take your theory seriously I must probe into them."

"Go ahead."

"Very well. My understanding is that the body—that of the drowned girl you buried last month—was not mutilated in any way? In particular, there was no injury about the face?"

The youth heaved a great sigh. "No. The coroner of course concluded that she had died of drowning. Scarcely a scratch was visible, as I recall. Except for the rigor of death, the girl's face was quite undamaged. But ah, what a difference, now that I look back! How could I have ever been deceived? Dead is dead, while Louisa is so, so essentially, unquenchably alive . . ."

Certain ineradicable memories, acquired in 1897, prompted me to break in with a question: "Were there any wounds, even small ones, elsewhere than on the face?"

Both men looked round blankly at my unexpected interruption. Then Armstrong responded: "Nothing of importance, as far as I know. Now that you mention it, it seems to me that the coroner did mention two small scratches, or punctures, on the throat. But I noticed nothing of the kind. Perhaps the mortician could tell you more about the details of the poor girl's condition—whoever she was."

Merivale was frowning at an Americanism. " 'Mortician'? You mean the undertaker? Ah, just so." The inspector nodded, then asked: "Once again, either at the time of the tragedy or since, have Louisa's mother or father ever expressed the slightest doubt that the body found on the bank of the river was their daughter's?"

"They have given no sign of any such uncertainty," Armstrong admitted.

"Even now?"

"Even now," Martin reluctantly agreed. It was his turn to sigh. "I talked with both of them just before we left the house. They both realize now that it was truly Louisa who came to us last night—but they insist on regarding her as some kind of ghost, or ectoplasmic form." The young American shook his head in pitying amusement. "They've both been taken in by this spiritualist nonsense."

And he continued to insist that his beloved Louisa was not dead, had never been dead, but that she had been somehow imprisoned or enslaved, and must be rescued.

Suddenly, pacing the platform and then spinning round on his heel to confront Merivale, he had a new suggestion: "It occurs to me that there's a simple answer, Inspector. If you doubt what I am telling you, have the body exhumed. If you cannot find the living woman, you know where the dead one lies. There must be, if we look for it, some difference discoverable to prove that that poor girl in the tomb is not Louisa Altamont."

The inspector growled something to the effect that, unless the girl's parents suggested such a course, he could not consider it.

I, for my part, endeavored to be comforting, insofar as that was possible without contributing to the false hopes Armstrong had so rapidly built up. The inevitable crash of disillusionment, when it came, would be violent indeed. With our adventure of 1897 in mind, I feared that exhumation might very well disclose inexplicable horror, and I was perfectly certain that nothing in the way of comfort was at all likely to result.

And yet I could tell no one openly that the conclusion I had drawn from the apparition was quite different from young Armstrong's—and from any speculative theory of Inspector Merivale's. While Armstrong had concentrated entirely on the essential presence of that white figure, I had carefully observed the mystery of its coming and going, the fact of its passing unhindered through locked doors or windows. Above all, I had noted the absence of any reflection in the mirror formed by the windows—and all I had observed had taken me back six years.

Abruptly the young American, seemingly unable to contain his excitement, and evidently despairing for the moment of making us see the glorious truth, announced that he was driving back to Norberton House at once and asked if the inspector wanted to return with him.

Merivale shook his head. "No, sir, thank you; I'm going to try to get an hour or two of sleep here at my inn. I'm fair beat, and I've already arranged for a room at the Saracen's Head." The distinctive signboard of that establishment could be seen clearly, swinging slightly in the morning breeze, not a hundred yards from where we were standing, down the main street of the village.

Armstrong did not delay, but left us with an impatient wave; in a few moments he had cranked his motor into roaring life again, and was gone, leaving a faint cloud of dust hanging in the village air.

In the ensuing silence, the inspector and I were left alone, at least for a few moments, on the platform at Amberley Station. There were indications that this time alone would be brief, for already the whistle of the oncoming train could be heard and the smoke of its engine was visible above some distant trees.

Merivale began by informing me frankly that he did not know what to make of the claim that Louisa Altamont might be still alive.

"See here, Dr. Watson, I'll put my trust in you as a steady, reasonable observer of last night's events. And as a student of the whole affair up to this point. No doubt Mr. Holmes, before he went away, shared with you all his thoughts on the subject?"

With that the inspector fell silent, assuming an expectant look I found quite irritating. I said: "I am afraid that Mr. Holmes does not always share his thoughts with me. As for last night's apparition, I never approached it quite as closely as did either Armstrong or the Altamonts—or Sherlock Holmes. And of course I was never acquainted with the girl in life."

"I see." Merivale, hands behind his back, leaned forward, scrutinizing me closely. Again, delicately stroking his mustache, he frowned as if he still thought I might be holding something back. "First, in the interest of thoroughness, let me be absolutely clear on one point. Does Mr. Holmes have any theory along that line . . . that Louisa Altamont might still be living?" His deprecating smile indicated what answer he fully expected to receive.

I did my best, in my exhausted state, to consider my reply carefully. I was constrained by the fact that, at some future point, it might become necessary, regardless of the risk to my reputation, to reveal all to the police. "I cannot say that he had ruled out the possibility," I responded finally.

Merivale's jaw dropped, and he stared at me in astonishment. "By all that's holy! You mean the young chap might be right? Then who was it that her parents buried here three weeks ago?"

Already I regretted my first reply. "Inspector . . . I will say this much: I believe you would be wise to delay any inquiries along that line until . . . until you are able to consult with Holmes himself upon the subject."

Merivale scratched his head, then smoothed his mustache. "Well, I suppose that's not much to ask; Lord knows, there are plenty of trails to follow that look more promising. Those two mediums, to begin with."

We briefly discussed other aspects of the case, including the mysterious jewel robbery, before my train pulled into the station.

Merivale's parting advice, as I climbed aboard, was to get some rest. "As I told the young man, Dr. Watson, that's what I intend to do myself. I had a full day yesterday and I'm about at my own limit. A couple of hours' sleep, then back to work. By noon I'll have twenty men on the job here, and I promise you we'll find Mr. Holmes if he's still in the area—and willing to be found."

I muttered something in response, and repressed an

urge to underline for the inspector the fact that neither Holmes nor I had yet turned fifty. Though Merivale had actually said nothing about my age, it seemed to me that in his urging me to rest, there was a certain almost-patronizing tone, that of a grown son or daughter looking after an aged parent. A strong implication that neither Holmes nor I were as young as we once were, and that in dealing with the twentieth century and its affairs, we must expect to find ourselves occasionally too exhausted to keep up.

In fact I dozed on the train, caring not what the other passengers in my carriage might think.

It was a little before noon when I disembarked from a cab in Baker Street, and saw the first newspaper headlines proclaiming that Sherlock Holmes had disappeared. Other sensational aspects of the previous night's events were also featured in large print.

MYSTERIOUS SÉANCE IN BUCKS
SHERLOCK HOLMES MISSING
FAMOUS DETECTIVE ABDUCTED TO OTHER WORLD?
"DEAD" HEIRESS STILL ALIVE?

It occurred to me that one or more of the servants at Norberton House had very likely been talking to reporters—and only then did I belatedly recall that Armstrong himself was a journalist, probably not loath to report on private matters to his London colleagues if by doing so he thought he could facilitate the search for Louisa.

I ignored the inspector's well-meant advice to get some rest. (And did my best to put out of my mind his insinuations, however well-founded, on the subject of age.) Instead I nerved myself for my next task, that of summoning a vampire. I fully expected that the experience would not be pleasant, though its exact nature still remained to be discovered.

~ 8 ~

On entering our old lodgings in Baker Street, I found two messages awaiting me. Both were notes in the handwriting of our landlady, Mrs. Hudson. The first one I happened to pick up was her record of a telephone message, received an hour before my arrival: Count Kulakov—Mrs. Hudson had spelled the name out carefully, in block letters—had telephoned to offer me his sympathy and would 'phone back at another time. After puzzling briefly over the question of who Count Kulakov might be, I could only conclude that he was an acquaintance of Sherlock Holmes and had already seen the early morning newspapers.

The second message I considered of vastly greater moment. It recorded another telephone call, this one from Mycroft, Sherlock Holmes's elder brother. Immediately this intelligence drove all thoughts of the unknown Count Kulakov from my mind.

And in my memory rang certain words Sherlock had said to me at the time of our adventure six years earlier, in the only discussion in which my friend had ever drawn back for me the curtain which concealed from the world the mysterious and terrible events of his own childhood.

On that occasion Holmes had said: "Watson, you must pledge me this instant, upon your honor, that you will never mention the subject of vampires to my brother Mycroft; it is the one thing that would undo him utterly . . . Mycroft's childhood must have been worse than mine, for he is seven years my senior, and must have seen more, and understood more at the time . . . the mere mention of vampires could destroy him."

Once more I scanned the message from Mycroft. It begged me to telephone him as soon as possible—and of course I moved to comply with this request at once, using the instrument in our sitting room.

The telephone rang even as I was reaching for it.

The voice on the line, though distorted somewhat by its passage over the wires, was undeniably that of Mycroft, and called up in my mind's eye a vivid image of the man himself: considerably taller and stouter than his brother, yet bearing a strong family resemblance.

Mycroft had seen the morning papers with the news of Sherlock's disappearance, and from his agitated manner it was soon evident that certain elements in the story had strongly suggested to his clever brain the horrible truth—that vampires were involved.

"Watson, tell me the truth—what is happening?"

"Mr. Holmes—" I began.

"Watson, I beg of you, put an end to this damned formality between us! How long have we known each other?"

"I—"

"I'll tell you. Almost fifteen years have passed since my brother introduced us. That was at the time of the Affair, as you called it, of the Greek Interpreter."

"Is it really fifteen years, then?"

"It is indeed. Consult your records if you doubt the fact. No doubt you would find it difficult, and perhaps confusing, to call me simply 'Holmes,' as you and Sherlock cling so obstinately to that form of address between yourselves. But this is an emergency, and 'Mr. Holmes' is no longer acceptable. Therefore, from now on I intend to call you 'John,' and you will call me by my Christian name as well."

"Mycroft, then," I responded. But my heart sank when I considered what I ought to say to Mycroft next.

He was too impatient to wait be addressed. "It is true, then, that Sherlock has disappeared?"

"I fear so."

"Does the matter really stand substantially as the newspaper stories have it?"

"I have not yet read them—I have seen only the headlines. I am afraid—"

"Then the most startling particulars are true—I mean, that he has been carried off by—how does the newspaper put it?—by 'some mysterious agency'? Following—what does it say?—'an attempt to communicate with the spirits of the dead'?"

"I suppose the stories are substantially correct," I admitted. "Although I have not read them yet. The attempt was made to reach one spirit only," I amended—and again could not think of what I ought to say next.

"The spirit of the recently deceased young woman, Louisa Altamont?"

"Yes. At the request of her parents . . . of her mother in particular."

"And you are telling me that this attempt to reach beyond the grave . . . in some way succeeded?" I could sense him waiting with a feverish concentration for my answer.

"I . . ."

Mycroft's keen brain—his brother considered him his intellectual superior—evidently read volumes into my sheer clumsy hesitation. "I beg of you, John, tell me the truth. Tell me all you know about the 'mysterious agency' that carried Sherlock off."

"It was a human agency, of that much I am sure."

"One man?"

"I believe so, yes."

"A man, I take it, of phenomenal powers—of a truly extraordinary nature?"

"Yes, Mycroft. Yes."

There came over the wire what sounded like a despairing sigh. "John, I am going to ring off now. I am coming round to Baker Street to see you." This announcement, to anyone who knew Mycroft's fixed habits, was startling in the extreme. "I have in hand another matter or two of the greatest urgency, requiring my attention first. But you may expect me within the hour."

Mrs. Hudson, who had also seen the newspapers, was naturally disturbed by my confirmation of the fact that Holmes was missing. But, as she reminded me with determined cheerfulness, we had weathered many a crisis in the past; and this latest difficulty did not delay her orders that my bath be drawn at once, and that a hearty breakfast be made ready for me when I came down to the sitting room shortly after noon.

Freshly bathed, shaved, dressed, and fed, I felt my energies somewhat renewed. Still I had to force myself to put aside my worries concerning Mycroft, and all other matters not bearing directly on the problem at hand, and concentrate upon the effort now required of me, to establish contact with Prince Dracula. This task had been the reason for my return to London.

To begin with, I had no idea of where the prince might presently be found, no reason to believe that he was even in England. As far as I was aware, Holmes had maintained no steady or regular contact with Dracula over the six years since our first encounter. But years ago my friend had had the foresight to inform me that a definite summoning procedure had been arranged, at the same time warning me that it was to be used only in case of emergency. The necessary information, Holmes had assured me, was filed, indexed by means of code words I was required to memorize, among his papers in our lodgings. Duplicate materials were stored in the vault of the Capital and Counties bank.

As I began my search, I could not rid my mind of my worries regarding Mycroft. And in fact the man himself arrived, and was shown up to our rooms while my preparations were still under way.

As Sherlock Holmes had once remarked upon a similar occasion, I could not have been more startled to see a planet departing from its orbit, so proverbial was the fixity of the man's daily routine. The morning of each business day saw Mycroft leave his rooms in Pall Mall for his (deceptively small and unassuming) office in Whitehall; the evening saw him walk back to his lodgings; and he was seen nowhere else, save in the Diogenes Club, which was just opposite his rooms.

One glance at the materials I had begun to arrange upon the table—the old book, the mirror, the candle, and the tied-up lock of graying human hair—sufficed to reveal the truth of the matter to him at once.

"So," he murmured abstractedly, rubbing his massive, clean-shaven chin with a broad, trembling hand, as he observed these preparations. "So, it has come to that again."

Regarding my visitor, I beheld a man now in his middle fifties, his hair now substantially more gray than dark, a change from the last time I had seen him, a year or two earlier.

Mycroft was, as I have already noted, a much larger and stouter man than Sherlock. His body was absolutely corpulent, but his face, though large, had preserved something of the sharpness of expression which was so remarkable in that of his brother. His eyes, of a peculiarly light, watery gray, seemed always to retain that faraway, introspective look which I had only observed in Sherlock's when he was exerting his full powers.

So far I had of course held to the pledge requested of me by Sherlock regarding his brother and the mention of vampires; but now it was Mycroft himself who had raised the dreaded subject, and I could only suppose that a total refusal on my part to discuss it might strike him even more terribly than the truth.

Before 1897, I had considered vampires (on those rare occasions when the word, the idea, had crossed my mind at all) as nothing more than tropical bats—any further interpretation of the word was utter rubbish, the material of lurid fiction and superstition. The events of that year of Her Majesty's Diamond Jubilee had disabused me of my basic misconceptions on the subject—but in truth I now did not know what to think.

However, I judged it necessary to give Mycroft the facts, putting as optimistic an interpretation on them as possible. He appeared much perturbed, though not at all surprised. To my relief, the news at least did not cause him to faint, or to collapse. In a voice that quavered only slightly he assured me that, while garlic might sometimes be an effective repellent, the efficacy of crucifixes and holy water must be regarded, for this purpose, as mere superstition.

"I am aware of that, Mycroft," I assured him patiently.

"Are you indeed?" He dabbed at his broad brow with a handkerchief. "It somewhat relieves my mind to hear it."

Impulsively my visitor went on to discuss briefly the history of the Holmes family as it had been affected by vampires. The main problem (it pains me even now to set the matter down; therefore I pass over it quickly) had been the vampirism, developed after her sons were born, of Mycroft's and Sherlock's mother.

This conversation on Mycroft's part was conducted, understandably, with intense emotion; and he then begged me to allow him to take himself away, before there was the least prospect of Prince Dracula actually appearing in our rooms. I had the impression that he would not have been surprised had his distant cousin arrived upon the scene in a dazzling flash and a cloud of smoke, like some stage representation of Mephistopheles.

When Mycroft had gone, I returned without hesitation to the task I found myself required to do. Finding the information and the necessary materials concealed among my friend's private archives had been actually the work of only a few minutes, since I had fortunately remembered the essential code word by which the items were indexed. Putting the information and materials, once obtained, to their proper use proved considerably more difficult.

Until now Holmes had given me not the slightest hint of what his special procedure for communicating with Prince Dracula might be, and I in my reluctance to think about the matter at all had not endeavored to find out. I was somewhat relieved on discovering that the details, which were distasteful, were not as bad as I had feared: The summoning involved the reading aloud of a few Latin verses from an old book, and the simultaneous burning of a lock of what appeared to be human hair—the latter provided with the book—before a mirror. This performance, strongly suggestive (to say the least) of magic, even of witchcraft, was most uncongenial to my nature. Yet I dared not even hesitate, as the matter had already been unavoidably delayed. Holmes's old chemical workbench provided me with the space and the small flame that I required.

Bolting our sitting-room door on the inside, I began. So repugnant did I find this business to common sense, so mocked by the warm summer sunshine at the window and the mundane noises of the street outside, that three or four times during the course of the brief ritual I found myself on the verge of damning it all as foolishness, consigning to perdition the book, the hair, and the small mirror which also played a part, and seeking some other means to locate the man I wanted. Only the certainty that I was following Holmes's instructions, which had been given in deadly earnest, and the knowledge that I had not the faintest notion of any alternate method of procedure, caused me to persevere.

My task was soon completed, but no immediate result was visible. I confess that while pondering the situation, wondering if I had erred somewhere, I fell asleep in my chair from sheer exhaustion. When I awakened, at seven upon a clouded summer evening, my neck and limbs were stiff, and for a moment or two I could not remember why I found myself once more in this familiar room rather than at home with my wife in our recently acquired lodgings in Queen Anne Street.

Memory soon returned. I glanced again at the clock, which ticked remorselessly upon the mantel. Approximately nineteen hours had now elapsed since Holmes had disappeared, and still there was no news of him. And no response to my summoning. I wondered again whether I had mishandled the ritual in some way.

Thunder rumbled over London, and I had just closed the window against a first spattering of rain when there came a brisk tapping at the bolted door. I am certainly not the most imaginative of men, but I found it necessary to steel my resolve before walking to the door and undoing the bolt.

Even so, a moment later I was trying to conceal my disappointment. The opened door revealed no figures more impressive than those of Martin Armstrong and Rebecca Altamont.

"Watson—good to see you again—I don't suppose that Mr. Holmes is here?" Armstrong looked about anxiously as he came in. It was plain from the young man's appearance—haggard, disheveled, and unshaven—that he had had little or no rest since I had left him in Amberley and that he was now in the last stages of exhaustion.

"Certainly he is not," I replied. "I have not heard from him. Have you just come from Norberton House? What can you report from there?"

Both the young American and Miss Altamont began to speak at once.

The most important item of information they brought with them was the sad but not surprising news that Abraham Kirkaldy had died of his injuries.

"It's a case of murder now," Armstrong said solemnly.

Maddened by the lack of any progress in organizing a search for the living Louisa, by what he considered an obstinate refusal to face the facts on the part of the authorities, Armstrong had boarded the train to London to confer with me again, preferring not to try to discuss the subject on the telephone. Rebecca Altamont, concerned about this mood of desperation on the part of the man who was to have been her brother-in-law, had insisted on coming with him. Her first look at me was a silent plea for help, and I endeavored to convey a silent reassurance.

Armstrong, stumbling and stuttering in his weariness, and now distraught by his renewed fears for Louisa, still had not slept. Somehow, between conversing with his companion and attempting to compose an article on last night's events for his American newspaper, he had kept himself from nodding off on the train.

"Even my friends in Fleet Street, Watson—for example, a London editor I know—even he cannot seem to understand. He now complains that I 'phoned him an unsupported story. I can tell he doesn't really believe me about Lou being still alive. All anyone will tell me now is that I ought to rest. But how can I rest, Watson? How—?"

"At least you can sit down," I advised him gently. "You

ought to save as much of your strength as possible for when it will be needed."

"Yes, that's true—true enough. Let me rest, then—for a few minutes only." Moving with the uncertainty of an old man, he lowered himself to the sofa. "Any word as yet from Mr. Holmes?"

Patiently I repeated that there was none. Meanwhile Armstrong, having allowed himself to sit down, was almost at once reclining at full length on the sofa, as though he had been drawn into a horizontal position by some irresistible force of gravity, though scarcely conscious of its operation. Only moments later he was sound asleep.

Bending quietly over my visitor—who now, by default, seemed to have become my patient—I loosened his collar, took his pulse, and concluded a brief examination. None of this disturbed the young man in the least. Obviously he had succumbed to total exhaustion, both mental and physical.

"Let him sleep," his fair companion pleaded in a whisper.

I straightened, nodding. "Of course. But there is no need to whisper. It would not be easy to rouse him now if we made a deliberate effort to do so." Then, fixing the young lady with my professional gaze, I added that she looked very tired herself.

Miss Altamont, sunk wearily in an armchair, dismissed my comment with a wave of her hand. "Dr. Watson, what has really happened to my sister? Do you know?"

"I was hoping that you would be able to give me some information on the subject," I hedged.

"I cannot," Rebecca responded sadly. Then she cast on the recumbent form of young Armstrong a glance in which pity and some stronger emotion were perhaps mingled. She shook her head. "He is certain that it was Louisa who came to us in the library last night, but I am not sure even of that.

While we were on the train coming here, he . . . he looked so pitiful that I pretended to fall in with his ideas."

Clearing my throat, I made an effort—perhaps a rather clumsy one—to turn the conversation another way. "I wonder, Miss Altamont, whether your parents did not raise a strong objection to your coming to London in this way?"

Her gaze came back, as if from a great distance, to settle wonderingly on me. "Why should they do that, Dr. Watson?"

"I meant . . . that you should travel such a distance accompanied only by a young man who is really not a close relative."

I believe it took her a moment to understand. Then she dismissed any such Victorian misgivings with another wave of her hand—I got the impression that Rebecca Altamont had had a great deal of practice in this gesture. As for any moral concerns that I, or her parents, might have regarding her traveling about unchaperoned, she gave me to understand that we were now living in the twentieth century and there was no need any longer to worry about such things.

I think it was in that moment that I for the first time truly began to see myself as old.

Meanwhile my young visitor had promptly returned to the subject from which I had sought to distract her. "I don't know, Dr. Watson, if that was really my sister who came into our house last night or not. It was certainly no ghost or spirit, as our parents believe. But if it was Louisa—then I tell you that something dreadful has happened to her. She has been terribly changed."

Some relevant response on my part appeared to be called for. "Changed? In what way?"

"I don't know! That's part of the terror of it." In another moment the girl had broken down in tears. I thought that she herself could not be far from collapse.

Then she appeared to rally, and stated firmly: "Nothing has made any sense, really, since the day Louisa drowned."

Her eyes sought mine, as if anticipating and challenging my reaction to what she was about to say. Then, drawing a deep breath, she added: "Since the day I saw those pale hands reach up out of the water to overturn the rowboat."

~ 9 ~

The walls of our sitting room at 221B Baker Street have been privileged to hear many a strange tale, but perhaps none quite the equal in its implications of that which was related to me by Miss Rebecca Altamont upon that fateful summer evening. It was then that she revealed for the first time the full story of her experiences on the day her sister had been so tragically torn from the bosom of her family.

"Until now, Dr. Watson, I have held back certain things—one thing, really—I thought I saw that day. Because I doubted my own sanity, and I feared that others would doubt it even more. But now, when some people seriously believe that séances can bring us the truth—and others are convinced that our dear one whom we all thought dead is only hypnotised—oh, I cannot bear it any longer, I must tell someone!"

I took my visitor's hand and patted it reassuringly. "If you have any revelation to make, I hope you will tell me. You may find me a more receptive audience than you expect. More than that, you may help us all to find a way out of this ghastly business."

The young woman sighed, and sat back in her armchair. "You've heard the statements I gave, and Martin gave, at the inquest. They are substantially true as far as they go. But mine, at least, did not go far enough. Now let me tell you everything.

"You've seen the Shade now, Doctor—it's always a fairly placid stream, no more than twenty or thirty yards wide anywhere within several miles of our house.

"We'd brought a picnic basket with us, and most of its contents had been disposed of—we'd been nibbling pretty steadily. And we were singing, off and on—Louisa had brought her banjo.

"Martin of course had been doing almost all the rowing, though each of us girls had taken a brief turn. Everything was going peacefully and pleasantly . . . and then it happened." Miss Altamont paused at this point, her blue eyes searching mine as if for reassurance.

"Go on," I urged, as cheerfully as possible.

"You won't call for attendants and have me taken to an asylum?"

"Most assuredly, I will not."

"You say that very convincingly. Well, call them if you must; still, I must tell someone.

"I was sitting with Lou in the stern, both of us naturally facing forward, looking past Martin toward the prow. What I thought I saw then . . . it was only the briefest impression, and for days and days I have tried to convince myself that I must have been mistaken . . ."

"Yes, go on," I urged again. Encouragement seemed necessary.

Briefly the girl still hesitated. But then she plunged ahead. "What I thought I saw was . . . first, hands. Large, human hands coming up out of the water, one seizing the very front of the boat on each side, like this." The girl raised her own small hands in demonstration. "And then . . . then I had the distinct impression of a man's head and body coming up, just on the left side of the boat as I sat looking forward."

"A man? Who?"

"I don't know; it was only the briefest glimpse, if it was not entirely an illusion, but I have no reason to believe that it was anyone I'd ever seen before. My impression is of longish red hair, and a red beard, both looking dark because they were wet—and I can remember, or I think I can, that his lips were parted, showing his white, sharp teeth. And his eyes . . . they were green, I think, and when I try to remember, something about the memory always makes me think of dead fish, or of something drowned . . ."

Briefly Miss Altamont buried her face in her hands. When she looked up again, I asked as gently as possible: "Was there anything else you noticed about him?"

"Only that he was—he appeared to be totally unclothed, and his skin was everywhere very pale—I may have only imagined all this, you understand."

"I understand."

"I suppose Louisa might possibly have seen him too, because she uttered the last sound I ever heard from her lips, a kind of little gasp, or shriek—although that may have been only because the boat was going over. I cannot rid my brain of the thought that the man was really there, and that he tipped it. If so, it was incredible."

"Surely any man might tip a rowboat?" I asked in soothing tones.

Miss Altamont dabbed at her eyes with a small handkerchief. She nodded. "Yes, an ordinary man could do it gradually, by throwing all his weight on one side and forcing one gunwale under water. But whatever happened was nothing like that. What happened still does not seem possible. We were in the center of the stream, deep water, and I don't see how the man's feet could have been planted on the bottom.

Yet he—if he was really there—he flipped that heavy rowboat—you have seen it—like some child's toy."

I nodded reassuringly. "Do you think that Martin might have seen this man too—if, as you say, he was really there?"

"He might have seen him." The young woman shook her head. "But he has said nothing to me about it. Of course, at first Martin was facing in the opposite direction, but he might possibly have seen him when the boat capsized . . . Dr. Watson?" A new tone had come into the girl's voice. "Is it really possible that you believe me?"

"I have no reason to doubt, Miss Altamont, that events might have taken place very much as you describe them. I only wish that you had told us sooner."

Her blue eyes opened wide. My reaction was evidently not at all what she had anticipated. "How strange!"

"My belief? Well, as I have grown older, I have learned that there are many strange things in the world. Are there any more details that you can give regarding this pale man?"

The lady shuddered. "As I say, in the next moment, we were all in the water, and I never saw this—apparition—phantasm—again. But Doctor, it haunts my dreams. And there I can see it clearly—that hideous, somehow dead-looking face. He has red hair, dark with wetting, all matted over his forehead. And he is glaring—no, not glaring, smiling, which is worse—at my sister and me with nightmarish malevolence. And in my dreams I see his body clearly too, those white arms, those white hands, arms and hands all very muscular, gripping the gunwales near the bow. He must have been immensely strong . . . if he was real." And once more my fair visitor shuddered.

A moment later she demanded: "But then who was he, Dr. Watson—if he was really there? What is the explanation?"

"That will have to wait. I cannot provide it."

In the meantime, there still had been no indication that my effort to communicate with Dracula would be successful. I hoped I somehow could get Miss Altamont out of the way before he did arrive.

When I had soothed the young lady as best I could, and while I was endeavoring to persuade her to rest, I closed and put away the old book, set aside a partially burned candle, and picked up the broken pieces of a small mirror which were now littering Holmes's chemical workbench.

"Have an accident?" my visitor asked abstractedly, observing my activities. She had arisen from her chair and was following me about the sitting room, unthinkingly, like a small child trailing a parent. "I've studied chemistry in school," she added, with the irrelevance of a mind wandering in weariness.

I muttered some evasive comment. Truly I was concerned about the young lady's welfare, for she looked little better than Armstrong, as if she might faint at any moment.

After persuading her to sit down again, I rang for Mrs. Hudson, who soon looked in. As I had hoped, she offered Miss Altamont the hospitality of her own rooms. She also sent Billy, the young page, with a blanket and pillow for Armstrong, and for me some later editions of the newspapers, which were still making much of the story of Holmes's disappearance. By this time other news had forced the story from the headlines, and now the supposed supernatural aspects of the matter were receiving somewhat less play.

With Martin Armstrong snoring comfortably on the sofa, in a manner indicating he would be there for hours to come, Rebecca, obviously losing the struggle to keep her own eyes open, was soon persuaded to take advantage of Mrs. Hudson's kind offer of hospitality, and avail herself of a few hours' rest in our landlady's rooms.

* * *

I had awakened from my own sleep at seven in the evening, and by now the long summer twilight was well advanced.

My energies had been somewhat restored by a few hours of uneasy slumber, and now by a second meal provided by Mrs. Hudson. Having already done all that I could do in the way of calling for specialized help, I resolved to return as soon as practical to Amberley, there to aid the search for Holmes in whatever way was possible. I thought it would be possible to catch a late train before midnight.

Once back in Amberley, I intended, despite Ambrose Altamont's warning, to arrange to see Sarah Kirkaldy, privately if at all possible, and question her. I had gathered before my return to London that she was not to be held at the local police station, but kept more or less under house arrest in her room at the Altamonts'.

Remembering that there was a telephone at Norberton House, I naturally thought of calling there before I boarded a train again, to discover whether there might be any fresh news of Holmes, or other developments in the case.

The voice of Ambrose Altamont, when I heard it on the other end of the line, sounded coolly sympathetic regarding the mysterious fate of Sherlock Holmes. But our former client was still intent on, if not obsessed by, the return of his daughter from the dead (as he saw the matter) through psychic materialization.

"I see now, Dr. Watson, that there are truly greater powers in heaven and earth than I had ever dreamed of."

"Indeed?" I inquired sharply. "You have been given some fresh evidence of this?"

There was a crackling pause along the lines. "Of course—my daughter's appearance at the séance. You were there and witnessed her return. What did you think I meant?"

"Sorry," I murmured. "Perhaps I did not hear you clearly. You were saying?"

"Of course I pray that we will all see Mr. Holmes again, in this world. But I fear we ought not be surprised if we do not." Altamont's manner remained distinctly cool, and when I mentioned that I contemplated a quick return to Amberley, he only grunted, issuing no invitation for me to return as a houseguest.

In turn I assured him—rather stiffly I suppose—that his younger daughter was safe, and presently in good hands. I thought I detected a kind of start on his part when he heard this, suggesting that he had not known, or had entirely forgotten, that Rebecca had gone to London.

Scarcely had I replaced the telephone receiver in its cradle, when Billy appeared, to announce a mysterious caller who was urgently and (I gathered) even abusively demanding to see Dr. Watson, alone. The young page reported indignantly that the man had declined with an oath when asked whether he would send up a card or any written note.

For some reason the name of the unknown Count Kulakov sprang immediately to mind, but my first glance at my latest visitor laid that theory to rest. The caller was a poorly dressed, rough-looking man, who at first displayed a smiling, nodding manner that appeared incongruously obsequious. Something about his clothing reminded me of Holmes's description of the mysterious man who had watched us through the window at Simpson's.

My uncouth visitor started visibly on catching sight of the recumbent figure of Martin Armstrong on the sofa. "Who's that?" he demanded. The man spoke in a thick foreign accent, which I took to betray some origin in Eastern Europe.

"That's none of your affair. If you have some business with me, you had better state it."

He glared at the page. "When we are alone."

I signaled to Billy. When the boy had left us, the man,

smiling and nodding again, said: "Your friend Mr. Holmes need your help. Even now he in great danger."

A moment later, evidently seeing my suspicions plain upon my face, my mysterious caller took out of his pocket and handed to me a worn briar pipe that I immediately recognized as belonging to Holmes.

While I thoughtfully turned this piece of evidence over in my hands, the messenger insisted that if I really wanted to help Holmes, I must come with him at once, without a moment's delay. "It is your friend himself who tells you this."

"He did not write a note for you to bring to me?"

"Why you want notes and writing?" My nameless visitor shook his head decisively. "He cannot write."

"What prevents his doing so?"

This question was answered with a frown and a gesture of impatience. "I tell you, he may be dying and need your help. You are to talk with no one, leave no writing, but come instantly with me."

Scrutinizing once more the gnarled old briar pipe with a silver band around the amber stem, I had no doubt that it was one Holmes had had with him on our journey to Amberley. It had very probably been in his pocket at the time of his disappearance.

The messenger was watching alertly, and I decided to defy his orders openly.

"What are you doing?" he demanded, seeing me take pen and paper at my desk.

"I am leaving a message—whether you approve of the act or not."

Under his scowling supervision, I jotted down a few words for Mrs. Hudson, briefly outlining the circumstances under which I was being called away and instructing her to notify the police if she did not hear from me again within six hours. I folded and addressed the paper, and left it in a prominent position upon my desk.

Then, with great misgivings, but seeing no other course of action open to me, I went with my strange guide down to the street. At our door a four-wheeler stood waiting. The driver, his face muffled by hat and scarf, leaned down from his high seat to exchange a few words in a low voice with my escort. Obeying an impatient gesture from the latter, I opened the door of the coach and climbed in.

On putting my head inside, I was surprised to find one seat already occupied, by a second man who seemed in every way a fit companion for the first, being dressed in the same rough style, and looking as desperate and dangerous. The first man now climbed in after me and closed the door.

The cab started with a lurch, on the instant the door was slammed, and I heard the repeated crack of the driver's whip, showing that we were to maintain a rapid pace.

Immediately I began to question my escorts, who both sat facing me. One held his right hand in a pocket, and the other held his hand under his coat, suggesting that weapons might soon appear. The windows of the coach were covered with some opaque fabric, so that I could see nothing of our route.

"Where are we going?" I demanded, in as firm a voice as I could manage. "Where is Sherlock Holmes?"

"You be with him soon enough," said the man who had been waiting in the carriage, now speaking for the first time. He grinned, displaying white teeth in a face dark with grime and stubble.

I simply nodded, and inwardly made ready for the desperate personal struggle that now seemed unavoidable. I thought my chances would be better if I could delay it until I had dismounted from the coach.

A minute or two before the end of our ride, which, to judge by the time elapsed, had covered about two miles altogether, the sounds of surrounding traffic began to grow more remote, as if we were leaving well-traveled thoroughfares behind us. At the same time, we began jolting and bumping over some surface notably rougher than even the worst of the ordinary London streets.

After a brief interval of this lurching progress, the carriage stopped abruptly. Immediately one of the men riding with me opened a door and jumped out. A moment later, I was bidden to dismount, and stepped forth to stand in heavy shadows upon the uneven footing offered by an expanse of broken pavement. Inadvertently I put one foot into a deep puddle.

The buildings nearby loomed dark and silent, and their jagged outlines against the lighter sky assured me that I was standing amid ruins. What little I could see of my immediate surroundings strongly suggested that we were in some impoverished part of London, among structures which had been condemned or were actually in the process of being demolished. Dark, half-ruined walls reared their uneven outlines on every side, and the alley, or mews in which the coach had stopped was half-blocked by piles of rubble, among which I heard the scurrying of rats. Whatever these desperate men had in mind, no passersby were likely to interfere with it.

The second man had come out of the coach close on my heels, and the two exchanged a look before turning to confront me.

I determined to put as bold a face on the matter as possible. "I demand to know what you have done with—"

But my guides—rather my kidnappers, as I now fully realized, with the clarity of something like despair—had finished pretending to answer questions.

"Imperialist pig! Your hour has come!"

"Die, monarchist! Capitalist swine!" With that the speaker, who was now standing some four or five paces off, drew a pistol. Meanwhile his comrade, actually within arm's length of me, fetched a short bludgeon from inside his coat.

But before either form of attack might hit home, or I could attempt to strike a blow in my own defense, interruption came from an unexpected quarter. The coachman, who had remained silent and unmoving in his high seat, suddenly lashed out with his long whip. The weapon writhed and struck like some great serpent from atop the carriage, wrapping itself solidly around the gunman's wrist. The latter cried out in astonishment, and his weapon discharged harmlessly, sending a bullet into one of the half-ruined walls by which we were surrounded. In the next moment a harder pull on the whip had yanked him off his feet with terrific force.

At that instant I could see no more, because the man with the bludgeon raised it, rapping out an oath at the same time, and I managed to grapple with him only just in time to save myself from being brutally clubbed. Whether I or my opponent would have prevailed will never be known, for in the next moment a darting black shape had come to my defense, swirling down from the coachman's high seat to pounce like some winged predator upon my attacker.

A moment after that, my immediate antagonist had been wrenched out of my grasp. His body now hung in the air, dangling incredibly like that of a snared bird, held prisoner in the iron, one-handed grip which had been fastened on the back of his neck by the tall, lean coachman. The latter was now standing almost within arm's length of me, and his hat had fallen off, revealing a shock of black hair. Some yards behind him, the bully who had drawn a pistol lay sprawled facedown, as if dead, upon the broken pavement, his useless weapon at his side.

Almost before I had begun to struggle on my own behalf, the fight was over, and for the moment I was safe.

I think my last doubts regarding the coachman's identity had been dissipated even before he used his free hand to loosen the scarf which had until now effectively concealed the lower part of his pale, clean-shaven, and somehow shockingly youthful face.

I was gasping from the brief exertion, and needed a moment or two in which to regain my breath. "Prince Dracula! I had begun to fear that my summons failed to reach you."

"Most diplomatically phrased, Doctor." Dracula's well-remembered voice was deep, his English precise and elegant, though still marked with the accents of Eastern Europe. Simultaneously he let his prisoner down until the man's feet just touched the ground. "I really came as quickly as I could. Unhappily, when your summons reached me I was not in the close vicinity of London—though fortunately I was at least in England."

"That is fortunate indeed for me."

"My apologies, Doctor, for any inconvenience my tardiness may have caused you. But I was unavoidably detained—ha, would you?"

This last was addressed to his prisoner, who, with some breath restored, had summoned up fight enough to attempt to kick the prince. Dracula, pinching the fellow's neck in a way that rendered him unconscious, allowed him to slide down, to sprawl at full length on the broken pavement. Then my rescuer went on unconcernedly to explain that he had reached Baker Street at about the same time as these messengers, and from the moment of his arrival had been suspicious of such a thuggish-looking trio of callers—their number had then included their own driver on the coach.

"Naturally," my rescuer concluded, "I felt it necessary to make sure that I understood the situation before I interfered."

"No apology is necessary," I murmured. By this time my

respiration and pulse were beginning to return to their normal rates. "My thanks for your help."

"The determination was a matter of some delicacy." The prince went on to explain how, employing several of the powers naturally available to his race between the hours of sunset and dawn, he had invisibly followed and then secretly boarded the four-wheeler as it pulled away with my kidnappers and myself inside.

Crouching undetected behind the driver, making use of his preternaturally keen hearing to eavesdrop on such conversation as took place inside the vehicle, Dracula had soon convinced himself that his suspicions were fully justified.

"Then it was necessary first, to interview their driver as quietly as possible, and next to induce him to tell me where he had been told to drive the coach. I allowed him to make a quick and silent departure from the vehicle, while he permitted me to retain his whip, hat, and scarf.

"The fellow could scarcely wait to be off—it may have been something I said, or the way I looked at him. At any rate, I satisfied myself that he was only a hireling. Not worth a great deal of our attention. This man, on the other hand, may be worth talking to." The prince smiled, looking down with what appeared to be affection at the thug who lay at his feet.

"Where are we, then?" I looked about, but the night-filled ruins in our immediate vicinity shut us closely in, and the only sounds of traffic came from blocks away.

"Somewhere in the City, a little northwest of St. Paul's. The original driver told me that this was our general destination."

I realized that we could not be far from normal streets and traffic; and events proved that we were in fact no great distance from the site where the demolition of Newgate Prison, to make way for the new Criminal Court, was already under way.

Before we made our way back into the traveled streets, a decision had to be made about our prisoner, or prisoners.

The man whose pistol had been pulled from his grasp had now revived again, but only briefly. I went to attend him and saw that he had sustained a deadly fall upon the broken pavement, suffering a broken spine as well as other severe injuries. Before dying he found breath enough to rail at me again as an enemy of the people.

And briefly he accused Prince Dracula—hearing me address him as "Prince"—of being a servant of the Okhrana and a lackey of the Tsar.

"I have no notion of what the fellow was talking about," I assured Dracula.

He began to explain to me that Okhrana was the name of the Russian secret police.

"I am aware of that, Prince." I had now retrieved my hat and was dusting it off. "What I do not understand is what possible connection there can exist between politics in eastern Europe, and spiritualist sittings in central England."

He shrugged. "You do not know how you have managed to acquire such exotic enemies?"

Quickly I outlined my reasons for summoning help, and the situation in which Holmes had disappeared.

. . . but let me not bother to record the good doctor's somewhat awkward answer. He was at a certain psychological disadvantage at the time: feeling grateful, as well he might, and honor-bound to express his gratitude—but, in general, firmly disapproving of my way of life. Once more, let me take up the narrative.

As Watson in his workmanlike prose has already informed us, the two of us, standing victorious among the ruins, faced the question of what we ought to do with our sole surviving foe.

In my expert judgment, then and now, a successful interrogation would certainly have been possible. But, now having heard Watson's story, at least in outline, I feared that nothing our prisoner could say would lead us immediately to our chief enemy.

However, wishing to leave no stone unturned, I tried. Dragging the wretched survivor to his feet again, I demanded of him: "Where is Sherlock Holmes?"

There was no answer at first—then only an obscene, ranting defiance—until I did something that produced a real, if still unhelpful, response: "I don't know! Aaagh! Don't know!"

Here I thought it wise to assure Watson—he was already starting to look a little green around the gills, and I think was on the verge of protesting my methods—that his immediate presence was not required. I, Dracula, were I left alone with this would-be assassin, expected no serious difficulty in inducing in him a most talkative mood. Within a few minutes he might be expected to pass on to us every scrap of information in his possession regarding the identity of his immediate employer.

But, more important, I feared it might be wasted effort; already I was convinced that all this man could tell us was not going to be enough.

Watson murmured uncomfortably that he was not sure that he understood.

With pressure—relatively painless—upon certain nerves, I rendered my captive unconscious and let him slide once more to the ground. Dusting my hands fastidiously, I took time out to explain: "He will remain so for many hours, unless I rouse him . . . but you see our problem, Doctor, do you not? Even if this fellow should be stimulated to a high pitch, one might even say a frenzy, of enthusiasm to be helpful to our cause, I am morally certain that he really does not have the information we consider vital. To obtain that, it will be necessary to find and interview one more link in the chain at least. This process might well occupy us for a day, or for several days, before we could come to grips with the one who ultimately dispatched these men to kill you. And meanwhile, Cousin Sherlock . . ."

"Our main concern must be for him. I quite see the difficulty, yes." Watson was wiping sweat from his forehead. He turned his head this way and that, obviously wishing he could be somewhere else. I remember thinking that he looked somewhat older than he had at the time of our previous encounter in 1897.

At last he came up with what he considered an appropriate response, satisfying the demands of honor as well as the exigencies of the immediate tactical situation. "In the circumstances I have no compunction about simply leaving these fellows here. In their present condition they can do little harm. And fortunately they have provided us with transportation. I think, Prince Dracula, that if you will come with me, we have ample time to catch the early train to Amberley."

~ 10 ~

Before going to Victoria Station, I thought it best to stop in Baker Street to pack some personal things—or perhaps more accurately, to rearrange them—for my journey. The fact was that I had not yet unpacked from my previous trip to Amberley. Also I wished to leave word with Mrs. Hudson regarding my current plans and situation, and to examine any messages that might have arrived while I was gone.

Dracula, who continued in his role of driver, declined my invitation to enter the house. As we parted in the dark street outside, he assured me that I would find him there when I came down, and also cautioned me—rather unnecessarily, I thought—that I might well find it unsafe just now to go about in public without a bodyguard.

Entering the house, I ascended straight to my room to pack, without stopping to look into the sitting room; but on my way upstairs I encountered both Mrs. Hudson and Billy—each of whom had been anxiously awaiting my return—and heard from them that the exhausted young couple were still asleep in their respective rooms. I hastily scribbled short notes of encouragement, one to be given to Armstrong and one to Miss Altamont as soon as they awakened, including the information that I was on my way back to Amberley.

My preparations for the trip were soon complete, being confined to essentials. In addition to the routine items which a traveler might be expected to carry on any journey, I brought along a well-stocked medical bag, and my old service revolver. In the circumstances I thought it wise to load the weapon with a few of the cartridges, fitted with wooden bullets, which had been especially made at Holmes's order in 1897. The gunsmith was the blind German Von Herder, the same artisan once so well known for his skill at building deadly air guns. The wood, a waxy greenish-brown, was *lignum vitae,* very hard and too heavy to float in water. Against vampires these bullets were vastly more effective than any metal projectiles. For six years I had retained this ammunition as a curiosity, never thinking that we might again require it for a serious purpose.

When I came down to the street, Dracula, still in his character of driver, was waiting as he had promised. I noticed that the prince now wore a different hat, of dyed and woven straw, the sort of broad-brimmed head covering which any person of his race would find useful if not essential against prolonged exposure to even the tempered English sun. In my absence the carriage had been moved to a different position at the curb, and on entering it again I discovered a carpetbag which had not been in the vehicle before. Evidently this was my new associate's baggage for our journey, obtained somewhere, along with his new hat, during the few minutes I had been absent. Surely, I thought, he could not have gone far to get these things. It occurred to me for the first time to wonder whether Prince Dracula might have as many lairs or refuges in different parts of London as did Sherlock Holmes himself.

It was near midnight when we arrived outside Victoria Station. As I was handing my companion's carpetbag out to him, I both heard and felt a slight crunching of its contents, and the thought flashed across my mind that they must consist at least partially of dry earth. Dracula, I realized, must be carrying with him, as part of his regular baggage, a supply of his native soil. This substance was not, of course, to be consumed, but served as a necessary adjunct for vampirish sleep; to a man or woman of his race—or tribe, or species, if either of those classifications is more accurate—the soil of one's homeland is every bit as much a necessity as food or water is to us.

There seemed nothing better to do with our captured vehicle than to abandon it just outside the station. An hour later, my new associate and I boarded the next available train to Buckinghamshire. It carried us out of London in the very early morning, more than twenty-four hours after Holmes's disappearance.

Fortunately, at this early hour, we had a carriage to ourselves, illumined by a dim electric lamp. Long before the great metropolis had fallen behind us, I had begun to relate to Prince Dracula in detail the facts of that last and dreadful séance in Norberton House, and its violent aftermath.

Dracula, seated opposite me, his body swaying in what seemed to me a faintly reptilian fashion with the motion of the train, was paying close attention. The prince studied me intently over a pyramid formed by his pale, long-nailed fingers—a gesture which emphasized his resemblance to his missing cousin—and interrupted once to express his contempt for séances in general.

"I have no patience with such spirit gropings, whether the perpetrators know they are employing trickery, or have convinced themselves that the effects they produce are genuine."

"No?" Perhaps illogically, I was surprised.

"No." He shook his head decisively. "In my experience, Doctor, men and women who have died the true death are thenceforward permanently and effectively separated from all the things and people of this world. It is my opinion that no amount of concentrated mental effort by one's fellow humans, sitting in a darkened room, is going to change that fact. Now, I shall be obliged if you can begin at the beginning—or wherever you think best—and state your reasons for believing that at this moment, Cousin Sherlock is personally in great peril, and has not merely immersed himself in one of his eccentric modes of investigation."

I began with the story which had been told us by our client, Ambrose Altamont, and added the results of our subsequent investigation, giving as much detail as I could immediately recall. My auditor listened attentively, and almost without further interruption, only nodding soberly from time to time. At the conclusion of my tale I yawned uncontrollably, feeling a certain relief in having unburdened myself of my fears and having done my duty, as I thought, to the best of my ability.

The prince seemed to concur. "I believe you have done well to call upon me. Regrettably, I cannot be sanguine about our chances of getting Cousin Sherlock back alive—but at the very least, Doctor, we will take a thorough vengeance upon his enemy." My companion smiled, in a way that he evidently meant to be reassuring. "Now you should get some more sleep."

Dracula's voice as he uttered the last phrase seemed to reach me from a considerable distance. He had already drawn the blinds over the windows to shut out as much as possible, the rays of the newly risen sun, and in the dimness of the compartment, nothing but his eyes seemed clearly visible. The rocking motion of the train, the steady tumult of the engine, and the muffled chatter of wheels on rails were irresistibly lulling. I seem to recall beginning some formal protest; and then the next thing I remember is that pale and powerful hand upon my shoulder, that oddly reassuring voice informing me that we were pulling into Amberley.

I found myself notably refreshed by the brief slumber. There had been some delays en route, and the time of our arrival was midmorning, only a few hours earlier than on my previous trip with Holmes.

While on the train, the prince and I had decided to postpone, or to omit altogether, any social call at Norberton House. The omission would put off the whole question of whether I was to introduce my new companion to the Altamont family, and if so, under what name? In any case I had not been invited to return as a guest of the Altamonts, and could expect no better than a cool reception on their doorstep.

Instead, Prince Dracula and I proceeded at once to secure lodgings at one of the local inns, with which the village and its surrounding neighborhood were fortunately well provided. A number of journalists and high police officials were already staying in the neighborhood because of the continuing investigation, and the promised inquest into the death of Abraham Kirkaldy. We heard that the latter function was currently being delayed at the request of the police, because at least one important witness—the reference was to Sherlock Holmes, no doubt—could not be found.

At any rate, when my companion exerted all of his considerable charm upon the landlady, we were able to get rooms at the Saracen's Head, where Inspector Merivale was also staying—I thought that for some reason the name of the establishment particularly appealed to the prince. At the time of our arrival the landlord informed us that the Scotland Yard man was out in the countryside, continuing to lead the search for Holmes and for Louisa Altamont.

We assumed that Armstrong would soon return from London, and would again be staying at Norberton House.

The question of an exhumation had been raised earlier

by Armstrong, but I thought there was no possibility of his convincing either Louisa's parents or the police that such a procedure should be undertaken.

Shortly after our midmorning arrival, we were exposed to rumors current among the villagers, to the effect that Mr. and Mrs. Altamont were eager—the husband now even more so than the wife—to arrange yet another séance. The couple was determined this time to have no disruptive skeptics in attendance.

We learned also that rather than being under any kind of house arrest, Sarah Kirkaldy was still the cherished houseguest of the Altamonts. One version of the story among the villagers was that Sarah's grief at her brother's death had become so intense that there were fears for her reason; another account had her suffering an attack of brain fever.

By now, of course, the police had questioned the young spiritualist exhaustively. But by all reports, the Altamonts were offering her their protection and gave every indication of being ready to use their wealth and position to the utmost, if necessary, to defend Sarah, who had, as they thought, restored them to communication and even to direct contact with their departed daughter.

The fact that her brother had been fatally attacked during the last séance certainly tended to indicate that the Kirkaldys had been innocent in whatever crimes might have been committed.

To both Dracula and myself, the present attitude of Sarah Kirkaldy was unclear. It seemed very likely that the bereaved family would want to hold the new sitting in secret, as free as possible from police surveillance.

It seemed to us also that the elder Altamonts, anxious to convince the young people that their elders' view of the situation was correct, would want Martin Armstrong as well as their younger daughter to attend the next séance;

and young Armstrong might very well prefer to be there rather than to go poking into the mausoleum where, as he now believed, some stranger had been laid to rest.

But we had not come to Amberley to engage in speculation. I even resented Prince Dracula's suggestion that I might want to stop for food before commencing our search for Holmes. However, we took some sandwiches and a flask of coffee along, as well as my usual medicinal supplies of water and brandy, and my revolver and my medical bag.

At a stable near the station, we hired a horse and trap. When we climbed into our rented conveyance, Dracula took the reins and asked me for directions; he wanted to begin at the mausoleum in which Louisa had been entombed.

"There is no reason to suppose we will find Cousin Sherlock there, but I think it a likely spot at which to pick up a trail of one kind or another."

"Then let us begin there, and quickly."

Dracula was obviously somewhat uncomfortable in the late-morning sunshine. Once or twice I could see him grimace as if in pain when a shaft of brilliance came stabbing through between the longer intervals of cloudiness. But, demonstrating the attitude of an old campaigner, he pulled down his wide-brimmed hat, put on some gloves, and dismissed any reference to his discomfort as he led the search for Holmes.

As we rode I explained to my new colleague that I saw several reasons to act on the assumption that Holmes had been kidnapped by a vampire—not necessarily Louisa.

"I shall rejoice to hear them."

"Very well. First, Sherlock Holmes is, as a rule, quite capable of defending himself; no ordinary opponent would be likely to carry him off so quickly, almost without an outcry."

"Assuming he has indeed been carried off, and did not

choose to vanish—it would not be the first time he did that, as you are well aware. What else?"

"A second reason is that people of the . . ." I paused to clear my throat; a certain word still tended to stick there. "That vampires were, and are, certainly involved."

"You are certain of this?"

"I am certain." And I gave my reasons.

If I had expected a defensive reaction I was wrong; my companion only nodded. "It is most likely that you are correct. But proceed, Dr. Watson."

"In the first place I am certain that the girl in white, appearing at the séance, was indeed a vampire, whether or not she was truly Louisa Altamont. And where there is one vampire—"

"—there is likely at least one more. Very good, Doctor. If we assume that you are correct, and that Miss Altamont acquired her nosferatu status rather abruptly about three weeks ago, then it is very likely that another of my kind—her lover, or her attacker—is still currently near at hand."

As yet, I had not actually visited the Altamonts' family burial ground, but I had heard enough from Armstrong to be reasonably sure of its location. The cemetery lay on the bank of the Shade, somewhat less than half a mile in straight-line distance from the bend in the stream where Louisa's drowning had taken place.

We reached our goal after a drive of less than half an hour from the inn. The ancient churchyard was enclosed by an iron fence which, along much of its extent, was almost hidden in luxuriant shrubbery. The graveyard had its own entrance from the road, and the area inside the iron fence was rankly overgrown, with a look of not having been properly maintained for years. In certain places the lush grass and wild flowers had recently been trodden down by human feet and heavily crushed by wheels and horses' hooves; there was plenty of evidence that over the last few weeks the place had been repeatedly visited.

A small, ruined church or chapel, apparently older by several centuries than any of the visible graves, looked down from a small hill upon the cemetery and the wooded banks of the Shade, and lent something of a romantic aspect to the scene. Not much was left of this ecclesiastical structure but a few crumbling walls and arches, spotted with lichen and entwined with ivy, sweet honeysuckle, and woodbine.

But our first goal was near the middle of the cemetery. There stood the Altamont family mausoleum, a moss-grown structure as big as a small house, round which the indications of recent visitors were heaviest. This mausoleum was readily identifiable by the family name carved in the stone, and it, like the ruined chapel, was partially covered by the tall climbing vines.

Dismounting from our rented trap, Dracula soothed the restive horse, with a few murmured words and a stroking of the animal's neck. He then silently approached the sepulcher on its most shadowed side. The prince leaned against the stone wall, first with both hands and then, after removing his hat, with his pale forehead. After remaining in this position for a moment or two he turned away to inform me calmly that he had detected definite evidence of vampire activity within. He added that he perceived no trace of Holmes still living, in either the breathing or undead state.

I shuddered inwardly to think of my old companion becoming a vampire, or imprisoned in a tomb.

The prince, frowning, put on his hat again and backed away a step from the Altamont mausoleum, looking about him keenly.

"We must expand our search a bit, I think," he remarked, and started to walk slowly away. Then he turned back to me as if in afterthought. "You were certainly right about one thing, Doctor. There is a young girl who even now is sleeping—quite breathless, but not truly dead—inside these walls." And he stretched out a long arm to touch the old stone once more with a white hand.

I could not entirely repress a shudder. "Louisa Altamont?"

Dracula shrugged. "Very likely. I cannot tell her name. Later, perhaps we will awaken her and ask. But that will best be done after sunset; and first we must find Cousin Sherlock, while we have grounds for hope that he is breathing still."

Several other charnel houses stood scattered about the half-acre, which, a century ago, must have been an active country churchyard, small but yet well tended. None of these other mausoleums were quite as large as the Altamonts'. Some were older and some newer, but in general, none showed any sign of having been disturbed for years, or even for decades. A variety of smaller stone monuments and headstones shared the area and the same condition of general neglect.

Prince Dracula made the round of graves and tombs, evidently testing each, through some procedure that was invisible to me. His search was without result, though he paused several times, once for a full minute, to stare down at a tangle of vines, long undisturbed, beneath his feet.

During this part of his search, he bent swiftly and, with a grunt of speculation, straightened up, holding an object that glinted a bright yellow in his hand. It was a golden pin, set with some greenish stones which I took to be not emeralds, but perhaps jade, aquamarine, or garnet.

"That," I announced, "may well be one of the pieces of jewelry taken from the house on Wednesday night, while the sitting was in progress or shortly afterward. All were moderately valuable. But why is it here?"

Dracula only shrugged, handed the golden thing to me, and once more concentrated upon his search.

I inspected the pin briefly before dropping it into my pocket for eventual delivery to the police. It was a family heirloom sort of thing, and no ordinary burglar would have thrown it away; on the other hand it certainly did not represent the kind of treasure whose loss might be expected to provoke a thirst for vengeance lasting for more than a century.

I considered this find a possibly helpful development. But of course it could not be allowed to distract us from our main goal.

Dracula seemed already to have forgotten it. "None of the others who lie here are restless," the prince murmured at last. Then he raised his head, fixing his gaze in steady contemplation of the ruined chapel standing on its little hill nearby.

Moments later, we had climbed the wooded hillock together and Dracula was leading the way into the now-roofless structure. Scarcely had he taken three steps across that old pavement, which still bore in places broken fragments of mosaic decoration, before he paused in an attitude of listening, one hand upraised in my direction, commanding silence.

The pause was only momentary. Quickly my companion darted ahead, and as quickly stopped. "Here, Doctor Watson. Under the floor!" He stamped his foot lightly on a stone slab that must have weighed at least a quarter of a ton. "Sounds of breathing. And a heartbeat, slow but still strong."

If there was indeed a cavity beneath that ancient floor, the mass of stone was too great to resound hollowly from the impact of a boot. I hesitated. "Then we must get tools—"

"You need bring only the tools of your profession, from the trap. Be quick!" And already the prince was crouching, digging and probing with nervous, bony fingers at the edges of the slab. Stone flaked and crumbled under those long nails which seemed able to bite and penetrate with the force of steel tools.

Hesitating no longer, I ran, stumbling through weeds and over gravestones, back to the trap, and as quickly returned with my bag to the chapel. In those few moments Dracula had made astonishing headway in loosening the stone, which did not appear to be mortared in place, but fitted almost exactly the space in which it lay. Barehanded he had chipped away an opening beside it, and was now lying at full length on the old pavement, reaching with one thin arm underneath the slab, which as yet he had not attempted to remove.

He chuckled—a thoroughly delighted and unpleasant sound. When he spoke, his voice sounded much more pleased than outraged. "As I thought . . . very pretty . . . a snare for the unwary. Any incautious effort to lift the stone would cause it to slip and fall straight down upon the victim in the cavity beneath."

I shuddered. "How did you know there was such a snare?"

His head turned slightly and a dark eye glittered at me, while the visible portion of his body, excluding the arm beneath the stone, remained utterly immobile. Again I was struck by something distinctly reptilian in the man's aspect.

At the same time his voice remained very human, and indeed gentlemanly. "Because, Doctor . . . it is just the sort of thing I should have arranged myself . . . in our opponent's place. Ah, there we are!"

As soon as the mechanism of the snare, whatever its exact nature, had been disabled, the prince gave a little cry of triumph, then withdrew his arm from beneath the stone and crouched beside it in the position of one about to lift a heavy object. Before I could offer to help, there came a moment of apparently effortless exertion, and the immense stone slab rose on one side—a feat that, I am sure, would have tested the strength of three or four ordinary men.

Revealed was a little crypt or cavity, not much bigger than an ordinary coffin, and nearly filled by the form of a man who lay upon his back, eyes closed, his limbs tightly bound with rope.

"Holmes!"

Scrambling down into the pit beside my friend, I seized a thin white wrist. A moment later, to my immense relief, I could detect a pulse. "Holmes! Holmes, speak to me!"

To my indescribable joy, those pale eyelids fluttered open; the dry lips stirred. In a moment I had uncorked my flask of brandy and water and was lifting the victim's head. My friend drank avidly, and coughed, and then could speak.

His voice was so weak as to be almost inaudible. "Watson. A timely arrival. I . . . was confident that . . . that you . . ."

"Of course, of course. You must not exert yourself just yet. Breathe deeply."

"The blessed light of day," Holmes murmured feebly. "There for a while, Watson, I feared that I might never see the light of day again."

~ 11 ~

Holmes, in his debilitated state, evinced no particular surprise at Dracula's presence. Turning his head slightly, he murmured a word or two of greeting to his cousin, to which the prince responded calmly.

Even before we had lifted him from the earthen-floored pit, he gave orders that we must thoroughly search the narrow space in which he had been confined, looking for any evidence that Louisa Altamont had at least briefly—after her supposed drowning, but before her funeral and burial—been confined in the same place.

"You have reason to suspect this?" I demanded.

"Logic suggests it, Watson. I was unable to search properly myself. Do look carefully. Perhaps a ribbon or some other small item from her clothing—"

We lay Holmes at full length on the crumbling medieval mosaics of what had been the chapel's floor. I then went back, as commanded, to search the pit, but could find nothing useful. Meanwhile, Dracula's sharp nails worked like metal picks, his pale, resistless fingers tearing to shreds the ropes that bound his cousin. As he did so the prince muttered something about psychic vibrations—these were quite imperceptible to my no doubt cruder senses, but to the prince they indicated that indeed a vampire had recently been here.

"No," he amended this opinion. "I believe there have been two vampires, one of them only a young girl."

But further investigation would have to wait. In a moment the bonds had been completely torn away, and Dracula, lifting his cousin as easily as a small child in his arms, carried him to our waiting carriage, where I wrapped him in a robe.

Before leaving the site, Dracula insisted on taking a few moments to lower the great stone slab back into place, and to replace most of the fragments he had broken free around its edge, leaving to a casual inspection no visible sign that a rescue had been effected. Holmes agreed that this was a good idea.

We drove at a good speed back to our inn—at Holmes's request, keeping as much as possible to little-traveled roads. My patient, drawing deep, grateful breaths of the fresh air, already sounded a little stronger when he announced his wish that the fact of his rescue should be kept secret from the public for as long as possible.

By the time we reached the inn, Holmes was actually able to stand unaided, and, with a little support, to walk into the building, through a rear entrance. Dracula suggested carrying his cousin up and in through a first-floor window, directly into our reserved rooms, but such heroic measures proved unnecessary. We managed to reach our quarters by normal passages, without encountering anyone.

In only a few hours, when food and drink and fresh air had been allowed to begin their cure, Holmes had rallied wonderfully, though something of a chill still lingered, as he said, in his bones. At dusk, he was seated in his dressing gown, warming his hands and lighting his familiar briar pipe at a fire in our sitting room. When his pipe was drawing satisfactorily, he agreed to reveal to us exactly what had happened to him on the terrace of Norberton House.

I recalled that Holmes had still been present on the terrace when Abraham Kirkaldy was struck down, slaughtered by a blow from the hand of a strong vampire, as irresistible as that from the paw of a lion—and Holmes confirmed that he had seen that happen.

"But after that, old fellow, I was not able to see much. Will you tell me what occurred after my forced departure?"

"Of course." I now briefly outlined for him the later events I had witnessed on the terrace and in the garden. Dracula, though he had heard substantially the same story from me earlier, sat listening with great attention.

When I had finished, Holmes said: "Gentlemen, we are dealing with two vampires here—I believe with no more than two. One of these, I am now certain, is the unfortunate Louisa Altamont."

Here my friend glanced at his impassive cousin. "I say 'unfortunate' because she has been brought to her present state not by her own choice, or even by an accident precipitated by excessive passion. Rather the young woman is the victim of a deliberate attack."

Dracula stirred at last from his pose of rapt attention. "And the other nosferatu?" he inquired in a soft voice. "The one who carried you away?"

"That one, I am morally certain, is also her attacker. But let me tell you from the beginning the story of my own abduction."

Holmes went on to outline, in a few words, what he had been endeavoring to accomplish by dashing out onto the terrace at the conclusion of the séance: "I was determined to save Mrs. Altamont if I could, and also the breathing men who could not understand what sort of enemy we faced. I considered that they were all in danger of the same fate which had befallen Abraham Kirkaldy—if not of something worse."

"Thereby exposing yourself," I commented, "to a greater danger still."

Holmes made a dismissive gesture. "It is true that the intruder at the séance might have slain me on the spot—he might have slain us all. But it is obvious now that he had in mind something more than the mere slaughter of those he considered his enemies."

Then Holmes related for us in some detail what he had actually seen, felt, and heard while being seized and carried off by a single adversary of immense strength. "I must tell you, gentlemen, that it is not an experience I should care to repeat.

"Naturally my first reaction, when I felt his grip upon me, was a spontaneous attempt to resist; but that effort was both short-lived and unsuccessful, as my opponent quickly proved himself fully capable of pinioning both of my arms with one of his own. In that fashion he carried me, held at his side like an infant, while he beat a swift retreat from the vicinity of Norberton House.

"As there was no longer the slightest doubt about the nature of my antagonist, my immediate and overriding fear was that he might choose to drink my blood . . ."

Holmes paused for a moment. "I am, as you know, no weakling in ordinary circumstances, yet I could do nothing physically against a vampire. I regret that his identity remains a mystery—though to judge by the few words I heard him speak, and by a few other clues I noticed, it is certain that he is not English."

"I am glad to hear it," I murmured, and felt rather than saw the gaze of Prince Dracula turn toward me.

Holmes resumed his tale. "Not knowing why I was being taken prisoner, I fully expected death at any moment. Realizing that any continued physical struggle would be useless, I next endeavored to influence my captor by making him aware that I understood the basic truths regarding the existence and nature of vampires. By this means, I hoped to suggest to him the possibility that he might find me more useful alive than dead . . . but my attempt at cleverness was ignored about as thoroughly as my physical struggles had been."

"It is a miracle that you survived."

Holmes nodded at me. "I tell you, gentlemen, it would have been less frightening had he gagged me, or threatened me to keep me silent. But I received a strong impression that he was indifferent as to whether I might cry out. I sensed that nothing I might say or do was going to influence my captor in the least."

Holmes went on to describe how he had been taken to a secluded glade along the riverbank. There his limbs were bound, quickly and efficiently, and he was thrown down upon the grass and questioned at some length.

"I saw no point in trying to deceive him regarding my identity. Still, I am not even sure that he recognized my name."

This, I surmised, had probably stung my friend's pride as sharply as had being carried away like an infant.

"What else did he ask you?" Dracula inquired.

"There were several commonplace questions about the Altamonts, and how long I had known them. These I answered truthfully, not seeing that there was anything to be lost thereby. But—and this is interesting—when he moved on to Ambrose Altamont's reasons for hiring me, he doubted my still-truthful answers. He would have it that my real purpose in their house and at the séance had been to protect 'the treasure,' or 'the jewels'—he used both phrases several times.

"Steadfastly I denied any knowledge of a family treasure. I admitted having heard the apparition in white speak of it during the séance, but said I had assumed that her claim had been made at her new master's prodding.

"Then—after perhaps an hour, though really it might have been considerably less—my captor abruptly seemed to lose interest in me."

"Lose interest!"

Holmes nodded. "That is the impression I received. Though unfortunately I was not entirely forgotten. Again my kidnapper picked me up, throwing me over one shoulder this time, and carried me some little distance through the dark wood.

"Already the faint traces of dawn were visible in the east. No doubt the approach of daylight contributed to his decision to postpone any further questioning, and it gave me hope that at least my uncertainty regarding my fate was not to be much more prolonged.

"Not until we were climbing the slope surrounding the abandoned church did I recognize my surroundings. With scarcely another word to me, my enemy brought me to the place where you found me. Effortlessly he lifted the stone slab and packed me away beneath it.

"I can only describe his manner in doing so as if it seemed to him that I might be too valuable to be thrown away, but at the same time, he could not for the life of him think of anything useful to do with me at the moment."

Fervently I repeated a sentiment I had already expressed: "It is amazing that you are still alive!"

"For that I have you gentlemen to thank." And Holmes solemnly nodded to each of us in turn.

Dracula rubbed pale hands together, as I have seen his cousin do on occasion, in the manner of one who looks forward to some task he is about to undertake. "Tell me," said the prince, "more about this man we are looking for. I confess that I am intrigued. About this insane Russian, if that is really what he is."

Holmes shrugged. "There is not much more that I can tell. I am not even completely certain that I shall recognize him when I meet him again. The darkness was very nearly absolute in among the trees where I was questioned, and I was cast to the ground in such a position that my face was turned away from him. And as we know, the face, even the voice, of the vampire may change from one day to the next, much more than that of any breathing man."

I interrupted at this point to say that perhaps I could provide some physical description of the enemy, and now I repeated to Holmes another episode I had earlier recounted to Dracula: Rebecca Altamont's revelation of what she had seen, but had not previously disclosed, on the day her sister had been lost.

Holmes, who did not appear to be much surprised, listened with great attention. "So, he deliberately capsized the boat to get at his prey! The faint marks on the prow had suggested as much to me; but I could not be sure. The maneuver required him to expose his naked body to the daylight, if only briefly—even for an angry vampire, such a tactic seems bizarre, does it not?—but there can be no doubt that it is the same man. Did Rebecca Altamont hear him speak?"

"Apparently not."

My friend arose from his chair and paced the floor, and I was glad to see this evidence of his returning strength. He said: "Overturning the boat suggests a certain cleverness—it allowed him to make off with the older sister, and use her for his own foul purposes, while leaving everyone else with the impression that she had been accidentally drowned. But then why take the risk of allowing himself to be seen? Surely he might have tipped the boat while remaining hidden. Why? Why? Mere bravado? But that would be inconsistent. Real lunacy is a more convincing explanation." Holmes paused, and sighed. "Watson—"

"Yes?"

"A criminally insane man is terrible enough when he is breathing. When we add the immense physical strength of the nosferatu, and the other powers they possess—this is a fearful business indeed."

Holmes was excited and expressed his urgent wish to question Rebecca, and his concern for her safety.

Presently, seating himself again, he resumed the narrative of his captivity. "Our criminal's accent is Russian, I should say. Though I have some small knowledge of the language, I cannot be absolutely sure—perhaps his native tongue is some antique dialect of Russian. That would suggest that he is of considerable age. Definitely he is a native speaker of one of the Slavic languages; with years, perhaps centuries, of intermittent practice in the English tongue, yet still the traces linger."

"Holmes—"

He turned to me with an inquiring look.

"Holmes, is the name 'Count Kulakov' familiar to you?"

He thought for a moment. "No. Who is he?"

"I ask because a man of that name 'phoned to Baker Street and left a message of sympathy for me."

"Sympathy? Because of my supposed demise?"

"I assumed that was the reason. The name sounds Russian, and your mention just now—"

"Quite so." My friend was frowning. "Count Kulakov. But no, I am acquainted with no one . . . well, we shall see."

Dracula, who had been listening intently, asked: "And you really can give no reason why you were spared?"

"I cannot. Perhaps, as I half-seriously suggested a moment ago, it was out of a mere uncertainty as to what to do with me. During the hour or more that I was in the immediate presence of my enemy, I am sure that there were intervals, some lasting a full minute, when he was not entirely aware of everything about him. Could I have freed myself from my bonds during one of those periods, I might have been able to escape. But the cord was strong, the knots were skillfully tied, and I was not allowed time to overcome them."

"You say he was 'not entirely aware'?"

"That is understating the case. The actuality was something more frightening; the word 'catalepsy' comes to mind. It was rather as if my antagonist were functioning in a trance, or under some kind of posthypnotic suggestion."

Dracula and I were both intrigued by the medical possibilities, and the prince urged his cousin to give us more details.

Holmes did his best to provide them. The foreign vampire had sat immobile for minutes at a time, staring at nothing, as far as Holmes had been able to discern, except the very darkness of the night. "Again, the suggestion of real insanity looms. Had he been a breathing man, I should have strongly suspected epilepsy, or drugs."

At this, Dracula shook his head doubtfully. "Among us, both epilepsy and drug use of any kind are practically unheard of." The prince paused before adding, with evident reluctance: "Unfortunately, we do have cases of insanity." He paused again before admitting: "And they are not particularly rare."

Holmes turned toward his cousin. "Prince, he may have given us a valuable clue. There was a certain name he uttered—I do not think it was his own, but he pronounced it more than once. Does the name 'Gregory Efimovitch' mean anything to you?"

Dracula shrugged minimally. "Male. A Christian name and patronymic, according to the Russian style of address."

"Of course. But—?"

Our vampire colleague shook his head. "No. As the name of an individual, it means nothing to me. No more than does 'Count Kulakov.' Well, possibly they are the same."

Holmes returned to the question of Louisa Altamont. His brief observation of that young woman when she appeared at the séance had been enough to convince him, even as I was convinced, that she had definitely passed into the nosferatu state. But my friend had seen nothing of her; indeed, he had seen or heard no one but his captor during the period of his captivity. He was keenly interested when Dracula reported that Louisa's tomb was occupied by a living member of that race.

"We must call upon her, Prince." Holmes consulted his watch. "Tonight, if at all possible."

" 'Call upon her'?" I asked, puzzled.

"In her tomb, Watson, in her tomb!" Even as I shuddered inwardly, I took comfort in the fact that my companion had so far recovered as to display a flash of his old impatience.

Prince Dracula took the suggestion with perfect calm. "To arrange a conversation with the young one who now sleeps among her ancestors should not be too difficult. It may be that in the process, we will encounter the one who put her there as well." He smiled. "If so, that problem at least may be rather quickly settled."

The detective now turned his attention to me and requested that I give him a more detailed account of the events in and near the house following the séance. I complied, describing as fully as I could the savage attack on Abraham Kirkaldy, my conversations the next morning with Armstrong and Merivale, and the subsequent attempt to murder me in London.

Holmes reacted with considerable alarm upon hearing a partial account of my communications with Mycroft.

He beat a fist softly upon the arm of his chair. "But this I did not expect! I must telephone—no, I prefer not to appear in public just yet. Let my survival remain a secret, if possible, for a little longer. Watson, you must find a telephone at once. Call Mycroft and reassure him regarding my safety."

"Cousin Sherlock," interposed Prince Dracula, "before you do that, allow me to make a suggestion."

~ 12 ~

The prince proceeded with a formal request for our opinions on a plan that had suggested itself to him. This involved returning to the chapel and there setting up an ambush in force, with the object of trapping the slayer and kidnapper when the latter sooner or later returned to the hidden crypt. But Holmes immediately though diplomatically expressed grave doubts regarding the likelihood of success and soon we had all agreed that the idea was untenable. After all, Holmes had lain in confinement from very early on Wednesday morning until around midday on Thursday, and the villain had not returned to the crypt during that interval. Given his evidently uncertain mental state, it seemed perfectly possible that he might never go back at all.

With that decided, our next step was to communicate with Mycroft. Knowing the extreme regularity of the man's habits, I felt confident of being able to reach him at his desk at the ministry—or at the Diogenes Club during the evening, from a quarter to five till twenty to eight. After that, he was sure to be found in his rooms just opposite the club, across Pall Mall.

The Saracen's Head, like most other inns, boasted a telephone. But since the instrument was located on the ground floor, any conversation conducted there might be uncomfortably public. Other 'phones were sure to be available somewhere in the village—at the other inns, and at the railroad station if nowhere else—but I felt that a similar problem would surely arise whichever one we attempted to use.

The prince, always at his best when faced with an immediate tactical problem, quickly suggested a scheme to enable me to conduct my call to London without being overheard. Dracula proceeded me downstairs and went into the public room, from whence, a moment later, I heard his voice raised in unfamiliar tones, calling jovially for a round of drinks for the house. With bewildering facility, he had adopted the character of a commercial traveler. When I presently followed my ally downstairs, all potential eavesdroppers were concentrating eagerly upon a story of amatory adventure, as thoroughly improbable as it was distracting. This tale was scarcely concluded before it was followed by another. In using the telephone, my only remaining problem would be the occasional wave of boisterous laughter emanating from the pub down the hall, which might interfere somewhat with hearing.

Reasonably confident now of privacy, I put through my call and had the satisfaction of promptly reaching Mycroft—the further satisfaction of remembering to call him by that name, and of being able to assure him that his brother was now safe.

"But," I added, "he wishes to remain for a time out of view, and so has sent me to the telephone."

"Thank God!" came the heartfelt sentiment across the wires. "Sherlock has come through what must have been a terrible experience. Can you tell me whether the precise nature of it was . . . was . . . ?" It seemed that there were certain words Mycroft could not quite bring himself to say.

"It was, I regret to say, of the kind that we discussed in London. But he has come through it well."

"Thank you, John, for your honesty." Again the voice on the other end was quavering. "Is there anything I can do?"

"There may be several things." We conferred briefly, quickly agreeing that there was no immediate need for Mycroft to come to Amberley.

"I was not looking forward to the journey. Tell me, what does Sherlock request?"

"First, that you gather and pass along any information currently available on any unusual activity you can discover taking place in the Russian immigrant community in London."

"A large order." Mycroft sighed faintly, a sound of relaxation indicating, I thought, that the fact of his brother's current safety was sinking in, and that he was looking forward to being able to resume his own regular activities, which consisted almost entirely of the gathering and ordering of information.

After a moment's thought, Mycroft continued: "Just now we have in London the unity conference of the Social Democratic Party, which includes in its membership Russians as well as many other nationalities. The gathering has just moved here from Brussels, with the encouragement, not to say prodding, of the Belgian police. There are several prize rascals to be found among the delegates, along with a number of sincere reformers. Actually, I was studying the dossier of one of the men only this afternoon, trying to decide in which category he belongs."

"Not," I asked, "that of a man named Gregory Efimovitch?"

"Who is that?"

I did my best to explain. There was a slight pause at the other end of the line. "No, John," Mycroft answered presently. "The information on my desk concerns one Vladimir Ilyich Ulyanov, age thirty-three. A writer of revolutionary propaganda, under the pen name 'Lenin.' I don't see how this Ulyanov, or Lenin, can be your Gregory Efimovitch."

Nor did I. Mycroft, provided with such details as I could offer, promised to do his best to ascertain whether anyone prominent in the revolutionary intrigues, on either side, bore that particular Christian name and patronymic. Currently, the appellation was as unfamiliar to him as it had been to any of us.

Sherlock had given me several additional requests to pass along to Mycroft: First, pursuing the idea of a mysterious treasure, my friend wished to learn the origins of the Altamont fortune—not a difficult task for one who, like Mycroft in his position of power behind the scenes, had the whole resources of the British government at his fingertips when he felt it necessary to call upon them.

Second, Sherlock had also inquired whether there were any Russians or other Eastern Europeans known to be living or visiting in the vicinity of Amberley.

Our 'phone conversation was soon concluded, without either of us mentioning directly the once totally forbidden subject of vampires. Still, I felt justified in concluding that Mycroft had successfully adjusted to the facts of the situation and was bearing up better than his brother would ever have predicted.

Perhaps I had better explain to my readers that Mycroft Holmes, though he received very little publicity or recognition, at times almost *was* the British government. I thought it perfectly possible that in that capacity he might already have some information regarding Count Kulakov.

This supposition proved correct. Within two hours Mycroft had 'phoned back to me at the Saracen's Head, to pass along the information that several months ago a Russian gentleman named Alexander Ilyitch Kulakov had taken a country house within a few miles of the Altamonts' estate.

While I was engaged in this second call, Prince Dracula had once more entered the public bar and resumed his role of entertainer. Still, I refrained from saying openly on the telephone that we were facing the definite possibility that this Kulakov and our mysterious vampire were one and the same.

"Is there anything more you can tell me about him—Mycroft? It may be vitally important."

"Yes, John, actually there is a fair amount of information." And Mycroft relayed to me the suspicions then current in British intelligence circles, that the Russian count was quite likely mixed up in the conflict between terrorist revolutionaries and the Okhrana, or Tsarist secret police. Each of these parties was known to have agents in England. Some people, men and women, were double agents, trying to play both sides.

"And his personal description, Mycroft—his appearance?"

"I have never laid eyes on the man myself. But he is described as tall and well built, about forty years of age. Has red hair and beard and greenish, peculiar eyes. He seems to be heir to some remote but extensive Siberian estates that were his father's and grandfather's before him. Another—"

"Red hair," I repeated. "And beard. Tall and powerful. Even green eyes."

"That is the description I have been given."

Mycroft had more information at his fingertips. The Russian count had apparently come to England unaccompanied save for a faithful servant or two. Our own intelligence service supposed him, and doubtless his servants as well, to be involved, in some way hard to determine, in the ongoing duel of secret agents between the monarchy and the revolutionaries.

There was still more. Mycroft had discovered a dossier

on one man bearing the given name and patronymic of Gregory Efimovitch, who had attained a fair degree of prominence in the intrigues among Russian exiles, and Mycroft had already set in motion an investigation to determine his current whereabouts.

"Can we establish any connection," I asked, "between this man and Kulakov?"

"So far I cannot. But sooner or later we will discover the link if it exists."

Presently I rang off the telephone, looked in at the public bar to let my colleague know the latest call had been completed, and preceded him back to our rooms to report to Holmes.

On my arrival upstairs I found my friend in conversation with Martin Armstrong and Rebecca Altamont, both of them much restored in appearance from the last time I had seen them.

Armstrong and Rebecca Altamont had each awakened in Baker Street shortly after noon that day, Thursday, and had been promptly handed my messages by Mrs. Hudson. After our landlady had provided them with a hasty meal, the young people had come rushing back to Amberley on the first train available. The two appeared at the Saracen's Head at seven o'clock on Thursday evening, after having stopped first at Norberton House to bathe and change.

They came to our inn partly with the intention of seeing Inspector Merivale, who also occupied a room there. Further, Holmes had said he wanted to see Armstrong, and I had sent a message to Norberton House—where any request from me was rather coldly received—asking the young American to call on me.

On the arrival of Armstrong and Miss Altamont, Holmes had ordered tea to be served in our rooms, and I found him entertaining our visitors there.

Prince Dracula, now once more relieved from his duties in the bar downstairs, looked in, and I had introductions to perform. "This is Mr. Prince," I said, using an alias we had agreed on earlier, "who has come down from London with me. He is another associate of Mr. Sherlock Holmes."

Prince Dracula had been looking forward to a well-earned sleep, in his own room, during the day's remaining daylight hours. But he was also eager to meet these people who were so deeply involved in our mystery. "How do you do?"

I thought that Rebecca Altamont colored slightly when Dracula bowed and greeted her with continental politeness—an assured manner which clearly indicated his noble origins.

Later, I heard from both Martin Armstrong and Miss Altamont, that they on seeing Dracula for the first time, had taken note, as I had myself, of the strong resemblance between the cousins. Though neither of the young people said anything at the time of their introduction, both, as they told me later, were ready to believe there was some family connection. Still, I thought the present likeness not as great as it had been six years earlier; my friend, I realized, had aged perceptibly in that interval—the change was more noticeable in the hours immediately following his confinement—while Holmes's distant relative impressed me as looking even younger in 1903 than he had in 1897.

Both Miss Altamont and Armstrong, of course, were delighted to learn that Holmes had managed to avoid serious injury while in captivity. Soon the young man eagerly demanded of my friend what news he might have of Louisa.

Holmes shook his head. "There is no news directly; I did not see her, or hear her name mentioned."

The American's face fell. "But you know now who her captors are? They must be the same men who held you."

"Very likely. But as yet, I can tell you nothing on that score."

Rebecca broke in: "At least you can tell us whether my sister is still alive? You now have evidence of that?"

Holmes looked very grave. "I am afraid I cannot promise you an answer on that point either."

Armstrong leaped to his feet. "What do you mean? God! Don't tell me the scum have killed her after all? Or that they have . . . have . . ."

"I said that I can promise you nothing. But perhaps I can show you something that has a bearing on Louisa's fate. Can you come with me tonight?"

"Of course—wherever you wish!"

"Am I to be excluded?" demanded the young woman.

"By no means." But then Holmes turned to face Armstrong fully, and my friend's expression was grim. "In return, Mr. Armstrong, I require complete candor on your part. Will you now tell us the full story of how the rowboat was capsized?" Holmes's expression had grown still more ominous. "I am convinced that in your earlier account of the matter to us, you omitted certain details of great importance."

At this key point, our conversation was interrupted by the arrival of Inspector Merivale. Soon Armstrong, in the presence of Scotland Yard, admitted that there was something he had not told.

While Rebecca Altamont, her face suddenly pale, sat back in her chair, the inspector demanded: "Why did you say nothing about this until now?"

Armstrong looked pleadingly from one of us to another. "Gentlemen, it was so strange a thing that I couldn't bring myself to mention it. But now—now that we know Louisa's still alive—why, it's plain that whatever is going on must be very strange indeed. And this odd piece will fit in with the rest somehow." He turned an appealing look in my direction. "Do you see what I mean, Doctor?"

"If you will tell us everything you know," I advised him, "your meaning may be easier to grasp."

"Of course." Martin Armstrong drew a full breath and seemed to pull himself together. "Gentlemen—Becky—I now confess that at the time—just as I turned in the moment of the boat's capsizing—I thought I did catch just a glimpse of something very strange.

"As we began to go over, I twisted my head around, looking over my right shoulder . . . and I retain the distinct impression of a pale hand, or at least of human fingers, grasping the gunwale on that side. Then a few moments later, when I was under water, I felt the sense of some stranger's body near me there. But I hope you will understand, so brief and fragmentary were these impressions, so unsupported by either logic or common sense, that ever since, I have discounted them as the result of nerves, or actual hallucinations."

Holmes demanded: "And you have never mentioned to anyone—to Miss Altamont here, for example—what you thought you saw?"

Armstrong shook his head violently. "How could I? Rebecca would have believed me mad."

"Perhaps not," the lady herself said, shaking her head.

The young man went on to explain that the sense of some mysterious presence had not appeared to him to offer any genuine explanation of the upset. At the moment of crisis, of course, he had given little thought to causes, but expected it would be relatively easy to make sure that both girls were safe.

We urged him to tell the whole story again, this time as truthfully as possible, and he agreed. When he had come up, gasping, to the surface after his initial plunge, Armstrong had immediately seen Becky struggling to stay afloat; he swam to her and guided her to shore, which was the work of less than a minute.

"Then Becky and I looked at each other. And both of us said the same thing at the same moment: 'Where's Louisa?'

"There was the rowboat, now floating almost placidly, drifting upside down. There were the two oars. I seem to recall seeing a floating banjo and a picnic basket. But no sign at all of Louisa. I wondered, was she on the other side of the boat, or had she come up underneath it?"

In a strained voice, Martin went on to tell us that he had stripped off his light summer coat, which was already sodden, and then his shoes, and in light summer trousers and shirt-sleeves, plunged back into the stream. Quickly, he made sure that no one was trapped under the boat. He came out from under it and dived again, thinking that surely, surely, his fiancée's head must appear above the water at any moment . . .

"I did find her hat—did I mention that before, gentlemen? Yes, her hat, in the water . . . but that was all."

Time dragged on, the horrible minutes following the capsizing of the boat lengthening into a full hour, and extending themselves endlessly after that . . .

Rebecca, of course, had summoned aid as quickly as possible. But dusk, which was gathering at the time the boat tipped, had deepened almost totally into night before there were answering shouts and lights coming through the trees.

"We searched on, of course, through the night. Men and boys from the neighboring houses and farms, as well as from Norberton House, looking along the shore and in the water. Gradually, we all lost hope. No one found . . . found her . . . until broad daylight. By then, the girl, whoever she was, had been dead for hours. Her . . . her body lay on the bank, nearly a mile downstream." Briefly overcome by emotion, the young man had to pause. "Oh, God! Oh, God, when I thought that was Louisa—"

In the morning, as we already knew, there had been the limp, white, unbreathing body to be taken up, carried home and mourned over. Drowning was the obvious cause of death. As we had earlier learned, there had been no visible injuries—certainly no more than a few scratches, including the two small marks upon the white, still throat.

Within a day or so, an inquest had been held upon "the poor girl, in the full belief that she was Louisa," and her body had been duly interred.

When Armstrong had concluded his story, Rebecca Altamont took his hand and did her best to comfort him; and I remember that at the time, it crossed my mind that when grief and terror had been surmounted, there might be the chance of a more tender attachment growing between them.

Presently the young American, recovering himself a little, proposed a plan in which several of we men would return in the same rowboat to the scene of the catastrophe, and one or more might strip and jump into the water to try the experiment of tipping the craft over, just to see how difficult it was, even where the river was shallow enough to allow more or less solid footing on the muddy bottom.

"If it proves really impossible to capsize the boat that way," he concluded, "then perhaps I was hallucinating after all."

No one answered that directly. I could see Dracula smile faintly, no doubt at the thought of himself going for a bathe in the bright morning daylight. In a moment, the prince murmured that he would decline to take part in such an exercise. "Running water and I are not always on the best of terms," he added. "Not to mention my tendency to sunburn." I could see that this refusal and comment both rather puzzled the young American.

Holmes commended Armstrong's plan of reenactment as worthy, possibly useful. "But unfortunately there is no time for it now; there are other matters which much more urgently require our attention."

Armstrong blinked at him. "Of course. And I still insist that the first of them is finding Louisa, wherever she may be, and thereby putting an end to this nightmare."

At this juncture Holmes suddenly brought the name of Count Kulakov into the conversation. Both of the young people could immediately confirm that there was, or had been, a foreigner of that name living in the neighborhood and attending a few social events, though neither Armstrong nor Miss Altamont had ever met the man, or even seen him.

But Rebecca then went on to recall hearing Louisa say that she had met him, and did not like him.

"I remember she told me that on one occasion—months ago, before you two were engaged, Martin—he had paid her attentions that were not entirely welcome."

Armstrong frowned. He harked back to his stay in St. Petersburg and tried to recall anything he might have learned about Count Kulakov during that time. "I do think I might have heard the name somewhere—but where? Is there a possibility that he is somehow involved in this business?"

"A distinct possibility." Then, changing the subject again, Holmes asked if the Altamonts had any plans for another séance.

Armstrong and Rebecca, during their brief stop at Norberton House before coming to see us, had already been apprised of the intentions of the family there. Louisa's parents were naturally expecting them to keep those plans secret from any investigators who might interfere.

But Armstrong had his own agenda regarding séances. "If these scoundrels think they can somehow smuggle Louisa into the house again, and then whisk her away as they did last time, they're in for a surprise. The police are watching, too."

Holmes's continued questioning of Armstrong and Miss Altamont elicited the information that Sarah Kirkaldy was refusing even to talk about the possibility of another sitting. With her brother's body in a coffin in the parlor, that struck me as hardly to be wondered at.

The young couple also had information for us regarding the time of Abraham's funeral, which they were naturally expecting to attend. He had been struck down half an hour before midnight Tuesday and had died on Wednesday morning. The funeral and burial were planned for Saturday morning.

"Probably I shall not attend," Holmes mused thoughtfully. "Yet I dare not delay interviewing Miss Kirkaldy as long as that. Her own safety, I think, will not permit it, and even tomorrow may be too late." He shifted the direction of his gaze. "Mr. Prince?"

Dracula, as if he had been expecting to be called upon, smiled and nodded gently. He appeared ready to abandon his hope of catching a nap before sundown. "If you wish, Mr. Holmes, I shall be glad to visit Norberton House. Perhaps I can establish some rapport with Miss Kirkaldy. I will, of course, convey our sympathies to her on the loss of her brother—and it may be that she will tell me a few interesting things."

Shortly, the prince and Armstrong had gone off together.

Holmes's recuperative powers, as I have remarked before, were truly impressive. As nightfall drew near, only half a day following his rescue from the crypt, he was on his feet again, insisting in his masterful way that there be no delay in our investigation. When I remonstrated with him that he required rest after his ordeal, he snapped back: "I have lain inactive quite enough during the past forty hours, I assure you!"

Two items now had very high priority on my friend's agenda. One was the interview with Sarah Kirkaldy, which matter he fortunately had been able to entrust to his cousin.

"She must be induced to tell us all she knows about this evil man! He is, I have no doubt, her brother's murderer."

As for the other objective, Holmes, speaking to me privately, insisted that it was now imperative that we open the burial vault of Louisa Altamont and interview her as soon as possible—whether Martin Armstrong was on hand or not.

It struck me that six years earlier such an assertion, with regard to any young woman whose body had been put into a tomb almost a month ago, would have seemed strong evidence of madness. Now I could only accept Holmes's plan as a way of dealing with an even more terrible truth.

"We must admit the gravest doubts as to whether it will ever be possible for her to rejoin her loved ones. Still, it is essential that I speak to her without further delay. Murder has been committed. The expedition will, of course, be dangerous."

"If you intend to go at night, I should rather describe it as foolhardy!"

"Calm yourself, Watson. Naturally, the danger will be vastly greater after sunset, when our chief opponent will be more likely to put in an appearance. But I intend to go nowhere after dark until Prince Dracula has rejoined us. Then we shall have odds of at least three to one in our favor, and, I think—our ally being who he is—no need to be overly concerned."

Holmes had already made arrangements with Martin Armstrong for the young man to accompany us when we went to open the tomb of Louisa Altamont. Holmes hoped to be able to demonstrate to the still-hopeful fiancé the truth of what had happened to his beloved. Despite my friend's assurance to the breathing Miss Altamont that she should not be excluded from the revelation, he had no intention of bringing her on this first expedition.

Armstrong had agreed readily. He still had his own reason for wanting an exhumation: the hope to prove that someone else had been interred under his fiancée's name.

~ 13 ~

I accepted the assignment from Cousin Sherlock calmly, not anticipating that it would present any particular difficulty. "There is, of course," I commented, "the matter of my obtaining an invitation to enter the house. I expect that would greatly facilitate matters."

"Of course." Holmes nodded.

"Of course," echoed Armstrong, nodding too. Naturally he, being still innocent of the least bit of vampire lore, could not have understood my being so particular about wanting an invitation to cross a mere threshold; but he very quickly volunteered to introduce Mr. Prince to the Altamont family as his own friend, a man experienced in dealing with psychic problems. "I understand that it will be wise to refrain from mentioning any connection the gentleman might have with Sherlock Holmes and Dr. Watson."

Soon—the time was now eight o'clock, still full daylight on a long summer evening—Armstrong and I were on our way, chatting together companionably enough. I have several reasons for remembering with great clarity that particular summer day: One is the fact that it marks the occasion of my first ride in a motorcar.

For several years I had been looking forward to the event, realizing that sooner or later I should have to accustom myself to the horseless carriage. When the opportunity arrived, I dutifully equipped myself for the adventure in borrowed goggles and a long dust-coat, telling myself that this was only one more step in my never-ending adjustment to an ever-new and changing world. In fact the ride, with Armstrong at the controls, was neither as bad as I had cynically expected nor quite as exhilarating as I had dared to hope. The sheer speed (I suppose some thirty miles an hour, substantially beyond the twenty recently established as the British speed limit for cars) was no real novelty; in some of my four-legged forms, I could have outsped the machine, at least over a short distance. And flying on the support of one's own organic wings, another act to which I am no stranger, is in my judgment a sensation far superior to that of riding in any mere land-bound device.

The young American (as Watson so liked to call him) and I were on our way, terrorizing an occasional dog or cat as we shot through the village, shouting back and forth to each other over the roar of machinery and the rush of air. Talking in this way we touched on several matters, including the current disposition of Louisa's parents. I gathered that both elder Altamonts were eager, as only recent converts are wont to be, for more doings in the world of spirits. Father and mother were fretting in their impatience to see their departed daughter again. Though I gave Armstrong no assurance, I was convinced that very encounter could be arranged, but was far from convinced that it would be wise to do so.

According to Armstrong, there were even rumors (the servants had been gossiping) that the senior Altamonts, unable to wait, had tried to hold another séance last night, even without the help of an experienced medium. The result seemed to have been a complete failure. Well, I thought, things might have been worse.

Little daunted (if the rumors were true), Louisa's parents were supposedly planning another sitting for tonight, still nursing hopes of getting the grief-stricken Sarah Kirkaldy to cooperate. Perhaps, I thought, the elder couple were wondering why Sarah, considered an expert in other worldly matters, should be taking her temporary separation from Abraham so hard; one might have thought that her brother, being himself a medium, should have a particularly easy time in getting back.

I supposed that Louisa's parents would be inclined to blame any new failure, as they had blamed the old, on strange, malignant powers that had been somehow attracted to the scene by Sherlock Holmes and his associates, including the police. None of this, I thought, was very logical; but then, logic had never been the spiritists' strong point.

Looking toward the house from the long drive, as we came rattling and roaring up to the front door, I could recognize, from Watson's description, the terrace where the murder had taken place, and I observed how the broken French window had been temporarily boarded up. I supposed that any real clues to the identity of the intruder at the last séance had long since been removed, either by accident or by the police.

Shortly we were at the door, divested of our long white coats and goggles, standing in a cloud of our own slowly settling dust.

When we had been shown in to meet the master and mistress of the house, Armstrong, ready to embroider the truth and demonstrating a cool skill in the work, claimed to have met me during his most recent sojourn in St. Petersburg, where (allowing for my ineradicable central European accent) I, like Armstrong himself, had been one of the corps of foreign correspondents.

Old Altamont's handgrip was firm, but his eye was

wary. His formal greeting was followed quickly by a blunt question: "Are you an agent of Sherlock Holmes?"

I blinked at this, and considered my answer thoughtfully. Finally I responded: "I have met the man, and I respect him. Nevertheless, there are important areas of human experience—far from the realms of law, or chemical science—with which his knowledge and skill are sadly inadequate to deal."

"You are yourself a sensitive?" Mrs. Altamont inquired of me hopefully. I noted that she had somewhat modified her vivacious dress, as recorded by Watson, but had not gone back to mourning.

Again I pondered carefully. "Sensitive, in a psychic sense? Dear lady, I would be loath to make that claim. Still, I cannot deny that there have been in my life certain incidents hard to explain by any other . . ."

And so on. Soon Armstrong, taking advantage of a pause in the spiritualist chatter, somewhat belatedly informed our hosts that Mr. Holmes had returned from his adventure and was safe. The Altamonts were charitable enough to express what sounded like sincere satisfaction with this news. In their current mental state they appeared uninterested in any of the fine points, such as whether Holmes's kidnapper had been a spirit or mere flesh and blood.

Wading boldly into this confusion, Mr. Prince, who had already hinted broadly enough at his own psychic powers, presented himself to the bereaved parents as one who might be able to help them in their current difficulties. Though, as he admitted when asked straight out, he had never conducted a séance. He did not volunteer the information that he had never even attended one.

He soon overcame his hosts' suspicions that he might be some kind of investigative agent. Conversing in ever more familiar terms, but in increasingly hushed voices, we moved slowly through the house toward an unstated goal. Naturally today's first order of business for any visitor in this home was to view, with appropriate gloomy aspect and sad murmuring of platitudes, the body of young Abraham Kirkaldy.

All that was mortal of the youth had been embalmed, dressed in a new, fairly expensive suit, and coffined tastefully in a parlor amid comfortable-looking white-satin pillows and a great many flowers, awaiting interment on Saturday morning. Dead as mutton was that lad, as I could see at first glance. No question in his case of that mysterious undeath which walks by night and sups on blood—not that I had thought there would be, but it was as well that the expert should make sure.

The coffin was open—I had wondered whether it would be. The side of the head on which the murderer's blow had fallen was turned away from the viewer, and the hair was long enough so that when properly arranged, it covered, or almost covered, the extensive damage.

Within a quarter of an hour after my arrival, I was seated in a (different) parlor and pretending to sip at some no doubt excellent tea (readers should remember that my taste in liquid nourishment is sharply limited). By this time, I was hinting strongly that I should like to be allowed to speak with Sarah Kirkaldy. Naturally, I promised to treat the bereaved sister with great courtesy and tact. I gently dropped an additional hint that I just might be able to convince the girl to conduct another séance within a day or so.

I knew that Cousin Sherlock was at least considering encouraging another séance in Norberton House—tonight seemed out of the question, but perhaps on the following night—and in any kind of planning long-range enough to reach hours or days into the future, I had learned to defer to my breathing cousin's genius. If our enemy should then attempt another intrusive haunting, it would at least bring him within our reach, as well as allow us to make contact directly with Louisa Altamont.

Sarah, as her kindly benefactors informed me, was currently resting in the garden—the Altamonts mentioned in passing that the poor girl had developed, in the past two days, a great longing for the sunlight.

And so it was that in the formal garden of Norberton House, on that fading summer evening, I presently was introduced to Sarah Kirkaldy. She was sitting in a chair on the lawn beside a quiet terrace—on the other side of the house, let me hasten to add, from the terrace whose flagstones still bore some faint stain of her brother's blood.

Mrs. Altamont conducted me to her, and spoke in a hushed voice. "Dear, this is Mr. Prince, a friend of Martin's, come from London. He has some experience in these matters, and has kindly offered to see if there is anything he might do."

Sarah was garbed all in black, forming an odd contrast with the liberated plumage of her hostess. She put down her book (a trashy novel, I was glad to see) and arose from her lawn chair with something of alarm in her expression. I suppose she must have been thinking that almost the last thing she needed at that point was another psychic swindler on the scene—or worse, another genuine terror like Mr. Gregory, whose existence she had not yet dared reveal to anyone.

Mr. Prince, who even in 1903 enjoyed four centuries' experience in the craft of soothing nervous maidens, did his best to put this one at her ease. Speaking gently and diplomatically, pressing Sarah's offered hand, I was soon able to calm her, and to begin to allay her fears. When, after another quarter of an hour, the two of us were left alone upon the terrace, I (having found for myself a chair in the deepest shade) began an effort to persuade her to tell me of what must have been some terrifying contacts with the rogue vampire who had slain her brother.

"Miss Kirkaldy, you have my most sincere sympathy in the loss of your brother."

"Thank you, sir."

"I think he need not have died, and I have hopes that his killer will not remain beyond the reach of justice." Here I paused, waiting for some comment that did not come. "Do you know—when you insist that the drowned girl, Louisa Altamont, genuinely appeared at your séance—I am inclined to believe you."

Sarah stared at me. I had been presented to her as a psychic, and to her stubborn skepticism, that meant I was a fake—or would have meant that a few days earlier. No doubt her encounter, or encounters, with the vampire who was Louisa's rapist and Abraham's slayer had done something to shake her materialist faith.

Meanwhile Mr. Prince talked on. "What the world calls death is not always the true death, is it, Sarah? Ah, I really believe that you do not yet understand."

"Sir?"

"Please, Sarah? May I presume upon our short acquaintance to ask a favor?"

"Sir?"

"The favor is just this: My Christian name is Arthur. Will you use it when you speak to me? Somehow, as you must have noticed, I have already fallen into using yours." Pause. "For this, I make no apology."

She looked at me long, with the dappling of the day's last sunlight and leaf-shadow on her attractive face. I was distracted by the tiny pulsing, so gentle a movement as to be scarcely visible, of a soft blue vein beneath the tawny skin of her soft throat. Remember, I warned myself sternly, that you are here on business.

"Arthur," she said at last.

"Yes, that is much better. Whom do you fear, Sarah?"

"Fear?"

We sparred over that question for a little while, and then I let it drop; it was not going to be quickly or directly answered.

Sarah, perhaps mainly to distract me from any line of conversation that might lead to the man she feared, began to complain about how roughly and inconsiderably she had been questioned by Inspector Merivale.

I sympathized, listened to examples of the questions asked by the man from Scotland Yard, and managed to get answers to one or two of them where Merivale had failed.

I could picture him, towering and official, stroking his little mustache, trying to be kind and efficient at the same time. He'd demanded of Sarah: "Now, Miss. We have testimony that at your sitting, on the night Mr. Holmes was carried off, there came into the house somehow a young woman, dressed in white—"

"I told him 'twas Louisa Altamont."

"And what do you really believe? You can tell me, Sarah."

"I dinna ken nae mair. I dinna ken what t' think. I thocht Louisa Altamont had been dead for three weeks."

"Come on! Tell the truth!"

"Inspector Merivale, I dinna control what happens when we ha'e a sittin'."

And the official questioning had made little if any headway.

Our afternoon trailed on toward dusk. I was doing somewhat better than the inspector had done.

And Madeline Altamont, looking out through breeze-blown curtains at the quiet young couple in the gathering twilight, and much more observant than her husband in certain human ways, had noticed that Mr. Prince bore a distant resemblance to Sherlock Holmes.

In fact dear Madeline had even begun to suspect that their new psychic consultant was Holmes's illegitimate son, but for the time being she kept this suspicion to herself.

~ 14 ~

In our telephoning and in other matters we had taken such precautions as seemed reasonable to prevent the fact of Holmes's rescue being revealed prematurely to the general public. By this means we hoped to keep our chief enemy also in the dark regarding the true state of affairs, and to avoid such difficulties as would inevitably be caused by journalists swarming round. Still, we realized that it would be extremely difficult to preserve the secret for many hours or days, unless Holmes were to remain in hiding, or adopt some disguise. Neither alternative seemed attractive.

Despite our desire for secrecy, we had felt it our duty, before there was any question of a general announcement, to notify Inspector Merivale at least that Holmes was safe. We did so promptly, and Merivale then quietly called off the official search.

Merivale, having absented himself for a while on other business, returned at dusk to our rooms in the Saracen's Head; this was rather awkward, as at the time Holmes and I were only waiting for Dracula and Martin Armstrong to come back from Norberton House before we launched our clandestine operation to open the tomb of Louisa Altamont.

This time it was obvious from the inspector's expression, even before we heard his report, that the official investigation was not going well. No convincing motive for the murder of Abraham Kirkaldy could be attributed to any of the people known to have been at the séance. No suitable weapon could be located; whatever object had been used (something much harder, sharper, and heavier than a human hand) must have acquired bloodstains. The reports of witnesses, including my own, were confused and contradictory regarding the presence, at the time of the murder, of another outsider besides the mysterious girl or woman in white. Some who had attended the séance had seen nothing of the kind, while others, including myself, were absolutely certain that at least one additional intruder had been present on the terrace.

In this state of general uncertainty, Merivale had succeeded in getting the official inquest postponed for a few more days.

My own version of events, as I now repeated it once more for the inspector, was simple, even though possibly hard to believe. It was also substantially, if not totally, truthful. I gave it as my impression that one or more unknown trespassers had invaded the séance and that they were responsible for the violence; but I had seen only vague shapes and could give no description of them. To make amends, in a sense, for this unsatisfactory evidence, I was able to hand the inspector the missing jewels which Mr. Prince in my presence had recovered from the cemetery.

Holmes was now able to offer the police some corroboration of my evidence. He stated that he was able to give no real description of his abductors—he allowed the implication to stand that there had been more than one. As far as he was concerned, they remained shadowy figures, impossible to identify.

My friend then told the inspector a convincing tale—similar to my own evidence in being true in its essentials, though incomplete—of being questioned in the dark woods and then imprisoned in the hidden crypt under the abandoned chapel.

Merivale marveled at all this, as well he might, but could not very well dispute any of it. He naturally expressed a wish to see the abandoned chapel, and announced his plan of visiting it when daylight came.

"Must be a gang, by the look of it," said the Scotland Yard man reluctantly, still marveling at Holmes's story even before he had a chance to see the slab. "And the girl, Mr. Holmes? What about Louisa Altamont? Is she still alive or isn't she?" The question had the sound of a fervent plea for help.

Holmes slowly shook his head. "In my opinion, Inspector, there is nothing to be gained by searching for a living Louisa. It is a tragic business, but I fear that sooner or later, the family will have to reconcile themselves to the facts."

Merivale sighed. "As I thought, then. That's too bad. Would you have a word with young Armstrong, Mr. Holmes? I've tried, and Dr. Watson has tried, to convince him that his young lady's not coming back. Maybe if you . . ."

"I shall do what I can. I have already had a talk with Mr. Martin Armstrong."

"Excellent."

We had earlier received by telephone from Mycroft enough evidence to at least cast strong suspicion upon Count Kulakov. Holmes now suggested that the police begin to take an interest in the visiting Russian. At the same time, Holmes warned Merivale that the gentleman should be kept ignorant of the fact that the official police were interested in him.

"I strongly advise against making an arrest, or even bringing the man in for questioning. I doubt very much that you would find it possible to subject him to the penalties of the law."

"He enjoys diplomatic immunity, you mean?"

"Something of the sort."

Merivale seemed doubtful, but acquiesced and outlined a plan for assigning one or two good men to keep a watch round Norberton House at night.

"There's another matter to be considered," the inspector offered next. "We have to consider who played the part of the spook at both séances. The Altamonts continue to swear it was actually their daughter, materialized out of the world of spirits; and young Armstrong, too, believes it was really his fiancée, though he keeps the business on an earthly plane. If we must consider that impossible, can we rule out Sarah Kirkaldy herself as the mysterious ghost in white?"

Holmes nodded thoughtfully. "It seems to me we can. There I believe we are on somewhat firmer ground. My associate, Mr. Prince, has already spoken with her."

Shortly after dark, Mr. Prince returned to the inn, having accomplished his assigned task of interviewing Sarah Kirkaldy. Dracula, looking younger and more energetic now that the sun was gone, appeared behind Inspector Merivale's back to signal me through one of the windows of our upstairs sitting room. I made some excuse and joined the prince in the adjoining room.

Dracula wanted to inform me, out of Merivale's hearing, that on his way back to the Saracen's Head he had detoured to the private cemetery. There he had managed to pick up another piece or two of the recently stolen jewelry, and had also found evidence that our chief enemy—Count Kulakov, if our suspicions were correct—had revisited the old chapel in our absence. This evidence took the form of rampant, raging vandalism—headstones and a decorative stone bench had been smashed and the pieces scattered about. In any case, we might as well give up all hope and pretense of keeping the secret of Holmes's survival.

While the inspector was still in our sitting room at the Saracen's Head, I was called downstairs to take another telephone communication from Mycroft in London. The chief news Mycroft offered was that no connection whatsoever could be traced between the Russian exile named Gregory Efimovitch, and Count Kulakov, or to anyone else in Buckinghamshire—"though perhaps there is one to that fellow Ulyanov I mentioned."

Even more dashing to our hopes for a solution, Mycroft's Gregory Efimovitch had been in jail in Liverpool for the past several months.

After returning to the inn, and there holding a brief private talk with Watson, I, Prince Dracula, enjoyed a short private chat with Inspector Merivale of Scotland Yard. Something about me had evidently interested the inspector when we were introduced. I could have wished that this second meeting might have taken place in more doubtful lighting, and under circumstances denying the inspector any chance to examine me closely or engage in prolonged conversation—but only the last of those conditions was fulfilled.

I had been introduced to Merivale, as I had been presented to Armstrong, to Rebecca Altamont, and to others, as Mr. Prince, one of the members of the small organization that the great detective had begun to put together in recent years—particularly since Watson had moved out of the Baker Street lodgings.

Merivale, as he talked to me now, appeared a little dubious about Mr. Prince—or would have been dubious had not Sherlock Holmes solemnly vouched for me.

On hearing that I had just come from Norberton House, the inspector naturally wanted to know whether I had spoken to Sarah Kirkaldy there, and if so, what I might have found out from her.

"Yes, I was privileged to talk to the bereaved girl—she is a sweet soul." Out of the corner of my eye I beheld Watson, who had just entered the room, staring at me. What had possessed me to make Mr. Prince such a cloying individual in the eyes of Scotland Yard, I really do not know. "Her brother's funeral is Saturday."

"Right, and I plan to be there. How about you, Mr. Holmes?"

Holmes, who had now come in as well, shook his head. "My plans are as yet uncertain."

Merivale was determined to interview the young woman yet again. I did my best to discourage him from the effort, without seeming to try to do so.

Despite my warnings to myself, I was already beginning to take a personal interest in Sarah. Ah, was ever woman in such humor wooed? Was ever woman in such humor won?

Richard the Third. Shakespeare. Remind me to tell you a story about him some day. I mean the poet, not the king. Though our careers did somewhat overlap (he died, I think, in 1485), I never met that monarch. I hear myself beginning to babble, but never mind. I told you at the start that certain aspects of this tale of séances tend to make me nervous—and we are getting closer to them.

Ah, that Edwardian summer! The delights of young love—no, of course I hardly qualified as young myself—but all the more delightful to my aging bones was the experience of youth, the gift of Sarah's warm young skin, and later her blood, and our shared laughter. Yes, during the following nights and days, I did that much for Sarah Kirkaldy: taught her how to begin to laugh again, gave her strong armament with which to face the fear and murder of the world.

It was a vintage year in many ways.

In 1903, motorcars were becoming commonplace in Britain—where there were already more than eight thousand such machines—and in much of the United States, where that very summer, the Ford Motor Company was being organized and the Wright brothers were hard at work preparing for their first successful flight, eventually to take place on 17 December.

In Switzerland, twenty-four-year-old Albert Einstein, no doubt enjoying a feeling of security by reason of his newly attained degree in physics and his steady job at the Swiss patent office, was in the process of marrying a young lady he had met at the university in Zürich. And in all quarters of the globe, the æther was being frequently disturbed by experiments with wireless telegraphy, carried out by researchers of several nations.

While waiting in one of our rooms at the inn for Cousin Sherlock and Martin Armstrong to join us, so we could pay our nocturnal visit to the cemetery, Watson and I relaxed with separate newspapers. I had taken up a recent edition of the *Times* of London and was pondering some of the articles. I think I even read a few of them aloud to Watson.

I reflected upon how much my understanding of the British had—as I thought—improved since my first visit to the islands some twelve years earlier (see *The Dracula Tape*), and yet how much I still found in their ways to marvel at.

The pages of today's edition alone offered much food for contemplation:

> EGYPTIAN HALL—England's HOME OF MYSTERY. Established 30 years. Manager, Mr. J.N. Maskelyne . . .

I read no further under that heading, being already confronted with quite enough mystery.

CAUTION—A.S. LLOYD'S EUXESIS—for shaving without soap, water, or brush . . .

PERRY & CO.—ELECTRIC LIGHT FITTINGS

Money Spent on Education Is the Best of Investments—

LATEST INTELLIGENCE—THE SOMALILAND OPERATIONS. Prisoners and deserters state that a British force is at Galadi and that Mullah has moved from Bur to Gumburro with his footmen . . .

With regard to the above item, the modern reader may note that the more things change, et cetera . . .

At Bangor petty sessions yesterday Mr. Horace Plunkett was summoned for furiously driving a motorcar along Holyhead Road. Evidence was given by two solicitors that the motor car passed them at great speed and nearly upset their vehicle. They estimated its speed at 50 mph. A fine of 5£, with costs, was imposed.

The legal speed limit in Britain, I remembered, had recently been increased to 20 miles per hour.

THE AMERICA CUP TRIALS . . .

TO THE EDITOR OF THE TIMES: SIR—I fear the 60 hours rain which we enjoyed on June 13, 14, 15 has utterly destroyed the prospects of partridge shooting for this year, at least in the southern Midlands . . .

BUER'S PILES CURE—gives instant relief . . .

CRYSTAL PALACE—MASSED BANDS—GREAT CONCERT . . .

WEATHER—Generally fair to fine and warm, for the next three days . . .

TWENTY-FIVE POUNDS REWARD FOR EVIDENCE which will lead to the Conviction of Driver or Owner of MOTORCAR which, between 4 and 5 o'clock on

Wednesday afternoon, ran into and knocked down two polo ponies . . .

A BEAUTIFUL HOME, 45 minutes from London amidst delightful scenery on the Kent and Surrey borders, to be SOLD, comprising a choice family mansion and heavily timbered park and woodlands of 300 to 700 acres as desired . . .

I had always found the prospect tempting, of being able to enjoy such an estate in rural England. Alas, my previous attempt along that line, some twelve years earlier (again, see *The Dracula Tape*), had taught me that such dreams were only folly for Prince Dracula—or Mr. Prince.

COAL—LOWEST SUMMER PRICES . . .

EXEMPTION of DOGS from VIVISECTION
Petitions to Parliament for the above are now being issued post-free . . .

EMPLOYMENT-OF-CHILDREN BILL . . .

NERVOUS BREAKDOWNS, Neuritis, Neuralgia, Sciatica, Lumbago, Rheumatoid Arthritis, Rheumatism, Gout and Malaria speedily cured by the highly recommended Ultra Violet Electric Light Lamp and combined Double Light Baths and Currents of High Frequency and Ozone . . . LIGHT CURE INSTITUTE. HOME TREATMENT if required, Distance no Object . . .

At WORSHIP STREET, the two men charged with attempting to defraud Frederick Wensley of £2,225 by means of a trick—the sale of brass filings as gold dust—were brought up on remand . . .

SERIOUS ILLNESS OF THE POPE—A sudden change in the condition of Leo XIII caused great anxiety . . .

THE UNITED STATES (from our own correspondent)—The President celebrated the Fourth of July by announcing at Huntington, "There is not a cloud of a handbreadth in the sky. We are on good terms with all the peoples of the world."

THE ASSASSINATION OF A RUSSIAN GOVERNOR . . .

Why Don't You Try BISHOP'S VARALETTES for 25 days for 5s? They work wonders in all uric acid troubles . . .

A MEDICINE OF IMPERIAL REPUTE
WOODWARD'S
"GRIPE WATER" . . .

SEQUEL TO THE TSAR'S RECENT MANIFESTO—The optimistic hopes of many of the Russian Liberals that the Tsar's recent manifesto heralded a large extension of local autonomy will hardly be upheld by the publication of the reprint of the conference held at Tsarskoe Selo on May 16 . . .

"One seems to encounter the Muscovites everywhere these days," I remarked.

Watson, lapsing into the comfortable manner of one London clubman communicating with another, grunted from the opposite chair some comradely agreement. Since I had played so important a role in the rescue of Cousin Sherlock, he evidently was content at least to tolerate me. For the time being. Currently his boots were off and his stocking feet elevated on an ottoman, his upper half invisible behind his newspaper. I suspected that he was half asleep.

Need I say that my feelings toward that most unimaginative man were—and still are—mixed? But I had responded to his summons as quickly as I could, and with a sense of urgency, confident that the invocation had not been made frivolously.

I read on.

> CRICKET
>
> GENTLEMEN vs PLAYERS
> The second day's play in the Gentlemen vs Players match at Lord's yesterday presented in every way, except the weather, a great contrast to the first . . .
>
> CHURCH OF ENGLAND HOMES FOR WAIFS AND STRAYS . . .
>
> ST. PETERSBURG—A Wireless Telegraph station has been established at Port Arthur, with the object of organizing regular telegraphic communication with Russian warships . . .

I cast my newspaper aside. Watson's had now collapsed into a kind of tent, behind which he was snoring. Holmes came into the room shortly, and I, Dracula, began to argue with him, because I still felt real doubts as to whether Holmes's kidnapper should be regarded as the only villain in the piece. For all we knew, young Louisa Altamont might have yielded willingly to her fanged seducer, even before the boating "accident"—and that traumatic event, if carefully investigated, might bear some different interpretation.

My cousin the detective did not care much for my tentative hypothesis, though he conceded to me that it was entirely possible that a treasure had been stolen from our mysterious Russian-speaking vampire at some time in the past.

Presently abandoning the argument, which had never been very intense, I announced my immediate intentions, or some of them anyway, and nipped out of doors. Shifting quickly to bat-form under cover of the blessed night, I made my second visit in a few hours to Sarah Kirkaldy, who, I must confess, was beginning to seem more and more attractive. Tut-tut, you say. With Brother Abraham still laid out in his coffin in the parlor downstairs?

Actually, I refrained from any romantic endeavors on

that night. I found Sarah keeping vigil by the coffin. For a while, I peered in through a window at this touching scene, then flew round the house, making an estimate of its security, before deciding that my seduction of Sarah had better wait. Maybe at least until tomorrow night.

While looking in the parlor window I also observed, briefly and more chastely, Rebecca Altamont, who like a good girl was reading another book—I could not make out the title—and keeping the bereaved Sarah company in her deathwatch. That dutiful young woman was spending most of her time with her parents now, trying to shield them from further hurt.

I thought that the younger Miss Altamont, too, stood at some risk from her family's mad enemy. I decided that tomorrow Mr. Prince must find an opportunity to warn Becky, as he had already warned Sarah, of the dangers of taking the night air unaccompanied. Of course rebellious Becky, if she knew Mr. Prince to be secretly associated with Mr. Holmes, would probably spurn the warning.

Even postponed for one more night, such early wooing would have to be classified as very impetuous. But certainly there was good reason not to leave Sarah unattended. I would go to her, when I went again, with the genuinely altruistic motive of offering protective advice, and real protection.

Readily enough I imagined for myself the scene that might take place upon my finding her in her room, restless and unable to sleep . . .

At my blackguardly intrusion, her gasp, of outrage mixed with other things. "Where did ye coom from?"

"You called me, Sarah."

"I didna!" Pulling the bedclothes up ever more tightly under her chin. But her outrage was hollow.

"Perhaps it was your beauty alone that called . . . with such a voice that I was quite unable to resist."

Well, soon enough I would probably play out that scene, or one much like it, in reality. I wondered whether my new potential conquest had been in communication with our chief foe since the former disastrous séance. Or whether this Count Kulakov—if that was really his name—his mind wandering as Cousin Sherlock said it did, or else focused sharply on revenge, had forgotten about Sarah and her dead brother for a time. A blessing for them if it were so—but one cannot always rely on blessings.

When I, Dracula, felt that I had done all that could reasonably be done to enhance Sarah's security, and that of the household in general, I flew back to rejoin Cousin Sherlock and the worthy Watson at the inn. En route, I actually passed (without, of course, being noticed) Armstrong in his roaring Mercedes, bound for the same goal. On reaching the Saracen's Head, I looked in at the window of Inspector Merivale's room, where a steady snore informed me that the poor, tired man had retired early.

Gathered at our improvised headquarters, we felt reasonably certain that the last of the regular parties sent out to search for Holmes had retired or been recalled from the field, and as soon as Armstrong had rejoined us we equipped ourselves as best we could for the effort that lay ahead. The necessary materials included some tools suitable for breaking and entering. Even I might have trouble entering this tomb without them.

Let Watson tell the tale again.

Holmes had earlier remarked, and Dracula reminded us, that now the Altamont mausoleum qualified as a dwelling place, being inhabited by a living (though unbreathing) human; even should the doors stand wide open, those portals would be closed to any vampire lacking a direct invitation to enter.

Armstrong was familiar with the village and its environs, and was able to provide us with some tools. As we left the inn, the night was mostly cloudy, with little moon, which suited our purposes admirably.

In response to a question from Holmes, I assured him that I had indeed come equipped with my old service revolver.

"And wooden bullets?"

With some dignity I was able to reply that such necessities had not been forgotten.

Armstrong looked from one of us to the other as if quite convinced that we were both mad.

(Holmes told me he had considered waiting, tactfully, until Dracula was absent on some errand, to equip himself and me with implements intended for an even grimmer purpose: a wooden stake and large hammer. But Dracula would accept the need for such implements if tonight's investigation indeed led us to the resting place of the vampire rapist and murderer, and if the latter should, by some good fortune, be in his coffin. At any rate, it would be hard indeed to conceal from the prince any sizable objects that we were carrying.)

Our party was fully assembled near midnight. The four of us set out for the cemetery secretly; we now had a rented carriage big enough to hold us all, and Dracula himself harnessed our horses without disturbing the stable boy.

Young Martin Armstrong's impatience with the general failure to find any clue to the whereabouts of the living Louisa was reaching a dangerous level, nearing the point of frenzy. Despairing of ever obtaining official permission, he was ready to consider a rough-and-ready exhumation of the occupant of Louisa's tomb as one way of making progress.

He mentioned that he had been planning his own independent expedition along that line, but he joined forces with us gratefully. He understood, he said, the desirability of having other witnesses present besides himself when the tomb was opened.

Though the night was very dark, so that I supposed even the horses could scarcely see the road, Dracula drove the carriage without lights, and without apparent difficulty. In about twenty minutes we were dismounting, leaving the horses and the lightness vehicle at a little distance from the burial ground. Before we left the animals, which seemed skittish, Dracula soothed them somehow, and they started to crop the grass.

An owl flew hooting overhead as we once more approached the Altamont family mausoleum, its walls pale in the garish light of our electric torches. The sweet honeysuckle vine was now marked, somewhat to my surprise, by clustered, night-blooming, purple-white flowers. I stared intently and suspiciously at a small shape flying near these, thinking about bats, until Dracula assured me it was only a night-feeding hawk moth, by which these flowers were mostly pollinated.

I held a small electric torch, and by its light Holmes needed only a moment or two to pick the old lock of the iron grating. The fastening of the inner door to the mausoleum yielded almost as quickly to his skilled fingers. The process of opening these barriers was silent; all the locks and hinges had been oiled and repaired less than a month ago, at the time of Louisa's funeral.

Meanwhile Mr. Prince stood back a little, watching silently and with every appearance of tranquility, first with his hands in his pockets, then with his arms folded under his short cabman's cape. He might have been listening to the ordinary sounds of the night—insects, an owl, the murmur of the nearby stream—but I felt mortally certain that he was on guard, in a way that we could never be, against any attack by our chief adversary.

Not far away was the place where Abraham Kirkaldy

was to be buried—by the kind charity of the Altamonts, put under the soil in a simple grave. Tonight the open pit, edged by its pile of fresh earth, yawned at us, awaiting its tenant, and when we shone our lights in that direction provided us with an ominous reminder of mortality.

Having all, or most of us, crowded into the little building, we now turned our attention to the small crypt in the wall where almost a month ago Louisa's body had been laid to rest. A small brass plate on the door confirmed the exact niche. Another door to be opened, and the casket was exposed. There was, as was more commonly the case a few years ago, a double coffin, the inner vessel of lead and hermetically sealed.

Dracula, resting one hand on the outer casing, turned his head and assured us silently, with a slight shake of his head, that the inner coffin was currently empty.

Holmes and I exchanged glances, while Armstrong, more and more puzzled, not aware that any discovery had yet been made, or that any decision was being taken, continued to look on impatiently.

Sherlock Holmes sighed, and I realized that he had decided it would be best to open the coffin to demonstrate its vacancy to Armstrong. Though the young man was bound to misinterpret this discovery at first, yet it was a step on the way of preparing him for the truth which he might sooner or later have to face. I wondered whether Holmes also expected, or hoped, to find some clue or evidence in the coffin, even though it should be untenanted.

Dracula returned to his position as sentry outside the mausoleum, while I continued to hold the lantern, and Holmes got to work with hammer and chisel and wrench. The inner container was of soft sheet-lead and easily cut apart.

Armstrong, despite his stoutly expressed confidence in Louisa's survival, continued to exhibit thinly controlled anxiety while first the outer and then the inner container were being opened.

There were the white-satin pillows, showing a round indentation where a head had rested. But the head was gone, along with the rest of the corporeal tenant of the coffin.

"It is, as you see, empty."

The young American let out a great sigh of relief. "Gentlemen, we have proof at last!"

I, at least, started in surprise on hearing this comment. But I realized that to Armstrong, the empty coffin was resounding confirmation of his own favorite theory. According to him, Louisa had never actually been interred here at all—no one had.

"Look at the sealing on the coffin, gentlemen—there has been no grave-robbery here. The body we all mourned last month as Louisa's was taken away somehow at the last moment, and the coffin buried empty. With all that lead, no one noticed the difference in weight. The kidnappers have done a thorough job!"

Sherlock Holmes and Prince Dracula—the latter had now stepped back inside the door—exchanged a look, whose meaning I thought I could read perfectly: that it would be useless at the present time to attempt to give the young man anything like a full explanation of the true state of affairs.

In fact, none of we older men could be sure at this point whether Louisa was out roaming, foraging for animal or human blood, or whether our chief opponent had intelligently anticipated our investigation here and had therefore moved Louisa elsewhere. The latter was perhaps the safest, as well as the most likely, assumption.

We resealed the coffins, inner and outer, so that a close inspection of the outer would be necessary to tell that anything had been disturbed. We relocked the doors of the charnel house, and in general put things back as they had been. Then we took our departure.

Choosing a moment when Armstrong could not hear him, Holmes put into words the thought we others shared: "Her native earth lies around her for miles in every direction, and there are an almost infinite number of places where she may be hidden."

Even Dracula could not undertake to find her in any reasonably limited period of time.

~ 15 ~

May I, Dracula, remind the gentle reader that when undertaking to tell this story I gave notice that from time to time I would indulge in some imaginative, reconstructive narration? Here comes a sample now: I am about to recreate a scene at which I was not actually present. (Exactly how much testimony I might have had later from one or both participants, I shall leave you to judge for yourselves.)

Know, then, that Martin Armstrong, despite his brave statements to the contrary, had actually been troubled by the empty coffin—it was as if until now he had not really believed that his own bizarre theory was true, but had only been using it as a kind of psychic crutch to cope with the reality of death. But now he had to believe in it—or allow that something else must have happened which was even stranger. Uncomfortable with either possibility, the young American returned to his room in Norberton House a little after midnight and fell uneasily asleep.

Some hours later, in the midst of that deep satisfying darkness (at least I find it so) that comes not too long before the dawn, Martin had fallen into an unpleasant dream—he told me about it later. It seemed to him that he was struggling to row a huge, ungainly boat upstream, all the while feeling tormented and cast into despair by the knowledge that he was late—terribly, irretrievably, late for the most vital appointment of his lifetime.

He was roused from this dream, none too soon for the sake of his mental health, by a familiar voice, softly and persistently whispering his name; and he opened his eyes in predawn darkness to find his beloved Louisa sitting close beside him, right on the edge of his bed.

She was very close to him—in fact in actual contact. She even held a hand stretched out, as if she were about to touch his cheek, his throat, caressingly.

The next few moments were full of confusion for the young man. Before he became fully aware that he was not still dreaming, some part of his distracted mind could not help noticing the reassuring solidity of Louisa's corporeal presence. Her body, though slender as always, weighed down one side of the mattress with a more substantial effect than he would have expected. The window behind Louisa's head created an aureole of predawn sky light—the ghostly glow of stars and moon and cosmic rays—around the tangled paleness of her hair. At the moment, with this backlighting, Martin could see nothing of her face even though she sat turned directly toward him.

The night in general was very quiet, but somewhere in the background, far to the east, thunder and lightning played, a flare and sound too distant to have awakened him.

"Martin?" Louisa's voice, uttering his name once more, was small and lost, just as he had heard it at the séance. But he had no problem in identifying it as hers.

He sat up automatically, pushing back the covers, wiping the sleeve of his nightshirt across his eyes, reflexively expressing doubt as to what they showed him. "Oh . . . my darling. I knew you couldn't be dead. I knew it!" He paused. "Are you all right?"

Foolish question, because he could see how she was—

lovely, fresh, and warm, and still dressed in the cerements of the grave.

He strained to see her face, but that remained well-nigh impossible.

"Martin, can you help me? I'm caught in the most hideous nightmare. I can't go to Mother or Father—I don't dare—Becky's room's right next to theirs. If I can't turn to you, then there's no one."

"Of course, of course, love. You can turn to me, Lou. What's happened?" He was aflame with both fear and fascination, dying to know what had happened to her in the hands of the kidnappers. In the back of Armstrong's mind was the idea that he would have to have second thoughts about marrying a woman who had suffered a fate worse than death.

And even now, in his first awareness that she had come back to him again, there came a moment of revulsion at the sheer strangeness of this new Louisa. He tried to put the strangeness from his mind, to focus his attention on her beauty—but he could not entirely succeed.

"Marty," she repeated. "Can you help me?"

"Of course, Lou. What can I do to help?"

"I don't know. Help me out of this." And for a moment, Louisa buried her invisible face in her pale hands.

Armstrong choked, at about this point, and could think of nothing further to say. The only certainty in all the world was the total, unarguable awareness of Louisa's presence in his room, in his bed.

At last he managed, "You've got free of them now."

"Got free?" Her hands came down. Now he thought that he could see her eyes. And something about her teeth, as if she were smiling strangely.

"Free of the villains who took you away," the young man replied. "You're here. Safe. With me." But even as he spoke those words they sounded odd and hollow in his own ears, and he knew with part of his mind that they were not true. Whatever strange and terrible thing had happened to Louisa had not yet been put right; and neither of them were yet anywhere near being truly free.

"No, Marty, I'm not free. Not free at all. Whenever he calls me, I must go to him . . ."

"Who?"

Her answer sounded like words out of a dream: "I cannot say his name. That's been forbidden me."

But then she moved, sliding even closer to him, and for the moment none of those objections mattered, because she was here with him. She was genuinely here. In his arms—and, for the first time, in his bed.

Again Louisa was trying to speak, but his lips crushed hers to silence. Now both of his hands, as if they had escaped from his control and taken on a life of their own, were seeking her warm body under the pale gown. And he discovered with joy, with all the certainty of dreaming, that under the gown she was wearing nothing at all.

Overpowering delight—the unmatched, unhallowed delight of her sensual embrace! Nothing mattered but this; everything else could be put right, somehow, later . . .

Their two bodies rolled over on the bed. To Martin Armstrong the fact seemed unutterably strange, and at the same time irresistibly arousing, that Louisa should be biting at his throat.

Later—Armstrong having at last convinced himself almost completely that he was fully awake—they were lying side by side on the cool sheets. Louisa was more silent tonight than had ever been her wont before . . . before . . .

He cleared his throat. "Last night—no, only tonight, only a few hours ago—we even went to look at the place where we thought you were buried." Her lover was almost chuckling with amusement at the outrageous idea. "How could we ever have believed that you were dead? Of course the coffin was empty. Whoever it was we thought we had buried there . . . whoever it was, she had been taken away again."

"Marty?"

"Yes?"

But then, before she said anything more, the young woman stroked the young man's hair for a time in silence. At last she murmured: "I was buried there, Marty."

That got him to lift his head from the pillow and turn toward her. "I don't understand."

"I was put there, in the family vault. You, and Father, and Mother, and Becky, buried me. I can remember it, my funeral, and all the rest, like some bad dream. I was aware of what was happening. I just couldn't move."

"Don't talk like that!"

But Louisa's voice went on, dully, gently, as if the story she recounted had happened a hundred years ago. "When the boat tipped, Marty, he was there, and he carried me away. Dragging me with him while he swam at great speed underwater. I was under water until I thought I was going to drown—I was still breathing then—but at last he brought me to the surface for a while and let me have air."

"Don't talk like that, I said!"

Louisa paused, looking at her lover wistfully. She added: "It was later when I stopped breathing, after he had— How can I tell you what it was like? But when we were far downstream, he took me out of the water, and he drank my blood, again and again—until finally I wanted him to do it. And he gave me his blood to drink—he opened one of his own veins for me—and it was marvelous."

"Lou!"

"Then you found me, and said prayers, and put me into the vault—and it was warm and dark and pleasant there. But twice now, he has made me leave the cemetery by night, and go back to the house, and say things to Mother and Father about some treasure."

Martin breathed twice before he asked: "What treasure?"

"I don't know! I say only what he orders me to say. I went into Father's safe, and took out some jewels; but he was only angry when I brought them to him, and he threw them all over the cemetery . . . and then he would not let me go back to my coffin, where it was so nice and dark all day. Now I must spend the day in a place where there are many windows, but no curtains, and light comes through into the place . . . and it's so hard to sleep. Oh, Marty! Hold me! Love me!"

And Martin Armstrong did his best.

Ecstatic fainting blurred and prolonged itself, in some manner, into sleep. From a dream of still being embraced tightly in Louisa's arms, Martin Armstrong drifted slowly into wakefulness. Early summer daylight had arrived outside his window, where now all was birdsong and gray light. His body stirred slowly, full wakefulness coming only as he sat up with a jerking start. Louisa was gone, gone as if she had never existed. Martin himself was entirely naked, his nightshirt having been cast aside during the . . .

The dream?

Lurching out of bed, he stumbled to the bureau, where his shaving mirror was propped. It was the need to see his own face that drew him there, the feeling that some essential doubt had been created regarding his own identity.

And indeed, the reflection of his face looked strange enough, pale and gaunt, but after a single glance he hardly looked at it. What put the seal of reality on Louisa's life, on last night's encounter, were the two painless little marks on his throat. As if they had been magically transferred somehow from her throat to his.

Becky was right, he realized twenty minutes later, while knotting his tie preparatory to going down to breakfast. (His collar hid one of the little marks at least, and the other was not particularly noticeable.) Louisa still lived—perhaps now more intensely than ever before—but she had been drastically altered. The woman who had come to him last night (however that trick had been managed) was no substitute for Louisa Altamont, but rather Louisa Altamont transformed. The girl to whom he, Martin Armstrong, had once proposed marriage had not become a ghost—but certainly the young woman who had wantoned in his bed last night was not the same one who had accepted his proposal of holy matrimony. Last night's . . . last night's whore (in the privacy of his own thought, he could try how that word sounded, when applied to his betrothed) . . . that woman could not be identified with the sunlit figure in a summer dress who last month had smiled at him so lovingly just before the rowboat tipped.

Armstrong, still staring into the mirror, shivered faintly, uncontrollably. If it were still possible, in this day and age, to believe in demons, or in possession . . . in, in something that could take the outward likeness of the beloved . . . but of course such possibilities could not exist in the same world as automobiles of forty horsepower, telephones, and progress.

Breakfast was an ordeal. Martin Armstrong, desperately seeking an explanation for last night's experience, felt himself unable to say anything to Louisa's parents or sister about her visit.

Why had she not stayed with him? If not in his room, why had she not remained in the house, her own home, reuniting joyously with Mother, Father, Becky? Obviously it was because something terrible had happened to Louisa, something that compelled her to an awful exile.

Was it conceivable—a new and hideous idea dawned,

and grew with terrible force and swiftness—could it be possible that Louisa had been stricken with some loathsome disease? But no, she had come so willingly to his bed . . . Louisa wouldn't infect him deliberately, whatever else was going on. That fear declined, as rapidly as it had burgeoned.

But was it possible that she was mad?

After breakfast he announced that he was going out. Secretly he had decided that he would turn to Sherlock Holmes.

Once more, let Dr. Watson speak . . .

On Friday morning, Holmes and I were discussing, over bacon and eggs in our rooms at the inn, what our next move should be. At dawn, Prince Dracula, exhausted by long exposure to daylight on Thursday, had retired to his own bedroom and the occult solace of his native earth.

Ever alert against the possibility of eavesdroppers, Holmes and I conversed in low voices; bright sun and birdsong outside our window seemed to mock the terrors of the night with which we had to deal.

One subject of our discussion was the deliberate countermove made by the Russian vampire, in getting Louisa Altamont out of her original tomb and into hiding elsewhere.

Before retiring, Dracula had advised us: "Of course her new sanctuary need not be a grave in the ordinary sense. Anyplace underground, or any sheltered vessel aboveground, containing earth, will do. A buried lair need not even be connected by a clear passage to the atmosphere. Between sunset and sunrise, the solid ground is generally permeable to members of my race moving in mist-form."

Holmes and I, in planning our efforts to discover the new hiding place where Kulakov must have commanded or forced his fledgling vampire to make her nest, began with the assumption that Louisa's new place of concealment was almost certainly somewhere on the extensive grounds of the house Count Kulakov now occupied. Such an arrangement would give the master vampire a large degree of control over access to the site.

We had not got far in our planning before we were joined by young Martin Armstrong.

"Did you sleep well?" my friend inquired, looking probingly at the young man as he gestured for him to take a chair.

"Not very well, actually." Armstrong cleared his throat and tugged at his collar as if it bothered him. "I thought, Mr. Holmes . . . I thought that I saw Louisa last night."

Holmes leaned forward, galvanized. "Where?"

"When?" I demanded at the same time.

Armstrong seemed startled at our readiness to believe that he had really encountered his former fiancée. He needed a moment or two to confess, rather awkwardly, that Louisa seemed to have come to him in his bedroom.

Again he was startled when I immediately asked to see his neck. There were the two fang marks, small and painless; I made sure that Holmes got a look at them as well.

Under our probing questions, the story of Louisa's visit to Armstrong came out in some detail.

My friend's interrogation was incisive. "Did she let fall any clue as to where she is now spending the hours of daylight?"

"No . . . yes. She said something about there being 'many windows,' which struck me as strange."

"How very odd. Anything else?"

"She said: 'many windows . . . but no curtains. And the light comes through.' Something like that."

Holmes and I looked at each other, but neither of us could make anything of this at the moment.

Holmes insisted that Armstrong accompany us on our new search. My friend considered it of vital importance now that the young man be brought to a full understanding of his own situation, and Louisa's.

Before we started out, I gave orders to the innkeeper that Mr. Prince was not under any circumstances to be disturbed; then, going into the room where Dracula was sleeping, I looked at him with the idea of making sure that all was well with our colleague. I was also fascinated as a medical man and a mere spectator. Dracula, tired by days of exposure to indirect daylight, lay flat on his back upon the bed, fully clothed and with a flattish bag or parcel of some silk-like fabric, containing his earth, unfolded between his body and the coverlet. He was obviously in deep trance. I looked into his open eyes, sought to find a reflex, and tried to take a pulse. I should have thought him dead, had I not known better.

Smithbury Hall, the country house rented by Count Kulakov, was, as Mycroft had reported, some twelve miles from Amberley, an hour and a half by horse-drawn carriage. Holmes declined Armstrong's offer to drive us there in his motorcar, wishing to avoid the inevitable attention the noisy vehicle would draw in the quiet country.

Meanwhile a decision had to be made as to how and exactly where we were to begin our search. The mention of "many windows" had suggested to me that Louisa Altamont's new daytime quarters were inside Kulakov's country house. But, as Holmes pointed out, "no curtains" would seem to argue against that interpretation.

Having stopped in the nearest village to make local inquiries, the three of us reached the grounds of Kulakov's rented estate, which were guarded by a high fence. After circling the estate cautiously on narrow, lightly traveled roads at a considerable distance, we left our carriage in a quiet lane. Crossing the fence, we began a circuitous approach on foot, a cautious process of observing the house from a distance. Now and then we spotted a servant or two moving about, but until the afternoon there was no one else.

At about two o'clock, peering toward the house through gaps in a hedgerow, we saw two men who, even at a distance, wore the indefinable look of official plainclothesmen. They were going, on some business or pretext, to the front door. After a discussion, conducted through the open door with someone inside, they were turned away.

"Merivale," I suggested, "may be taking action."

"He may be right to do so." Holmes's attitude was gloomy, with little evidence of the wry humor he often displayed when things were not going well. "So far I can claim no progress at all worth mentioning."

It occurred to me, not for the first time, that Prince Dracula would have been of inestimable help to us in the last stages of our search for the new resting place of Louisa Altamont; but our ally was not available, and we could not depend upon him for everything.

It was late in the day when Holmes, Armstrong, and I came upon an abandoned greenhouse, standing isolated and hidden in a grove of trees at least half a mile from any inhabited dwelling. Though the sun was lowering, it was still bright, and we calculated there would be time to investigate before the fall of night made our presence here prohibitively hazardous.

As we approached the derelict structure, Holmes pointed with satisfaction at the rows of glass panes, many of them shattered, which formed a roof and walls supported by pillars of brick and wood.

"Had it not been for the mention of windows, I should have concentrated my efforts on finding an old grave, somewhere in another vault or churchyard. Maybe an antique barrow, with some Druid tinge about it, or an abandoned boat shed. But as matters stand, this looks promising."

Armstrong, who seemed to have given up hours ago

trying to make sense of the search in which we were engaged, only nodded. "What now?"

"We must get in, and quickly."

Both doors to the abandoned-looking structure were locked, and the quickest way in was to break yet another pane of glass.

Inside, cobwebs and rust only confirmed the idea of long abandonment. Digging and poking around in search of a hiding place, we came upon a large wooden toolchest, suitable for the storage of shovels and similar implements, and on lifting the lid of this, I uncovered Louisa.

Martin Armstrong, who had been looking over my shoulder, recoiled with an audible gasp.

There were no satin pillows here, nor even a nest of blankets, but only leaves and earth and mold in the crude wooden box, and the poor girl lying among them, looking as dead as Dracula had looked when we left him in the inn.

Holmes came to stand beside us, and we all three silently regarded our discovery. Louisa Altamont was still clad in her burial gown—now sadly soiled and torn, lacking the unnatural powers of preservation of the body that it covered. Her body showed a convincingly lifelike appearance, a startling absence of decay—and there was also some blood, recently dried, around the red-lipped mouth, even spotting the pink cheeks. The hair, in contrast to the once-white gown, seemed fine and clean, as if newly washed. As a medical man, I was of course amazed, though intellectually I had been aware that our explorations were almost certain to lead to some discovery of the kind.

My instincts on seeing Louisa Altamont lying in such deathly stillness were (as they had been in the case of Dracula) to seek for pulse and breath and heartbeat, and actually I did so, of course with no result. But Holmes laid a hand upon my arm and assured me that the young woman's condition was in itself perfectly safe and natural, for one in her new mode of existence.

Martin Armstrong had backed up a pace or two, and now sat on a crude wooden bench, staring in shock.

"That cannot be Louisa," he said at last. "But . . . it is."

"It is." Holmes laid a sympathetic hand on the young man's shoulder.

"Doctor?" The young man turned to me, moistening his pale lips. "This girl is dead?"

"No," I said, and shook my head. "I do not believe so, despite appearances."

Armstrong made a curious, awkward gesture with both hands. "But . . . she came to me last night."

"We understand," said Sherlock Holmes.

"But I do not begin to understand. If this is not she . . . then who is it?"

"I tell you," said Sherlock Holmes, "that this is Louisa Altamont."

My friend and I earnestly renewed our efforts to explain to this lover of a vampire what sort of changes he must expect.

"Look!" I exclaimed, pointing at the white face of the figure in the box.

The sun was now very near setting. Tree shadows had covered all the windows, and Louisa, already partially awakened, had turned her head toward her lover.

Armstrong jumped to his feet. He uttered a strange sound, compounded of fear, fascination, and something very like disgust.

Then he mumbled a few incoherent words, because suddenly Louisa was sitting up.

"Martin?" Her voice was soft and calm.

His only answer was a kind of moan.

Again, she who had been his betrothed called to him

lovingly, and he hesitated, alternately shrinking away from her and then starting forward.

When the young woman's red lips parted and I saw clearly her white fangs suddenly grown sharp, I moved between her and the man she had once planned to marry, to keep them from embracing.

Louisa, reacting to my interference and Martin's acceptance of it, gave a little snarling cry and suddenly leaped out of the crude nest in which she had sheltered from the daylight, so that both Holmes and I recoiled, and I reached for my revolver. But the vampire, who was still Louisa Altamont, had no aggressive intention. In another moment she had fled from our presence into the gathering dusk, thereby relieving us of any need to make an immediate decision on what we had ought to do with her, or do about her.

The figure of the girl did not change form, but ran barefoot at amazing speed into the nearby trees and disappeared.

We had followed her out of the building. Armstrong, speechless, with one hand to his mouth, could only stare after her, on his face the wildest expression of terror and shock that I have ever seen.

Now that the sun was gone, it was imperative that we conduct a strategic retreat, lest our enemy vampire appear and destroy us all at his leisure. Once night had fallen, granting our enemy the power of changing forms at will, my chances of getting in a good shot with the wooden bullets would be reduced almost to nothing.

Armstrong, in a daze, made no objection as we urged him to come away. Nor did any of us have much to say as we walked briskly back to the place beyond the fence where we had left our carriage.

Driving back to Amberley as twilight deepened and faded into night, we stopped to light our carriage lamps, and Armstrong suddenly began to talk.

The burden of his conversation was that of course such things, outside the settled and scientific order of nature, were simply not possible. Certainly not now, with the world firmly established in modern times, the twentieth century well begun. And "demonic" hardly seemed the proper word for the female who had come to his bed last night. Pagan and passionate, he thought, were apt descriptions.

Holmes was musing that the testimony of the victim herself now definitely indicated that she was the victim of a rapist.

And I, Watson, remarked indignantly that what was known of the girl's history and of her family made any other explanation unlikely.

Holmes said it was almost certain that the vampire who had kidnapped him must be the same one who had so brutally and lustfully attacked Louisa.

It was, of course, fully dark by the time we returned to the Saracen's Head. There we found our colleague Dracula fully awake, well rested, and waiting for us in our sitting room.

The mere fact that Dracula was sitting with a companion, engaged in quiet conversation, would have been surprising enough—but when that companion looked around and revealed himself to be Mycroft Holmes, our amazement knew no bounds.

"Calm yourself, Sherlock," said Mycroft, starting from his chair. "The prince and I have introduced ourselves and reached an accommodation—it was necessary, you know, that we should."

Never have I seen Holmes so at a loss for words as he was then. But in a few moments, he had recovered from the shock, at least so far as to be able to bid his brother welcome.

When we were all seated, Mycroft Holmes explained

that he had found himself unable to remain away from the scene of action any longer.

Taking a deep breath of air, he looked toward the window open to the summer night. "It is years since I have been in the country." But having done as much, he thereafter seemed indifferent to his location.

Mycroft had brought word from London concerning the connection of the Altamont family with pirates in the eighteenth century. Also, he had obtained historical confirmation of the fact that the family fortune had always derived chiefly from land holdings and that none of the strange events of 1765—at least some of which he had uncovered—had had any noticeable effect on it one way or another.

In fact, a transcript of the Admiralty trial of the pirate Kulakov had turned out to be available, and Mycroft had brought a copy of the relevant portions with him.

We marveled that Kulakov, in his sleepwalking indifference to what his enemies might do, was still using his own name in the society of 1903.

Mycroft remarked: "Well, this much seems to be true—if there was any actual treasure involved, and the Admiralty records seem to suggest there was, the loot was never recovered."

Mycroft had also brought with him more details of Count Kulakov's rented establishment, Smithbury Hall, which we had already inspected from a distance, and he confirmed that the police were starting to take an interest there. Two plainclothes policemen, calling at the door on some pretext, had been told by the man's servants that he was not at home and that they did not know when he was to be expected.

Holmes was more and more intently focusing on the Russian aspect of this affair. "Prince, if you thought that some member of this English family, or any other, had robbed you, at some relatively remote epoch in the past, what steps would you be likely to take to regain your property?"

The prince, sitting with one pale hand extended before him, appeared to be admiring his own sharp fingernails. Suddenly, out of nowhere, it occurred to me to wonder whether they might be retractable, like a cat's claws, and I shuddered slightly.

He flexed his fingers briskly and then forgot about them. "That would depend to a great extent upon what kind of property it was."

"Of course. Land would be very difficult to regain by anyone striving for justice—as I presume you would be—outside the formal channels of legality. Gold, for example, or anything that can be locked up in a small space, would be comparatively easy."

Dracula, when he had heard the tale of our discovery of Louisa Altamont, was confident of his ability to overtake this little child-vampire in hot pursuit, catch her and bring her back. But he was not sanguine about his chances of discovering where she might be now.

"Why did Louisa flee from us?" Armstrong asked the question.

Dracula replied that she gave every evidence of being under some very strong hypnotic influence, strong enough to overcome her natural inclinations.

I then asked: "Even in this . . . altered state, she is subject to the hypnotic influence?"

The prince replied: "Indeed, even more thoroughly, strongly subject to such influence, given a mesmerist—or a hypnotist, if you prefer that word—of overwhelming willpower and superb technique."

How were we to find Louisa again? And when she was found, what to do with her, her pallid form, her bloodstained lips?

~ 16 ~

Martin Armstrong returned to Norberton House late that evening, and lied convincingly enough to Becky and to the elder Altamonts about his day's activities.

A little later that night, when Armstrong had retired and was trying to close his eyes in sleep, Louisa drifted in uninvited through the window of his room and, as on the previous night, materialized sitting on the edge of his bed.

The idea of trying to resist her attraction crossed the young man's mind, but only briefly. The attempt failed before it had really started, and the couple passionately made love.

This did nothing to resolve Armstrong's feelings. He found himself sliding inexorably into a crisis of doubt, fear, and hesitation regarding his relationship with his beloved.

While the sensual attraction between the pair was, if anything, stronger than on the previous night, the young man's feelings of revulsion had also increased to the point where they could no longer be denied. He realized, with the night's first surge of passion spent, that these contrary emotions must be either wholeheartedly accepted, or overcome.

Armstrong was thinking, as most of us do most of the time, of his own future. Holmes and Watson had been trying to instruct him about vampires. For him to remain Louisa's lover in a permanent way, forsaking all others, would sooner or later mean setting his own feet irrevocably upon the path to vampirism, thus bringing upon himself the implacable enmity of the great mass of humanity—however many could be induced to believe in him.

Side by side with the great tree of passion, the faint seed of disgust, sown during Louisa's first visit to his bedroom, was growing rapidly.

He spoke the word to her during this visit: "Lou, you have become a . . . vampire."

"Yes. I know." She pleaded with her lover not to tell anyone, her parents least of all. They must not learn that she was coming to him in this way, the discovery that their daughter had become a monster—so they must view the matter—would destroy them.

Nor did Louisa's new master know that she was here, and she was afraid that he would find out.

She also feared Sherlock Holmes and his associates, though not as much as she feared Kulakov. She felt instinctively that Holmes and Watson, as preservers of law and convention, would pass the terrible knowledge of her state on to her family, and would separate her from Martin.

Dracula she feared as well, but in yet another way; he was somehow kin to the man who had enslaved her, even though he was Kulakov's enemy as well.

Armstrong was both angry at Kulakov and afraid of him, and wanted to see the man destroyed.

Louisa had had other reasons for returning that night to the home of her breathing childhood, and actually she had accomplished these before coming to see her lover: She had wanted to see Becky (without allowing Becky to see her), and also to gaze from a distance at her parents, whom Louisa loved but who, she thought, were now farther than they had ever been from understanding what had happened to their elder daughter, and what was going to happen.

On Saturday morning, at least some of the people who arrived at the cemetery for the burial service of Abraham Kirkaldy were astonished and outraged to discover the vandalism that had been committed by an angry vampire the night before.

But the service went on as scheduled.

Martin Armstrong was there, nervously wondering if the small amount of blood he had lost during the night had weakened him, and if one of the new fang marks on his throat might show above his collar. A police constable was at the service too, taking the place of Inspector Merivale, who was busy elsewhere that morning. The constable stood quietly in the rear with Mycroft Holmes, observing the mourners.

Also present were the two elder Altamonts—Rebecca, pleading weariness, had stayed home. There were only a few other people, most of them spiritualist enthusiasts who had known the Kirkaldys as mediums. These last and the officiating clergyman eyed one another uneasily.

Just as the coffin was being lowered into the grave, a soft rain began to fall. Sister Sarah, weeping for her brother for the last time, was supported by both of the elder Altamonts, who, in the freshness of their conversion to the spiritualist outlook, could not refrain from sometimes gazing at the young woman's tears in gentle wonder that she, so knowledgeable about commerce with the other world, should grieve so at a temporary separation.

Prince Dracula, Sherlock Holmes, and Watson were elsewhere that morning, having delegated Mycroft, who was considered no great shakes as a man of action, to represent them at the cemetery and act as their observer. The hunters considered it barely possible that Count Kulakov, if he were truly as mad as his behavior seemed to suggest, might put in an appearance at his victim's burial. But they thought that in the daylight, and surrounded by other people, Mycroft would probably be safe enough.

I, Dracula, at the time of Abraham's interment, was wistfully imagining myself enjoying yet another daylight rest at the Saracen's Head, my darkened room's one door not only snugly locked, but barricaded, so that no maid might enter and run screaming to announce the discovery of a corpse. But alas for my comfortable imaginings; the game was afoot in earnest, as Cousin Sherlock used to say, and such lassitude on my part was not to be. At the moment when the first shovelful of earth fell upon the coffin of Abraham Kirkaldy, I, in company with Sherlock and the faithful Watson, not to mention Inspector Merivale and a small army of police in horsedrawn vehicles, was just arriving in sight of Smithbury Hall.

But let Watson tell the next part of our adventure—

Sherlock Holmes had also been thinking about secretly promoting another attempt at a séance, hoping thereby to make contact with both Louisa and her attacker. He discussed this possibility with his cousin and me while we were on our way to Smithbury Hall.

Today's raid had been organized and was being launched at the instigation of Sherlock Holmes, acting with the advice of Mycroft. There now existed some hard evidence to tie the Russian count not only to a particularly vicious group of terrorists, but also to the Okhrana, the Russian Imperial Secret Police. Such ambiguity, even among the nobility, would hardly be unheard of in the intrigues of Muscovy. Although our British law and custom can and does tolerate political refugees of every stripe, engaging in violent conflict upon our soil is quite another matter.

This next spiritualist sitting had been arranged for Saturday. It would be conducted in Norberton House by Sarah, with Dracula overseeing matters, lurking alternately outside the house and inside, trying to set a trap for Kulakov.

To hold this new séance so soon was definitely against Mr. Prince's advice. Sarah had been forced or argued into it somehow by the overanxious Altamonts. I hoped it would not produce disastrous results.

I raised another subject with Holmes as we rode in the carriage. I found myself deeply shocked to learn that Martin Armstrong, even after understanding what fearful alteration the girl's nature had undergone, had apparently made no effort to break off his affair with her. Indeed, he was seriously, deliberately, considering what sort of future life they might be able to achieve together.

"We must do something, Holmes."

"I share your feelings, Watson. But by what right would we interfere?"

"By what right? It is our duty to act, as we would act to prevent a suicide, to save a madman from self-destruction."

"Is Martin Armstrong mad?"

"If he behaves in such a way. On the other hand . . ."

"Yes?"

"I was about to say, it would be unthinkable, Holmes, to return the girl to her parents in this . . . this . . ."

"Quite so." Holmes, with a sigh, turned to his relative. "To the best of my knowledge, there can be no possibility of reversion to the breathing state once matters have progressed this far."

"To cling to any such hope would be an utter waste of time." Dracula's face seemed carved in ice, as if he might have been insulted by the suggestion that such a change might be desirable. As for repealing Louisa's vampire-conversion, the prince assured us that everyone had better accept that as impossible. Dracula himself had never seen it happen.

Today, as yesterday, our first glimpse of our enemy's rented house came from a little distance away among the trees. Today again we had eschewed attention-drawing motorcars and were traveling in a small convoy of carriages.

Smithbury Hall was a relatively new building, constructed in Victoria's early reign, of yellow stone with white stone columns, and in a mixture of architectural styles, most of them flat-roofed. It stood on a gentle, grassy hill amid fairly extensive grounds, some thirteen or fourteen miles from Norberton House and perhaps half a mile from the abandoned greenhouse.

Our discovery yesterday of Louisa's "body" so close to the house would certainly have interested the police; but of course we had not told them of our find.

Naturally, we had preferred to launch our raid on Kulakov's rented manor in daylight, when it was at least probable that the count might be caught sleeping within.

But he was not to be found. Perhaps, we thought, he had somehow got wind of our coming. With Holmes and Merivale leading the way, armed with search warrants, we stormed through the house. Of course Holmes and I, if not the police, were well aware that the vampire could not be caught in such a way—but the police were ready and eager to lay hands on a man whom they conceived to be an ordinary criminal.

Though within a matter of minutes, a dozen policemen were tearing the house apart from roof to cellar, we were not really surprised at our failure to discover Kulakov; and Mr. Prince, once invited in, searched the attic, and particularly the cellar, with a thoroughness of which no breathing man would have been capable, seeking traces of a hidden earth, whether occupied or not. Actually, Dracula, while the police remained oblivious to his real activities, located two or three such dens, but all were empty.

Holmes, the prince, and I had already agreed that Kulakov had probably formed a careful, suspicious habit of shifting daily from one earth to another, and that one or more of his essential troves of Russian soil might be in close proximity to the place where we had finally found Louisa, and where we hoped to be able to find her again.

Today our raiders, like yesterday's disguised inquirers at the door, were told by two servants of Kulakov's, the only people inhabiting the house at present, that the master had gone elsewhere; he was in London, they thought. No, they could not say where, and they had no means of reaching him.

When the opportunity presented itself, Holmes and I, by prearrangement, slipped away from the main house without telling Merivale or any of his men, and made our way back to the abandoned greenhouse. Holmes had great hopes that there we should find Louisa Altamont in daylight trance.

Should we be successful in this endeavor, Holmes had worked out a plan of getting her away to a hiding place of his own choosing and then, later, with Dracula's help, working out some kind of viable future for the girl.

But such was not to be. Our departure from the area of the main house was not unnoticed by our enemies. Holmes and I were trudging across a grassy meadow, not yet within a hundred yards of the old greenhouse, when I happened to glance back and saw that we were being pursued.

I cried out immediately, and my companion turned. At the same moment a shot was fired from behind us, and a bullet sang past our ears. A small group of men in dark clothing, sprung seemingly out of the earth itself, were running after us from the general direction of the house. Even as we stared, our lead pursuer raised a pistol and fired again. I had drawn my own revolver now, and returned fire, with no effect. Remembering that the wooden bullets would tend to be inaccurate at long range, I turned and ran, with Holmes, toward the abandoned greenhouse.

As investigation later proved, the men who came after us were some of Kulakov's adherents, four or five revolutionary terrorists wanted by the police in London and other cities, who had been using another old shed on the grounds as a hiding place. They had failed to observe our intrusion yesterday, but today, when they had seen where Holmes and I were going, they had burst out of concealment in obedience to their master's orders and pursued us. Evidently their dark master had enjoined them to protect the old greenhouse from intruders at any cost.

"Run, Watson, run! We must reach Louisa Altamont before they do!"

I redoubled my efforts, and managed to stay close behind Holmes as we went pounding over the meadow, stirring up songbirds, and along the faint track of a farm road, toward the grove of trees in which our objective lay concealed.

Shouts of anger, and of momentary triumph, sounded from behind us, closing in, and I knew it was likely that our pursuers ran on younger legs than ours. Once more I turned, at bay, thinking at least to delay the foe long enough for Holmes to reach the greenhouse and what it contained. This time the enemy was closer, and I took more careful aim. My next shot dropped our first pursuer in his tracks, and caused the others to hesitate.

Beyond the men who were chasing us, a greater number of policemen, some in uniforms, were now running to our aid. Among the latter I saw Mr. Prince, his long legs outpacing all the others.

It was necessary for me to shoot a second of the gasping villains in our wake before the rest turned away, scattering with police in pursuit. I then ran again, gasping and tottering, after Holmes, who had gone on into the grove.

I found my friend inside the greenhouse, where he stood looking down into the great toolbox. Inside it lay Louisa Altamont again; but this time the girl was truly dead. She lay on her back with arms outflung, still clad in her once-white burial gown, the fabric now further torn and disarranged. Her blue eyes were open and unseeing, unbothered now by daylight; her white breast was transfixed by splintered wood in the form of the long, broken handle of a rake.

We were standing there, speechless with exertion and surprise, when light rapid footsteps announced the arrival of Prince Dracula, who came bounding into the sunlit space to stop suddenly beside us, and join us in silent contemplation.

I turned to him in puzzlement. "But, her body—I thought that it would vanish?"

The shouts and heavy footsteps of the police now sounded from just outside the building. Dracula put his lips close to my ear and whispered, almost pedantically and more calmly than I would have expected: "A new vampire when killed is hard to distinguish from a breather newly dead; only the bodies of old nosferatu like myself are wont to disintegrate spectacularly into dust and gas when their spirits achieve a true departure from this plane of existence."

Within a few moments Merivale and others had joined us, and were loud in their expression of outrage at what they saw. Louisa's death was of course blamed on the villainous terrorist gang, whose surviving members were now being rounded up among the estate's woods and fields. Holmes soon whispered to me privately that he was certain Kulakov must be responsible, that perhaps he had slain the girl himself before somehow making his escape, or perhaps she had been killed by one of Kulakov's servants, obeying his orders to do so if her discovery should seem likely.

By whatever hand had been accomplished, the killing

was going to be difficult to explain, especially to Louisa's shocked and horrified parents. The official theory, soon developed, was that Louisa had been held for weeks as a drugged kidnap victim in Smithbury Hall, and whatever body had originally been buried in her place had now been destroyed by the villains in an attempt to cover their trail. Louisa's body, at last truly dead, was soon taken away by a medical examiner who, fortunately or not, had no means of discovering the truth.

I foresaw that Holmes and Dracula and I would be spending the rest of the day in clearing up, or concealing, the details of this grim and distasteful business; what I did not foresee was the great shock which awaited us on our return to Norberton House.

The abduction of Rebecca Altamont took place in her own home, in broad daylight, on the same morning as the burial of Abraham Kirkaldy and the police raid on Kulakov's rented manor.

As we were able to reconstruct the matter later, there sounded a light tap on the door of Becky's sitting room, wherein she was reading. When the girl opened the door, the man who had tipped the rowboat was standing just outside, rubbing the back of his neck as if it hurt. This time he was fully clothed, and as on the earlier occasion, she had been given only the most fleeting glance. But she had no doubt that the green eyes were the same.

With part of her mind, but only part, she wondered whether she ought to try to scream . . .

In Kulakov's place, I should probably have left some gloating sign of triumph behind, some challenging message, boasting of this latest punishment I had inflicted upon my enemies, and threatening to do even worse. Kulakov did nothing of the kind; we were left to realize gradually that

Becky was now gone, taking with her the clothes she had been wearing and apparently nothing else.

Early Saturday afternoon, with the graveside service for Abraham Kirkaldy some hours over, Martin Armstrong was told of Louisa's death, and treated to a further serious talk, by Sherlock Holmes, on the subject of vampires.

After dark there was another short lecture on the same subject, this one by Dracula, and accompanied by a demonstration. These coordinated efforts gave Martin a more realistic view of what his own situation would have been, and Louisa's, had she lived. Then, his mind full of other problems, Armstrong required some little time to understand that Mr. Prince was a vampire too.

On the day after Rebecca's ominous disappearance from Norberton House, the coffin containing her elder sister's body was—for the second time this summer—on display in the best parlor. Louisa's parents—for the second time—wore mourning and held vigil at the dead girl's side.

It was easy to see that the mother and father had been driven to the brink of madness, if not beyond, by grief and uncertainty. They could hardly avoid the torturing hope that this too might be some mistake, that the girl would yet again come back to them, somehow. Madeline soon collapsed with what her physician diagnosed as brain fever, and Ambrose was reduced to maundering about the construction of this seeming Louisa-body from "psycho-plastic material," a term then much in vogue with certain mediums.

"This . . . this is not my daughter, gentlemen," said he, looking fondly at the body in the coffin, as he might have gazed at a photograph of Louisa, or a sculpture. "This is only a reproduction, created by psychic forces."

And Martin Armstrong, who had found in a drawer and put on again the black armband he had so recently taken off, was looking at his lover in her coffin—again.

This was the face he had kissed, the body he had embraced and hungered to embrace again. But was this really his Louisa, or was it not? The breathing, laughing, shy girl of boat rides and garden parties in the summer afternoons?

And, above all, whoever this woman was, was she really dead?

Even though Louisa might now be truly dead, Armstrong endured, repeatedly, a horrible nightmare about her being raped and transformed into a vampire. He was beginning to fear that he stood in peril of undergoing the same change, begun much more gradually and pleasurably, but with the same resulting alteration in his very nature.

The fears and doubts that had arisen when the young man was repeatedly visited by his vampire lover at night returned with redoubled force now as he watched her lying in daylight—dead?

Armstrong told me he thought that perhaps never again could he be sure of death.

He was pale and trembling as he gazed at that pale, strangely transformed face. Her beauty had now been enhanced, as sometimes happens in such cases, to a breathtaking perfection.

Going back to his bedroom, where there was a mirror, Armstrong shut the door for privacy and began to examine his reflection, which was still reassuringly visible, in search of any preliminary changes that might signal a coming transformation. He felt encouraged that none were to be found.

For a moment or two, he even forgot the fact that Becky was now missing.

Sherlock Holmes, in discussion with his cousin, agreed that Louisa Altamont had been innocent of any serious wrongdoing. She had been only a pawn used by Kulakov, and her death deserved to be avenged as much as that of any breathing victim's.

Dracula, going into greater detail on the subject of Louisa's mental state, reiterated his remarks to the effect that folk of his race and hers were even more susceptible to hypnosis than the breathing variety of people were. Indeed, their very existence as vampires depended upon their flesh being held enchanted, as it were, by their own or another's will. This explained how Louisa could have been compelled by Kulakov to plague her parents about some treasure—a treasure that seemed to exist only in the vampire's deranged mind.

Holmes and I were invited back to Norberton House by Ambrose Altamont, who wished to apologize for having treated us, as he now viewed the matter, unfairly.

The true death of their elder daughter, and the abduction of their younger, would perhaps have given a clear-thinking Ambrose and Madeline strong reason for welcoming Sherlock Holmes at last into their house, for apologizing for past mistakes, and for humbly sequesting my friend's help at last. As matters stood, however, Ambrose was now a broken man, reduced by the blows of fate to a mild and pleasant manner, living in a kind of contentment from one moment to the next, vaguely agitated by everything that happened, but freed of all terror and grief. He only wanted to explain, he said, that there was really no need to be concerned: What lay in the coffin in the parlor now was not really Louisa at all, but merely a psycho-plastic construction. His dear girl would be coming back to them again, once the proper procedure for a séance could be worked out. They would be holding another sitting, he assured us, as soon as his dear wife felt well enough to take part.

Madeline Altamont, we were told by her physician, had taken to her bed. She was, at the moment, beyond listening to any explanations at all, or expressing any hopes, and her recovery was doubtful.

Before we left the house, Holmes tried once more, speaking slowly and kindly and carefully, to explain the matter to Louisa's father. "The apparition at the séance of the girl in white was indeed your daughter, though at that time, she was not dead. What we are dealing with here is something more strange and terrible than death."

Involuntarily I looked at Dracula to gauge his reaction to this remark. His glance at me held a flavor of amusement. "But I quite agree, Doctor. Life is indeed more strange and terrible than death."

As we left the house, Holmes grumbled privately to me that this was not the first time a client of his had been driven mad, but that made the matter no easier to accept.

"By Heaven, Watson, I mean yet to get my hands on the fiend who has done this. And when I do . . ."

Meanwhile, my affair with Sarah was now well launched, with the seductive vampire (myself) continuing to visit the young woman repeatedly in her room at night, or in the grounds of Norberton House at dusk.

Watson, on discovering (I never did learn how) the fact of this affair, was outraged (naturally so, as he thought) and proved brave enough to tell me so to my face.

Considerations of honor and duty restrained my natural reaction to this meddling, and Watson survived the occasion unharmed. His good luck may be partially attributable to Sarah, who, with the wise idea of separating the two men, prevailed on Mr. Prince to escort her there and then to the little cemetery where her dear brother now lay beneath the freshly mounded earth. She said she wanted to bring more flowers to the grave.

"And will you help us hunt his killer, Sarah?" I inquired softly, when she had risen from her graveside prayers. (In recent days the value of traditional religion had risen sharply in her eyes.)

"Aye. But how am I t' dae that?" Her brown eyes burned at me.

"He laid a spell upon you, did he not? Meaning to force you to do his will?"

"Aye, he did that."

"Then traces of that connection probably remain. Will you trust me to put you to sleep, and let me look for them?"

Suffice it to say that the experiment was made, the thin red threads of mental influence traced to their source. Evidence obtained through Sarah, speaking in true trance, detailing her psychic visions, indicated that Kulakov had carried Becky off to the docks, not in London but in Hull, and from there had promptly taken ship.

Sarah's visions were also of pain and intermittent weakness. When Sherlock Holmes heard this, he said with characteristic insight that Kulakov probably still was, and had been for most of his long life, suffering from the discomforts of having been hanged in 1765.

Holmes delegated to some of his lesser associates a sustained effort to find and destroy all of Kulakov's earths in England. Several such hideaways were found on the grounds of Smithbury Hall, quite near the place where Kulakov had been keeping Louisa. But Holmes thought this search of only secondary importance.

Dracula, too, freely expressed his doubts about the effectiveness of the procedure. "It seems most unlikely that we should ever really be able to render them all uninhabitable. I speak from a certain experience. A dozen years ago, as perhaps you are aware, some Englishmen led by that idiot Van Helsing were attempting to do the same thing to me. They failed miserably, though they were not aware of their failure. Someday perhaps I will tell you the whole story.

"But the point to be noted just now is this: A vampire given time for preparation, and the chance to ship in a supply of his native earth, can so entrench himself in a foreign land that he becomes almost impossible to root out—without killing him."

Kulakov's prospects for regaining his lost treasure must have seemed to him as remote as ever. The evil vampire had killed Louisa with his own hands, or arranged for her killing. The count had seen his convert now as only a liability.

Further evidence obtained through Sarah's psychic contact indicated that the Russian vampire had departed from the docks at Hull aboard a fast steamer which, the port records showed, was bound directly for St. Petersburg. The vessel was Russian, and we thought that probably it was under Kulakov's direct control.

Holmes promptly cabled a friendly contact in the Petersburg police, to alert them to be on watch for Kulakov, though there were as yet no formal charges to be brought against him. The cable brought a prompt response, which seemed to promise cooperation; but we feared that Kulakov might have so much influence in the Tsarist government as to be effectively immune to the police.

And Mycroft Holmes promised us that he could arrange for a swift vessel, perhaps even one of the Royal Navy's new turbine-powered destroyers, to carry the band of hunters on to St. Petersburg, where the next act of the drama was to be played out.

Dracula remarked that he could feel a certain remote sympathy for Kulakov.

"Sympathy!"

"Yes, Doctor. Oh, he is my enemy now, and I will hunt him down and kill him. But I found myself in a somewhat similar situation, that of the hunted vampire, about twelve years ago, on my first visit to Britain, before I had met either you or my distinguished cousin.

"Perhaps I will someday tell you that story, Doctor."

~ 17 ~

Before departing for London and thence for Russia, Holmes and I paid a final visit to the home of the Altamonts. The sad condition of this once-intelligent and happy couple stiffened our resolve to see that justice was done.

Ambrose Altamont, still denying the fact that his older daughter was truly dead at last, now assured us that his younger daughter, Rebecca, was only visiting a friend and would return at any hour.

Altamont's back was bent now, like that of an old man. He peered at us timidly, and his voice and hands alike were quivering. "Surely Becky will be back with us by this evening. Then we will have our next sitting. You gentlemen are welcome to attend."

With our former client in this condition, and with Mrs. Altamont still prostrated by brain fever, there was obviously no point in our attempting any further explanations . . . either of vampires or on any other point. Instead, we nodded and smiled and said our good-byes, promising to call again, with good news, when we could.

At least, as I commented to Holmes a little later, Louisa's parents had been spared the ultimate shock of being present when their daughter was staked as a vampire.

* * *

Mycroft was as good as his word, and with the benefit of his powerful though hidden influence, discreetly exercised, our expeditionary force was able to obtain, quickly and quietly, the use of a fast steamer for the journey to St. Petersburg. The vessel provided was in fact the private steam-yacht of one of the Sea Lords—I think that even now I had better not be more specific regarding the vessel's ownership or the circumstances in which we obtained its use.

There had been some discussion of our using a naval vessel, but Holmes had promptly decided that would be inappropriate. "Owing to the essentially private nature of our business, a privately owned craft is preferable to a ship of His Majesty's Navy, which would inevitably attract attention, and would require some diplomatic prearrangement."

Another advantage of a private ship was that she could stand by unobtrusively in the Russian port, ready to carry us on the return voyage—but haste in returning should not be necessary.

The craft we were privileged to obtain had engines similar to those of the new turbine-powered destroyers, capable of making more than thirty knots. Most naval vessels of the time could sustain no more than half that speed.

During our voyage, Count Kulakov's motives and behavior were naturally the subject of intense discussion. So were those of Rebecca Altamont, the question being by what combination of force and guile she had been compelled to accompany him. Our party included Sherlock Holmes, Prince Dracula, Armstrong, and myself, as well as Sarah Kirkaldy, without whose genuine psychic capabilities we might never have been able to follow the escaping Kulakov with any accuracy.

While the Russian's vampirish bloodlust had played a part in his behavior, obviously his prime motive in his attacks upon the Altamonts was—or had been—revenge.

Even so, that left unexplained many details of his behavior. Nor was it very helpful simply to say that the man was mad, though that undoubtedly seemed to be the case. And there was still the matter of the mysterious treasure. Did it exist only in the fevered imagination of a deranged vampire?

"It will of course be difficult, or impossible, to arrest the man we seek, in Russia even more so than in England—but it would be useless to arrest him anywhere. Courts, fines, and imprisonment are meaningless threats to him. The only practical way to punish a vampire is by the application of direct physical violence."

We could not but agree with Holmes.

At the same time, of course, Rebecca Altamont was making the voyage with Kulakov. We were sure that she must be in some sense his prisoner, though we could not say by what combination of threats, actual violence, and mesmeric power he might be forcing her to his will.

At one point Armstrong asked me whether Becky, having made the voyage with her captor, would be unloaded in an earth-filled trunk, and whether she had been brought aboard his ship and spent most of the voyage thus confined. We all assured him that this was unlikely—unless Rebecca had already become a vampire. Such intimations as we could receive through the entranced mind of Sarah Kirkaldy indicated that this was not the case, but we could not be sure.

Our sea route to St. Petersburg took us through the North Sea, among the islands and peninsulas of Denmark, and past Copenhagen, with a brief stop there to see if a cable might have arrived from Mycroft—the wireless was not yet available on ships—before entering the Baltic. Our journey in itself was almost completely uneventful, leaving us plenty of time for discussion of vampirism and related phenomena. I realized only belatedly that the favorable winds and generally calm seas we enjoyed were at least in part a result of Prince Dracula's efforts in an occult way.

Whether Kulakov might be capable of exercising a similar influence upon the weather, we did not know; in any event, we gained a day or more on his ship during the voyage, so that we arrived at our destination only a day, perhaps only a few hours, after he did. We were elated to see that the ship on which Kulakov and his hostage had traveled—her name was plainly visible—was actually still at the quay, in the process of unloading cargo, when we arrived in St. Petersburg. This was indeed an encouraging sign, showing that our enemy and his helpless hostage could as yet be at no very great distance from the city.

With our own vessel berthed, we disembarked amid dense fog and intermittent rain, conditions almost identical to those under which we had left Hull. Under Armstrong's guidance we had little difficulty in finding our way about the Russian capital. Our party took rooms at the Hotel de l'Europe. Here our windows overlooked Nevsky Prospekt, the great boulevard which runs for two and a half miles through the city's heart. When the fog cleared, which it soon did, the view was quite impressive. We saw the avenue thronged with people under black umbrellas, both of its sides lined by palaces and churches, by business establishments and government buildings of all sorts.

There were an amazing number of uniforms to be seen among the native populace, and no immediate way for the stranger to know which type of costume belonged to high officials and which to mere minor functionaries.

The hotel stood on the north side of the boulevard, less than half a mile east of the Kazan Cathedral, whose colonnade had been copied from that of St. Peter's in Rome, and whose interior boasted the regimental flags and imperial eagles captured from the ravaged army of Napoleon. A block past the cathedral, one reached the luxurious shops of the Morskaya, where I almost thought I might have been in Paris.

Traffic here kept to the right, which added yet another minor strain to our difficulties.

A mile to our north and out of sight from our hotel, on the far bank of the broad Neva, there rose the sullen, dun-colored walls of the Fortress of Peter and Paul, at once a stronghold and a prison. Towering four hundred feet above those walls, and visible from most parts of the city, rose the slender golden spire marking the site of the cathedral contained within the fortress.

For three miles along the southern bank of the Neva ran a solid quay of pink Finnish granite, lined on its inland side by the Winter Palace, the Admiralty, the foreign embassies, and the palaces of the great nobles, the wealthy merchants and landowners.

Currently the Russian capital was a city of about a million and a half people. This made it not as large as London, but still to be classified as one of the great cities of Europe and the world. And from the bustle of commerce along the quays, and the evident respect shown toward the monarchy by most of the people, it was plain that their Majesties Nicholas and Alexandra were still secure on their thrones, despite the continual ferment of terrorists seeking to incite revolution.

The Winter Palace, a huge and, as one might expect, an imposing edifice, built in the eighteenth century by the Empress Elizabeth, was seldom occupied by royalty at this season of the year. The Tsar and Tsarina, as Armstrong informed us, were in the habit of spending their summers at Tsarskoe Selo, the Tsar's village, a construction of fantastic extravagance fifteen miles south of St. Petersburg. This miniature domain had been called "a world apart," and "an enchanted fairyland." Eight hundred acres of green lawn—well over a square mile—in the imperial park delighted the four daughters of the imperial family, Olga, Tatiana, Maria, and Anastasia, whose ages were eight to two, respectively.

The horse-drawn tram had not yet been replaced by the electric vehicle, and motorcars were much more a rarity than in the vicinity of London. Rubber-tired carriages were fairly common in the summer, and the main streets, at least, were all smoothly paved.

Now we put into action, as best we could, the plans which we had made aboard ship. We were each of us to seek out our professional contemporaries in St. Petersburg, and endeavor to find out what we could about our quarry.

Dracula mentioned casually that there might be in the St. Petersburg area some local vampires with whom he could establish useful contact. "Most likely it will be something indirect—I have a place to start, the name of a certain breathing friend of an old friend."

Zubatov, then head of the Tsarist secret police, acquainted with Sherlock Holmes at least by reputation, was obviously a powerful man, important either as friend or foe; and Holmes would pursue his own inquiries by that means.

Armstrong felt almost at home in Petersburg, having spent much of the previous winter and spring in the city in the course of his duties as international correspondent for his American newspaper. He had found the place interesting, and had enjoyed many aspects of the local society. Others, such as the official censorship, were extremely distasteful. But mainly he had suffered by being separated from Louisa, until, to his joy, he had been reassigned to London.

For my part I endeavored, though I met with little success, to establish some contacts among the local medical community, by means of shared interests or mutual acquaintances. One friend of a friend turned up unexpectedly—a Russian who had been doing research on plague, in Paris, but his knowledge of Count Kulakov, or of anyone who might know the count, proved to be nil. From my new acquaintance, I learned little more than that this city had been called "the Babylon of the Snows," or sometimes "the Venice of the North"—the latter because of the number of canals and natural waterways.

I learned also that in summer, cholera was always a serious concern. It was important to make sure that drinking water was boiled.

I was pleased to observe that telephones were as readily available as in most parts of Britain. All of the best hotels and other important buildings had at least one instrument installed, and I was told there were many thousands of subscribers in Russia.

Our business in the city was facilitated by the fact that several of our party understood the language of the city's common people. Holmes spoke a little Russian and understood more—this knowledge, as he explained to me, being one of the fruits of two years of travel in Tibet. And Prince Dracula soon demonstrated fluency in the tongue of Ivan the Terrible, though Holmes told me there was much that was old-fashioned, even archaic, in Dracula's speech. The prince said that he had never visited St. Petersburg before; I admit being somewhat awed by the realization that he was considerably older than the city.

Armstrong, during the past year having spent several months in St. Petersburg, had a smattering of modern Russian.

Of particular help to me was the fact that every cultured person in the capital spoke French, some of them by preference over their native tongue; in addition, a fair number spoke English.

On our first evening in St. Petersburg, some of our party visited a certain basement café called the Red Jingle, rather a bohemian establishment. Under a poster advertising last season's performances of Anna Pavlova, we discussed our next move.

We intended to learn who might be Kulakov's special friends and associates in St. Petersburg, and Cousin Sherlock had been able to come up with some clues along that line. Everything we had learned so far tended to confirm that our quarry probably did not have many intimate associates, here in Petersburg or anywhere else.

We still did not know whether Kulakov had yet forced his fangs upon his latest victim and hostage. Personally I thought it probable, though I admitted there might be reasons for him to do otherwise.

Meanwhile I was congratulating myself for having managed to bring Sarah along, though the stern demands of duty kept me from seeing anything like as much of her as I would have liked.

Getting a black look from Watson now and then, I condescended to assure the good doctor that he need not be worried about Sarah's becoming a vampire. With a little restraint on the part of both parties involved, such an outcome could be delayed for a long time, and most of my love affairs did not end in that result.

Gradually our slowly growing network of contacts in the city began, like a tangle of grapevine, to bear fruit. Within two days we learned that in the higher social circles where he was known, Kulakov planned to present Rebecca as his new wife, acquired in England. In recent years he had been known in St. Petersburg as a widower, his last reported wife having died some years ago.

Insofar as we could discover, it had never been the count's habit, before his latest trip to England, to mix much in St. Petersburg society, but he was on fairly intimate terms with a few of the nobility. Though appearing socially from time to time, he mainly kept to himself, spending most of his time on his extensive country estates.

Martin Armstrong was still being tormented by his mixed feelings toward the dead Louisa. His beloved was, or had been, one of the undead. Having some difficulty in believing that Louisa was now truly departed, Armstrong was also anticipating a similar outcome for Becky. He brooded sleeplessly upon her fate, the unbearable fact that from now on, she might be compelled to spend her days, or many of her daylight hours, sleeping in her tomb. And he had learned from the party of vampire-hunters the uses of the wooden stake.

Who would her lover be when she had become a vampire? Not Kulakov any longer—vampire and vampire do not bed together.

No, Becky's new lover would have to be a breathing man. And there could be no future in society—any form of human society, as Martin thought—for such a couple.

Sarah Kirkaldy, as Dracula's lover, had, by the time we left for Russia, been brought to a certain practical understanding of vampirism. By this time Sarah, though her grief for her brother and her desire for revenge were genuine enough, was beginning to wonder, perhaps to calculate, how such powers as had been revealed to her might be turned to a medium's professional advantage.

Every witness—there were not many—who reported seeing Kulakov since his return to St. Petersburg, said that the man gave evidence of some kind of mental or physical infirmity. We wondered whether this infirmity had provided him with one strong reason, perhaps really the only reason, to come back to St. Petersburg. "Is it possible that he comes here in hopes of getting relief from these symptoms?" I asked. No one answered.

The beautiful white nights, persisting well into July, made a favorable impression on the breathing visitors, but somewhat hampered the visiting and native vampires alike.

Holmes asked Martin Armstrong for confirmation that

Rebecca Altamont did not speak Russian. Then the detective mused that this lack would doubtless add to the girl's sense of helplessness and isolation, and make it harder for her to attempt an escape unaided, even if she were able to contemplate such a course.

In engaging our hotel rooms, we had particularly asked for a suite equipped with a telephone. In the first two days of our stay, the instrument seldom rang; but toward the end of the third day, I answered a call and heard, to my great astonishment, the voice of a distraught woman whom I could only gradually, and with some uncertainty, recognize as Rebecca Altamont.

I will not repeat in detail all that the mesmerized and terrorized woman said, or elaborate on my futile attempts to interrupt and offer her some hope. Suffice it to say here that she cursed us, one and all, for interfering with her happiness, and warned us to go home.

There followed a little shriek as the instrument was evidently pulled roughly from her grasp, and then a gloating postscript in an unfamiliar male voice which I soon realized must be that of Kulakov himself.

"Dr. Watson, I take it? Mr. Holmes is not available at the moment? Ah, too bad." Kulakov went on to give his own warning, to the effect that until now he had treated his prisoner kindly, but if Sherlock Holmes and the other meddlers did not promptly take themselves out of the country, he would soon begin to punish Rebecca Altamont for what he called our misdeeds.

"The exact mode of this chastisement I leave, for now, to your imaginations. And ah, I must not forget. Let this call serve as formal announcement that a wedding ceremony is in prospect; I think, though, that it will be delayed until my bride and I have reached the country. It is easier there to find a priest with a dependable, sensible attitude in these matters."

At that, I thought that the connection was about to be broken; but then the vampire remained at his 'phone long enough to deliver a parting shot. "Oh, and convey my good-will to the family of thieves, the infamous Altamonts. Tell them I will yet have my treasure back. And give them my congratulations—they raise such tasty daughters. It is too bad they have no more."

There was a laugh, then a sharp click at the other end of the line, followed by the impersonal humming of the wires.

Rebecca was being held hostage for our good behavior.

~ 18 ~

Reeling under the shock of the horrible threat directed at Rebecca Altamont, our little group met in a council of war to determine what our next move should be.

We were all horrified, of course, at Kulakov's new challenge; the most terrible aspect was his threat to carry his helpless hostage away to one of his remote country estates, where the lord of the manor customarily ruled as a law unto himself, unfettered by any of the constraints imposed by an urban society; and where we would find it much more difficult if not impossible to reach either the criminal or his victim.

Prince Dracula of course was something of an exception when it came to considering impossibilities. On being informed of Kulakov's challenge he announced stiffly that, even if we were to fail in St. Petersburg, he would probably consider that his honor required him to mount an extended campaign, spending years if necessary, to recover the girl or at least to take vengeance on her abductor.

We appreciated this attitude on the part of the prince, but at the same time we took rather less satisfaction from the idea of mere vengeance serving as a substitute for rescue.

We considered the idea of trying to communicate our proud defiance, and the grimmest possible warning, to our foe, but soon decided that the only good response would be effective action.

The more I saw of the city and its people, the more I found St. Petersburg a very foreign place to English eyes, despite its homelike fogs and dampness. But at the same time, the metropolis struck me as quite European—not Eastern or Asiatic—and exceedingly impressive.

The city sprawls over nineteen islands, most of them at the time of our visit green with summer trees, and for miles along the ragged, swampy edge of the mainland. It is divided down the middle by the river Neva, which seems to carry with its flow the smells of pure wilderness water and bitter cold. I was startled to learn that the broad Neva is only forty-six miles in length. It drains Lake Ladoga, which, in turn, is fed by a number of streams flowing out of the infinite northern forests.

The islands upon which the city is built included: the Island of the Apothecaries, with its botanical gardens; Kamerny Island, where are situated the Church of the Nativity of John the Baptist and the Summer Theater; Ielagin Island, with its palace and famous oak trees; Krestovsky Island, with a medieval castle, gardens, and yacht club.

These and other outlying districts are invaded in summer by city-dwellers hungry for space and fresh air. Restlessly seeking out our several professional contacts, we prowled joylessly among the cheerful throng dining in restaurants, eagerly surrounding the bandstands, and attending the café concerts.

The layout and architecture of the city were far less Russian than European, especially Italianate.

People still talked about the bicentenary celebration that had been held in and for the city only two or three months earlier, back in May, 1903.

We were all of us occupied in our own ways with seeking information in and about the city; I for one became well acquainted with its cabdrivers *(izvoshniki),* many of whom spoke French, or even English to some degree, and who were all alike attired in a sort of uniform, chiefly consisting of a long, blue coat, thickly padded and secured with a brightly colored belt. The summer outfit included a small top hat of a peculiar shape, making the wearer look, as I thought, like some fanciful creature from the pen of Lewis Carroll. The cabs, strangely, in a place where winters were so severe, were not tightly enclosed, and only leather hoods protected their passengers from rain.

Fortunately I could manage tolerable French, which most of the Russian nobility preferred to their native tongue; to my relief, that proved adequate to see me through most encounters in my pose of casual traveler.

Holmes, endeavoring to ascertain whether either of Rebecca's parents might have recovered sufficiently to be informed of the latest news about their surviving daughter, exchanged cables with Mycroft almost on a daily basis. The name of an intermediary in London was used, since it was judged desirable for several reasons to keep Mycroft's name out of the public eye as much as possible.

Had our situation in St. Petersburg not been so tragic and so desperate, I believe that Holmes would have thoroughly enjoyed his visit. He was now able to meet personally with men whom he had heretofore communicated with only by letter and by cable, and to exchange with the Petersburg police important information on a number of professional matters.

To an Englishman, the main streets of this city are startlingly wide and straight (the elegant Bolshaya Morskaya has signs in French and some in English over the windows of its shops), and many of the buildings which line them have imposing stone façades. The dampness and fog tend to make the English feel at home. Cathedrals and smaller churches abound.

The Bronze Horseman, a monumental statue of Peter the Great, celebrated by Pushkin in a famous poem, stands just east of the English Embankment, near the Admiralty. The equestrian statue, commissioned by Catherine the Great to honor her illustrious predecessor, shows Peter in Roman wreath and toga, right arm outstretched toward the west, making his bronze horse rear on a huge rock, trampling under its hooves the serpent of sedition.

With renewed determination, we pressed our search for our quarry and his prisoner relentlessly through the city, and even through the suburbs.

It was only after a nerve-racking delay, following several days of fruitless search and investigation, that we succeeded in locating Kulakov's townhouse in St. Petersburg. Our task had been rendered more difficult by the fact that the legal documents of ownership were in another name.

Carefully we approached the house, and observed it from front and rear. Wherever the master might currently be, at the moment he was clearly not in residence, no more than he had been in his rented country house in England. In fact, the Petersburg house and its small garden had the look of having been long unoccupied. Shortly after our discovery of the place, and even while we still had it under observation, a small squad of servants appeared and hastily plunged into the task of airing the building and evidently preparing it for occupation. Holmes, through his official and unofficial contacts, soon managed to learn that the count, while en route from England, had sent his housekeeper a cable from Copenhagen.

That night we four men approached the building stealthily, managed to enter without disturbing any of the servants in their sleep, and subjected the premises to a thorough search. It did not take long to convince ourselves that the prisoner we sought could not be here, and that therefore Kulakov himself was almost certainly still taking his daytime slumber elsewhere.

The terrible thought haunted us that the Russian pirate's hostage might already have been dispatched to some remote Siberian province, and was being borne hourly, by carriage or by rail, farther and farther out of our reach. Prince Dracula and Sarah Kirkaldy were still conducting their daily hypnotic sessions, and the evidence from these was against Rebecca's having been carried out of the city—Kulakov was still in the city, and there were times when he seemed to be looking directly at his captive. But still, the horrible possibility loomed.

Then, just when all prospects seemed dark, encouraging news came to us—by precisely what route, I will not specify, even now, after the lapse of some fourteen years. Evidence came into our hands that the woman we sought was being kept out of sight in the house of a certain eminent person who was perhaps allied deliberately with Kulakov, or perhaps was being forced, by blackmail or other means, to accommodate the vampire's wishes.

Taking counsel quickly among ourselves, we hunters decided to risk everything and enter the mansion in question, by stratagem if possible, by force if necessary, and to do whatever was required to rescue Rebecca Altamont—whether she was still breathing or had become nosferatu—from her evil captor. To this end, we joined our hands in a solemn pledge.

~ 19 ~

Moving in and around the great city of St. Petersburg, meeting at our hotel to exchange information, the members of our party continued, each in his or her own way, to press the search for Count Kulakov, for his prisoner, and for the mysterious Gregory Efimovitch, who seemed to have a dark, controlling influence upon our enemy.

Certain signs suggested that we were making progress—at least our efforts had provoked the count into trying to warn us off—but in other respects we faced great and terrible difficulties. Some of these problems were simply a result of the fact that we were foreigners.

Again it seemed necessary to make sure that all of our party understood the dangers we were facing. We were putting ourselves at a grave risk in our efforts to rescue Rebecca. Dracula dutifully advised us that we breathing folk, at least, were risking arrest and imprisonment, which in Russia could involve a fate more terrible than quick death.

However, we were in agreement that duty and honor alike forbade any thought of turning back. Whatever fate our enemy might inflict upon his helpless hostage if we persisted, there was no reason to think that she would be spared the same doom if we withdrew.

At last—whether it came through some mysterious local contact of Dracula's, or whether it was first established through Sarah Kirkaldy, I never learned—there fell into our hands the first real clue as to where and when we might reach Kulakov.

At last, to our great relief, we believed we had succeeded in identifying the house in the city where Rebecca Altamont was being held, almost a mile from the count's own townhouse. Having ascertained this much, we thought it safe to assume that Kulakov would not likely be very far from this other dwelling, or remain absent from it for any great length of time. We remained determined to take whatever chances were necessary to effect the young woman's rescue.

Unfathomable complications lurked in the fact that we still had not learned who the important Gregory Efimovitch might be. Holmes suspected the name might be that of some Russian mastermind who was engineering a deep plot.

We had received an indication that Kulakov expected to meet this mysterious individual on a certain night—and in the very house where Rebecca Altamont was being confined.

Welcome confirmation of our first clue came by another route: A servant, angry at master or mistress for some abuse and therefore susceptible to being bribed, had claimed to know the identity of the enigmatic Gregory Efimovitch, and had even affirmed that the man we had so long sought to identify would be in the palatial residence tomorrow night; but when our agent demanded to know who Gregory Efimovitch might be, more money was demanded. Before the matter could be resolved, the conversation was interrupted and the informant of our informant had been called away.

Sherlock Holmes in particular, as he paced through our connecting rooms in our hotel, fretted and pondered over this continuing lack of knowledge. Neither in Holmes's world of police and crime, in mine of medicine, nor in Prince Dracula's peculiar domain—that netherworld of the strange and the occult, straddling the aristocracy as well as the lower classes—could we locate any Gregory Efimovitch who seemed likely to be of particular importance to our quarry.

Holmes gave vent to his frustration. "It would appear that the man must be of the first importance—and yet he does not exist!"

"I trust that our lack of knowledge on the subject will not prevent our accomplishing our objectives," I observed.

He smote the table beside him. "We must not allow it to do so. But I fear the want will make itself felt!"

The house, or perhaps I should say the palace, in which we at last ran our quarry to earth was one of those great mansions in the district including Bolshaya Morskaya Street and several of the more important cross streets in the western portion of the city.

Even at this late date, it is perhaps wise for me to refrain from specifying closely the exact location of the house involved, or telling more about its ownership. Suffice it to say that it stood near the Court Embankment, and that not far away were the palaces of the Grand Duke Alexandrovich and Grand Duke Mikhail Nikolayevich. The Yusupov palace on the Moika Canal stood within a stone's throw. In the vicinity of the Winter Palace there were also the Stieglitz Palace, Shermetev Palace, Beloselsky Palace, Stroganov Palace, Marinsky Palace, Chernishevskaya Palace, Vladimir Palace, and many others.

On the appointed night, Holmes, Dracula, and I made our way to a rendezvous just outside the mansion. Martin Armstrong also was ready to play his assigned role, which consisted of having a hired carriage in readiness for a quick getaway, not far from the house.

Having staked out our several positions, we waited

until past midnight for Kulakov to appear, but without result. Possibly, we thought, he had entered without our seeing him; there might be another entrance than those we were covering. At length we decided to delay no longer; even if our quarry had eluded us, Rebecca Altamont presumably remained inside, and having come this close, we did not intend to leave without her.

At first, in planning our excursion, we had thought that the owner of the mansion might possibly be induced to invite us in, or some of us, if we simply presented ourselves at the door and sent in our cards as if making a social call. On the other hand, the chance of our being turned away had seemed very great, as did the likelihood that our attempt would alert our enemy.

In the end we thought another arrangement more likely to succeed. Ideally of course an entrance during the day was preferable, but as matters stood, the only feasible time seemed to be at night, when fortunately late revelry seemed the rule rather than the exception, and neither domestic staff nor invited guests would be likely to take much notice of an extra gentleman or two, who behaved as if they had a right to be there. At least we could hope that such would be the case.

One encouraging sign upon the night we watched the house was a series of carriages coming and going at the main entrance, testifying that an even greater and later celebration than usual was in progress.

The treacherous servant, to whom I have already alluded, admitted us through a side door.

The mansion's resplendent interior was in keeping with its outward aspect. Furnishings included ornaments of old English silver, inlaid chests, Renaissance bronzes, and carved wooden chairs and tables. One anteroom contained a set of furniture made chiefly from elephant tusks. The dining room, decorated with gilt cups and majolica plates, boasted a Persian carpet and a splendid inlaid sideboard, upon which stood a magnificent bronze and crystal crucifix—Holmes, in an aside, whispered to me that it was Italian, of the seventeenth century.

Once inside, and free to move about, walking boldly and taking care to avoid any appearance of furtiveness, we found ourselves in a mansion the equal in splendor and elegance of any to be found in England. The furnishings included old European master paintings, Chinese jade, vases of Dresden porcelain, and French and English inlaid furniture.

It boasted an oak-paneled dining room, capable of seating at least forty people at a single table, with red-velvet curtains and a red-granite mantelpiece. On passing into the house, I had observed that on the ground floor there were at least two kitchens, and the one into which I obtained a glance was walled with marble.

The servant who had admitted us spoke English fairly well, and as we came in, he whispered to us where Rebecca Altamont was to be found. He added that Count Kulakov had now arrived as well; I was about to turn away when the fellow appended, almost as an afterthought, the information that the Gregory Efimovitch, about whom we had been inquiring earlier, was now also present.

"Then you know who he is?" I demanded eagerly.

"Not I, no sir. But when I say the name to Sasha, who work in the kitchen, he laugh, and say he know who is this Gregory Efimovitch, and has seen his dealings with the high nobility. Then Sasha was called away and I heard no more. But I think the man you want has just come into the house."

We three intruders in evening dress glanced at one another with a heightened resolve, knowing that we might find ourselves confronting not one deadly enemy but two. Yet our first care must be to rescue the helpless girl.

* * *

Within five minutes of my obtaining entrance, I, Dracula, had settled myself in a rather large alcove, furnished with a couple of chairs, just off the main stairway, one level above the ground floor of this St. Petersburg palace. I had even lighted a cigarette and was pretending to smoke. Tobacco is a convenient disguise, and one that I have used before—it serves quite satisfactorily to reassure any suspicious observer that at least one is breathing, even if one has no great respect for the condition of one's lungs.

From where I sat, I could watch all three branches of the hallway that came together at the stair. When I had given our helpful servant gold, he had followed me upstairs and obligingly added a little information about what we would now call the layout. The hallway straight ahead of me was marked on both sides with bedroom doors. At the far end, it turned to the left, and after two more right-angle turns, came back into sight as the hallway on my left; my point, and it has a bearing on the momentous events that followed, is that either passage could be used to get from the stair to the room in which Miss Altamont presumably was languishing.

The unfaithful (but useful) servant disappeared, in the quiet way good servants do, and Holmes and Watson set out upon their quest, choosing to go by the central hall. I settled down in a soft armchair, to pretend to smoke, and meditate. A guest or two, coming up or down the stair en route to other parts of the house—the party had spread everywhere—glanced at this fellow seated in the shadows and enjoying a few solitary puffs, and went their way, thinking that he was only waiting for someone.

As indeed he was.

Having established his strategic outpost, the erstwhile Mr. Prince was waiting, as patiently as his nature would allow, for Kulakov, or perhaps for the still-enigmatic Gregory Efimovitch, to show himself. I did not intend the former, who had kidnapped and abused my own blood relative, nor perhaps the latter either, to escape from this party unscathed.

Of course my stated reason for taking up a position just when and where I did was to enable me to stand guard while my breathing colleagues attempted to carry out what was—at least, for them—the most important part of the operation.

Ah. Ah, God. Bear with me, please. I told you this would be upsetting.

Back to Watson for the moment . . .

Holmes and I, doing our best to play the role of party-goers on a random stroll, set off down the hall in search of the room where, as the treacherous servant had assured us, the lady prisoner was being held.

We located what we were sure must be the proper door, just as the servant had described it. A soft tap at the portal elicited no response; this was not particularly surprising. Our next task was to get into the room despite the fact that the door proved to be locked. Holmes pulled his set of picklocks from his pocket, while I stood by holding a small electric torch.

Overall our plan was simple enough, though we expected to face difficulties in its execution. We would escort the lady downstairs, carrying her bodily if necessary, and bring her straight out of the house to the carriage that Martin Armstrong had waiting in the street. If anyone stopped us or tried to interfere, our claim would be that our companion of the evening had fainted and needed fresh air; if that course failed, we would take such action as we could.

The lock was perhaps more complex than Holmes had expected, and its opening more difficult; but at length he uttered a small hiss of satisfaction, and the door swung in. My friend and I, entering the room as quietly as possible, found ourselves facing Miss Altamont, who lay supine upon the bed, clothed in a nightdress of elaborate lace. Her head was slightly elevated on velvet pillows, and her open eyes were staring at the flame of a single candle, which burned on a small table at the far side of the otherwise darkened chamber.

The girl made no response to our entry, or to our first reassuring words. Taking up the lighted candle from the table and approaching her more closely, I saw that her face was calm, expressionless, and her eyes fixed on the now-moving flame. More shocking was the fact that I thought I noted some of the characteristics of the vampire in her appearance; but I could not be sure. At least there were no fang marks visible upon her throat.

Naturally we had closed the door to the room behind us. Just as we were starting to lift Miss Altamont from the bed, it suddenly opened; a chambermaid had entered and switched on the electric light. In the next moment, the young uniformed servant, every bit as startled as Holmes and I, gave voice to a faint cry and drew breath for a louder effort.

Before she could scream again, both Holmes and myself were at her side. We had come equipped with a small bottle of chloroform, in anticipation of some such difficulty.

After putting the unconscious servant in a large wardrobe, and blocking the door to the cabinet with a chair, we at length succeeded, by blowing out the candle, in partially rousing the lady on the bed.

Meanwhile, from my post just down the hall, I, Prince Dracula, heard the outraged servant's faint outcry, but being something of a connoisseur of such noises, I dismissed it out of hand for what it was. No one else in the house, if they heard the cry at all, paid it the least attention.

Next I detected the sounds of four human feet casually approaching, bearing with them two sets of breathing human lungs, one male and one female. They were coming down the hallway on my right. I waited, confidently, to confront whoever might appear.

I waited, I say . . .

Ahhhhhh.

I warned you at the start . . . now you must be patient with me for a moment or two.

Thank you for your patience. Now we can proceed.

The unknown man who came strolling into my sight was accompanied by a woman equally unknown to me, who appeared to be jealous of her escort's attention and was trying to engage him in conversation. She was perhaps thirty-five or forty, attractive and bejeweled, obviously a member of the upper classes—and what suddenly riveted my attention was the fact that she was walking worshipfully at the side of a man who obviously belonged to a much different stratum of society.

I was startled, to put it mildly, to observe that the man who drew such worshipful attention from this countess—for such she might have been—appeared to be a peasant. His long shirt, boots, and trousers were peasant garments, though of fine fabrics never seen on any farm, and he looked about him with bold, piercing eyes. He carried with him, like a wave, strong olfactory evidence that his body had been long unwashed. I found this apparition disconcerting. He wore on a chain around his neck a large pectoral cross of gold.

This peculiar stranger was also carrying, in one massive, thick-fingered hand, some kind of crystal cup, half-filled with wine. He held the vessel not in the manner of one serving drinks, but of one consuming them. He savored the contents of the valuable goblet, then almost contemptuously tossed it away empty.

The Russian woman with him continued incongruously

and—some would say—shamefully hanging on the peasant's arm, and at one point, she addressed him as "Holy Father," which startled me again. Besides the large pectoral cross, there was nothing about him to suggest that he might be a member of the regular clergy.

I thought that there were only bedrooms down the hallway in the direction from which the couple came. The suggestion was inescapable, to my experienced eye, that this lout and his fair companion—I even wondered whether she might be the lady of this house—had just been engaging in debauchery. I am not very easily shocked, as you may well imagine, but here roaring peculiarities demanded to be noticed. She was hanging on to her consort, obviously tolerating his odor and his strange appearance, now laughing—with him, not at him—and taking obscene liberties with his person.

Perhaps I should mention, even though I am a gentleman, that the lady was somewhat the worse for drink.

The man said something to her again, speaking in crude, peasant-sounding Russian, and I caught the name of Kulakov. He seemed to be trying to explain to his companion that he had an appointment to meet Kulakov and have a talk with him.

Then suddenly the man broke off, having become aware of my presence where I sat pretending to be smoking in the shadows. At once he grew interested in me. Something about me—even in the dim light—caught his attention sharply.

Gently but firmly the peasant put his fair companion aside. As he released her, he made a gentle gesture with his broad hand, a wiping motion with the palm out. The hand did not touch the lady, but her eyelids sagged and she sat down on the edge of a big chair, then pitched softly forward to lie partially on a bearskin rug, in which position she fell asleep. Her fair breasts, almost escaping her low-cut dress, seemed to be menaced by the dead fangs of the white bear.

My gaze lifted to the eyes of the man, who was standing motionless, regarding me. I was being challenged. Deliberately I crushed out my cigarette upon the marble floor. Perhaps this burly, impudent peasant was going to try to stare me down. A great many years had passed since anyone had seriously attempted that.

My eyesight, as you might suppose, is excellent even in dim light. I saw before me a powerfully built man, perhaps a little above the average height—he was not really tall, but he carried himself like a tsar and gave the impression of being tall. His age was in the early thirties. He had long, dark hair parted in the middle, and a beard stained with the remains of several meals. His boots and clothing were cut in the peasant style but, as I have already remarked, made of richer materials than ordinary peasants ever see.

However, all these matters were peripheral, as was his rancid, goatlike smell. It was the man's eyes that really counted.

Taking a step or two toward me, he put out a broad, strong hand and said in his peasant Russian: "Blessings, Little Father. I am Gregory Efimovitch."

Something was happening; I knew that, even as I got to my feet, but was not alarmed. I suppose I must have murmured something in reply. He accepted whatever I said as a fair greeting.

The hypnotic spell that had already begun to engulf me was very subtle, so subtle that I—I, Dracula—was scarcely aware of it at first. In my own defense, I can plead that I was already tired and that many days' exposure to feeble northern sunlight had been a strain. At any rate, I must confess that I was well on my way to being overcome before I even realized that anything was wrong. To this day I am not sure whether I succumbed to a deliberate assault on the part of Gregory Efimovitch, or whether it was only the way he was, part of his nature . . . for him, as automatic as drawing breath.

Suddenly, whatever the cause, at the suggestion that I might be tired, I was tired, and felt strangely content to sit back in my soft chair and stare into the fire. Have I said there was a fireplace nearby? I don't remember for certain, but I think there was. The burly peasant's eyes seemed to be there in the fire, too, as well as in his head, their burning images now woven of the flames . . .

Oh, it was all very pleasant. I was drifting, a ludicrous sense of safety assuring me that I remained securely in control of the situation, though actually I was in the greatest danger. Dimly, as from a distance, I could see the peasant leaning toward me, hear him saying in his rough Russian: "I see thou art one of the lovers of blood, like Alexander Ilyitch . . ." To me, a stranger in evening dress and speaking like a gentleman, the peasant used the intimate form of address with serene self-assurance.

"Like Kulakov? A lover of blood?" I chuckled, struck by the perfect appositeness of the phrase. To me, his Russian phrase seemed as oddly ambiguous as does the Neo-Latin, or the Greek: hemophiliac.

"Why yes," I said. "Perhaps I am." Gently I licked my lips. Vaguely I turned my gaze to where the dead bear's fangs still menaced the woman lying on the rug.

But those great dark eyes irresistibly brought me back. "Why dost thou not tell me thy name?"

"Vlad Drakulya."

"Thou art of the Romany? No? Art thou a friend of God?"

I shrugged, then frowned. This was a serious question. "He and I are old acquaintances, at least . . . I fear we do not always get along as well as we might."

"Do not blaspheme." It was a command, delivered not

with anger, but with the serene confidence of spiritual authority.

Obedience was necessary, but still I shook my head. I had not thought I was blaspheming.

"It might be possible to cure thee, Vlad Drakulya."

"I am not sick."

"Thy body is in a strange and wonderful condition. I meant to cure thee of thy taste for blood. Dost thou want to be cured?"

Again I shook my head. "That would . . ."

"What?"

"That would cure me of my life altogether. And I wish to live. What is thy name?" Somehow only the intimate form seemed appropriate to use to this man, as I did not object when he used it to me. His arrogance did not offend, because it was so great that it transcended arrogance.

He shook his head; the deep-set eyes were amused. My responses were unsatisfactory, though perhaps not unexpected. He said: "I told thee my name: I am Gregory Efimovitch Rasputin."

As yet that last name meant nothing to me—nor to the world, not for a few more years. But I believe I smiled, because the Russian word *rasputin* carries strong connotations of sexual debauchery; rather as if an Englishman or American were to introduce himself as Gregory Porno, or Ephraim Smut.

"A *starets,*" I murmured. "One of Russia's wandering, holy fools." That began, at least, to explain his acceptance among some of the aristocracy. Such people were a tradition among them and perhaps still are. In 1903 ten thousand, perhaps a hundred thousand, of them were walking the highways and byways of the great country, from Poland to Siberia. Not one in a hundred thousand of them, though, the Holy Virgin of Kazan be thanked, more likely not one in a million, carried or now carries in his mind and soul anything like the power of Gregory Efimovitch to blast or to heal—or felt or now feels as little responsibility toward his fellow humans.

Gently and irresistibly he was saying to me: "Come with me to the balcony, and we will watch the sunrise together."

Some remote part of my consciousness assured me that the Christian name and patronymic I had just heard should have been familiar to me, and that it had a particular meaning of great importance, related to some matter on which I ought to be engaged. Yet at the moment it was not possible to pursue the thought . . .

. . . because it was absolutely necessary to comply with the suggestion that had just been made. It was one of those suggestions that simply left one no choice. In my time, I have made a few of them myself.

Willingly I got to my feet. Images danced before me, of the cheery, sunlit days (there were a few) of my childhood and youth. "Yes . . . it is a long time, it is very long, since I have watched the dawn."

I think that there were stairs beneath my feet, and I remember vaguely that my new guide and mentor, whose commands were always to be heeded, brought me out onto a small balcony, one of several on the eastern face of the large house, and I remember placing my hands on the rail of cold wrought iron that guarded the small space at waist level. And then I was left standing on the balcony, serenely awaiting sunrise, while Rasputin went back indoors, where (as I now realize) he soon caught sight of Kulakov, whom he had been intending to meet and speak with.

The two men began to talk. I heard most of it, recording it without understanding at the time, while my thoughts remained serenely concentrated upon the coming dawn. Shortly it became apparent from their conversation that Kulakov, suffering from his long-term disability, had returned to St. Petersburg primarily, or largely, in search of the one person he knew who could give him relief.

Rasputin was, and had been, treating Kulakov intermittently for certain chronic conditions: nightmares, mental anguish, and some psychosomatic condition of the neck, a lingering result of being hanged.

I got the impression that Kulakov had told Rasputin months ago that he was going to England to try to recover a treasure, stolen from him long ago. But the peasant had not sent the count to England to rape and murder and loot. It seemed that in some general way, Rasputin had suggested that Kulakov try to see that amends were made for old, rankling problems out of his past.

Sounds of revelry from distant rooms of the palace came drifting into the chamber where the two men were meeting. A gramophone was playing over and over a scratched record—the distorted voice of Mary Garden.

Someone down on the ground floor put a new wax cylinder on the machine—now we had Enrico Caruso. There was an outburst of uproarious laughter; perhaps there were gypsies down there, entertaining in the lower regions of the house, and I wondered in a detached way whether the gypsies had even brought a dancing bear with them, at least into the kitchen or scullery. Certainly a distant crash of falling furniture and crockery indicated that the party was getting out of hand.

Rasputin, however, plainly preferred to keep his distance from such goings-on. Though a peasant and a mystic, he moved upon a different plane from gypsies, with their innocuous spells and love potions. He said to Kulakov: "Where hast thou been, my friend? I have not seen thee for months."

Kulakov: "I have been to England. I told thee months ago that I was going there."

Rasputin said something that neither I (nor Cousin

Sherlock, who as you will see was also eavesdropping) could clearly hear.

"—I told you, Little Father, that there were people in England who had robbed me. I went to get back what was mine. Also, to make them pay for what they did to me."

Rasputin: "That was not what I advised thee to do. Dost thou love God, Alexander Ilyich?"

"I need help, Gregory Efimovitch. Help me. The bad dreams have come back, and I have trouble sleeping, and my neck hurts all the time."

The holy man told his patient to sit in the soft chair where I had been. "Consider the sun and stars, and He who made them. The pain will go. And the dreams, also. I see that thou art worried. But nothing in life is worth worrying over—it all passes."

Kulakov, the murderous vampire, as if drifting toward sleep, murmured something in a soft, childlike voice.

Then Rasputin spoke again. "Tell me about this treasure thou sayest is lost. What is there about it that is so important?"

And Kulakov, under deep hypnosis, told Rasputin word for word what had passed between himself and Doll, back in 1765.

There, I have told some of it. Almost the worst part, though that is yet to come. I must rest. Watson . . .

Sherlock Holmes and I, walking Rebecca Altamont between us down the hallway—toward the stair—from the room in which she had been confined, heard voices ahead and stopped.

The voices spoke in Russian, and of course I could make nothing of them. But for Holmes, the matter was quite different.

~ 20 ~

Of course at the moment our immediate problem was not to interpret a conversation held in Russian, but to convey Rebecca Altamont safely out of the house. We had garbed the young woman first in a robe over her nightdress, then in a light summer coat, chosen from a wardrobe not occupied by a chloroformed maid. We had put slippers on Miss Altamont's feet and had got her standing beside the bed. Then, despite her continued mumbled protests, we cajoled and led and half-carried her out of the room and halfway down the hall.

We had just rounded the last turn of the dim hallway before the stair when the sound of voices and the sight of figures just ahead forced us to pause, and seek concealment in a kind of niche containing the closed door of another room. As we were coming out of a bedroom like kidnappers, we chose not to try to brazen out the threatened encounter.

So far, the doors in this part of the hall had fortunately remained closed. Still, we could not remain indefinitely where we were, nor could we reach the stairway without passing directly in front of the large alcove where Rasputin and Kulakov were having their strange confrontation. I now observed that the alcove also contained some nameless lady of the Russian nobility, whose elegantly gowned form was lying senseless upon a bearskin rug. Both of the men ignored her completely. I could see her stir at intervals, a movement suggesting that at any moment she might regain sufficient consciousness to complicate our situation even further.

In this awkward situation, Holmes and I exchanged whispered comments. Neither of us could understand what might have happened to Prince Dracula, who had supposedly been on guard in the very alcove where Kulakov and the strange-looking peasant were now conversing.

We were forced to the conclusion that in one way or another, the prince must have been put at least temporarily out of action.

Within a few moments—though the time seemed vastly longer—Holmes succeeded in somehow positively identifying a figure visible through one of the windows which illuminated the stairwell, silhouetted against a brightening eastern sky. It appeared that our ally was now standing, strangely motionless and facing outward, upon a balcony on the next floor up. If Kulakov and his companion were aware that anyone was on the balcony, they paid that motionless figure no attention.

Shaking my head, I whispered: "What shall we do? Dracula stands like one mesmerized."

"That must be it!"

And we realized further that the rising sun, due to appear in a few minutes, must destroy our comrade in arms. The balcony faced the east, where the orb of day would soon appear out of the endless bulk of enigmatic Asia.

Clearly we could not allow this, if there was any way to prevent it, and Holmes whispered as much to me. Hastily we worked out a plan between us. While I remained with our young charge, supporting her, still dazed and uncooperative, on her feet, Holmes walked boldly forward—there was no other way to reach the stair or climb to the level of the balcony where the prince stood so serenely poised to watch the sunrise.

To judge by the growing brightness of the eastern sky, dawn could not be more than a minute or two away—the sun never goes very far below St. Petersburg's horizon at this season of the year. And today, for once, the morning promised to be cloudless.

The two men in the alcove at the end of the hall looked up sharply as Holmes approached. But his walk had altered, become the light, obsequious tread of a servant, and it must have seemed to them that a dark-clad footman or waiter had gone by with averted face.

Evidently Kulakov had not recognized his own former prisoner. Still, something about the briskly moving figure apparently jarred the former pirate into suspicions regarding his present hostage. Mumbling inaudibly, moving slowly at first, he started out of the alcove—glanced up the stair after Holmes, shook his head as if in doubt—then turned again, proceeding straight down the central hallway in the direction of the room where Miss Altamont had been confined. By good fortune, he had chosen the other branch of corridor from the one where she and I were waiting.

My opportunity, as I saw it, had come, and I did my best to take advantage of it. Quickly I resumed my efforts to persuade Rebecca to walk along the corridor toward the stairs. My urging had little effect on the girl, who remained no more than half-conscious. After a moment, I picked her up bodily in my arms and strode along.

Evidently Kulakov, once distracted from his conversation with Rasputin, needed perhaps half a minute to clear his mind fully of the light trance into which, under the ministrations of the healer, he had begun to descend. By that time Miss Altamont and I had reached the stairs and were making steady progress down them. They were broad, marble stairs, gracefully curved, and discouragingly well-lighted compared with the dim bedroom corridors above. Although at the moment the young lady and I had the way all to ourselves, the sounds of ribald merriment proceeding from the several doorways visible below us suggested strongly that that state of affairs could not last long.

Meanwhile the count, going to check on his victim, needed only a few moments to discover that she was not in her room. Alarmed, he dashed straight back to the stairs, where one look down showed him that his prisoner was being carried out of his control.

Kulakov came charging, leaping downstairs after us, roaring like the madman he was. The vampire did not change form, and it crossed my mind, even in the moment of crisis, that perhaps daylight was already too far advanced to permit him to do that. The first rays of the rising sun, striking in through the skylight far above us in the roof, produced a crystalline, slightly dazzling effect, but I knew well that here in the house we were too sheltered and shaded to allow me to depend substantially upon the sun for our defense.

My revolver was already in my hand, and as that dark, snarling figure came bounding downstairs toward us, reaching out with taloned fingers, I fired repeatedly.

Fortunately my aim was true, and at least two or three of Von Herder's heavy wooden bullets pierced our attacker's body.

The effect was devastating. Kulakov went tumbling past us down the broad curving marble stairway, his flesh, even as he fell and rolled, hissing and dissolving as though submerged in some vat of acid. In another moment the vampire's body had been claimed by the true death.

With all the noisy celebration still in progress, no one in the house paid much attention even to the sound of gunfire; a few heads looked round corners toward the stairs, and laughter ceased briefly, only to resume as loud as before.

The body, being that of an old vampire, dispersed in mist-form, clothing and all, before anyone could see it, and before I or my companions could be embarrassed by the necessity of explaining a corpse.

Rasputin had come out of the alcove and looked down once from the landing. I am not sure that he actually saw Kulakov die, but I believe that through occult knowledge or instinctive wisdom, the peasant understood what had just happened, and that he then simply and prudently took himself away. I can only say that the man's later notoriety, seemingly at its peak in this year of 1917 in which I write, does not surprise me at all.

Meanwhile, once Holmes had reached the balcony where the prince was standing, it became possible for my friend to invoke a certain name effectively, that of a lady to whom the prince had long shown sincere devotion. Also, I suspect that Holmes's studies in Tibet might have served him well when the need arose to break a hypnotic trance. He led an awakened Dracula indoors before the direct sunlight could do his cousin fatal injury.

By that time it was possible for them to see that Miss Altamont and I had safely reached the street; and moments later, Dracula and his cousin had joined their co-conspirators in the street and were running to board the waiting carriage with them.

Fortunately, with Kulakov's death, Rebecca Altamont quickly recovered from her hypnotized state and was soon able to cooperate actively in her own rescue. Soon we had succeeded in removing her to a place of relative safety.

We determined to cable this happy result to England as soon as possible, but then decided we had better not delay our departure to do so.

Meanwhile, in the course of our forced delay inside the house, Holmes and Dracula between them had by accident overheard a fairly detailed account, by Kulakov himself, of those peculiar events involving vampires, an execution, and stolen treasure in London in 1765. After a few minutes of intense thought upon these matters, Dracula's cousin did hastily dispatch a cable, this one coded, back to Mycroft in London.

Having done this, the detective, in a smug, elated mood, promised all of us, to our astonishment, that he had identified the pirate treasure and hoped soon to be able to explain where it had been hidden for the past one hundred and thirty-eight years.

Some hours after Holmes had dispatched his cable to Mycroft—in fact, as we were about to board our ship to leave St. Petersburg—he received an answer, this time in the form of a clear transmission. It ran as follows: MATERIAL FOUND IN PLACE DESCRIBED ALL SATISFACTORY HERE MYCROFT.

~ *Epilogue* ~

We were worried lest some powerful subordinate or ally of Kulakov's deduce that he was dead, and discover—perhaps from the splinters of a wooden bullet—the manner of his death, and then take measures to delay or prevent our departure. Moving quickly, yet deliberately to avoid giving any appearance of undue haste, we completed our preparations for taking ship from St. Petersburg.

Fortune smiled on us, and within a matter of hours, we were well on our way back to England, embarked on the same speedy private vessel which had carried us to Russia.

We were well out at sea, and had satisfied ourselves that no pursuit was to be anticipated, before we openly discussed every aspect of the case among ourselves.

In these circumstances, Holmes concluded his summing-up, including an outline of the chief events that must have taken place in 1765 to provoke Kulakov's thirst for vengeance and cause the mysterious disappearance of the jewels.

"Before giving my final explanation about the treasure, I believe it will be pertinent to explain the circumstances in which Louisa Altamont had apparently been drowned.

"Young Martin Armstrong has told us how he plunged

again and again into the pool where the boat had overturned, looking for the victim of an accident, never dreaming that a kidnapping had taken place instead.

"But actually, Louisa, her attempts to cry out strangled in her throat, was already in the grip of the vampire Kulakov, and was being pulled downstream, under water, at a speed that would have seemed incredible to anyone who did not understand the powers of the being who had seized her.

"Pulled downstream, around the next bend, then brought to the surface long enough for a few gasps of air—the last air she would ever breathe upon this earth."

While Becky had run for help, first to the nearest cottages and then to Norberton House, Martin, soon aided by other swimmers, plunged into the water again and again, screaming Louisa's name in an ever more hoarse and breathless voice. He worked his way some yards downstream and then came back, afraid that she was still under water near the place where she had fallen in . . . afraid that she was dead.

"But in fact Louisa was not dead. Kulakov had repeatedly forced himself upon her—in vampire fashion. This sexual assault took place first underwater and later upon the land. He also, in his half-crazed state, demanded that his victim tell him where the treasure, the family jewels, were hidden.

"Louisa of course knew nothing, or at least very little, about her ancestor's conflict with a piratical vampire more than a century ago. Pressed to reveal the secret of a supposed family treasure of whose existence she was unaware, she could only tell this man, this fiend, about a safe in her father's office, which held only some irrelevant legal papers and a few pieces of modern and comparatively inconsequential jewelry."

Holmes went on to recount how the missing girl, still fully clothed and in the powerful grip of her naked captor, was carried swiftly and silently away downstream, to where a rusted, moss-grown iron fence marked the border of the cemetery.

There Louisa had been brought out of the water, and there her wet garments were torn back from her throat, and the vampire's fangs pierced her white skin.

"But even that was not the worst. She was compelled to drink her attacker's blood." There was a shuddering reaction among the listeners. "With a long nail, Kulakov opened the skin on his own chest, and forced her mouth to that place."

After that, Louisa, bound as Holmes was later bound, had been hidden for some hours in the same secret crypt from which Holmes was later rescued. There Kulakov again attacked her repeatedly, so that in a matter of hours, she was well along in the transformation from breathing human to vampire.

That transformation was irreversible by the next morning, when Kulakov left the girl's body on the riverbank, to be discovered by the first searchers who came that way after dawn.

"Had he a conscious motive in so doing? I am inclined to the belief that he did not. It seems probable that one of Kulakov's periodic lapses of purpose, even of coherent thought, overcame him there on the riverbank at dawn. He had achieved a great revenge upon the Altamonts, but there was no ultimate satisfaction in this deed, and he was as far as ever from recovering the treasure.

"We come now to the treasure—a much happier subject."

Our little circle of listeners heartily agreed with that.

Holmes went on: "The key, of course, lies in what Kulakov—during the last minutes of his life—confessed to the man who was endeavoring to heal him—about what happened in 1765, on the morning after Kulakov was hanged."

Holmes went on to describe the scene as it must have taken place in the Angel Inn: ". . . Kulakov, in his confused state, still looking for his treasure and having no success, had heard the woman's despairing cries and had come back from the adjoining room.

"Doll had put on her clothes again. Gibbering and pleading in her terror, she tried to bargain with him. She spoke now in her native language, which Kulakov had learned to understand. She told the Russian that she knew where the stolen ornaments were hidden, and that she would give them all to him in exchange for only a few pounds of her native earth.

"Somewhere among the hundreds of ships in the great port, which had brought in by accident soil, plants, vermin from the farthest reaches of the globe—somewhere among all those far-traveled hulls, surely, surely there must be one whose cargo or bilge or windblown planking contained a few pounds, a few handfuls even, of that stuff more precious now to her than any gems or lustrous metal.

"The Russian, with his understanding clouded by the multiple stresses of strangulation and rebirth, heard her out. Then he had a question of his own. He whispered it in English: 'Where are the jewels? They are not here.'

" 'Are you not listen to me? I tell you where the treasure is, I swear, when you have help me find the soil I need. The jewels are not here. But they are all safe, in place you know, where you can get them!'

" 'I know.' The pirate looked down at the red mess on the floor. '*He* gave them to his brother, who has them at his country estate, somewhere out of town. His brother, who helped him to betray me.'

"In near despair the woman clutched his arm, her long nails digging in, a grip that might well have crushed the bones of any breathing man. Once more she spoke in her own language. 'Will you not listen to me, Kulakov? I need my earth! By all the gods of my homeland—by whatever gods you pray to in your Muscovy—I swear that if you help me find the earth that I must have, the treasure shall all be yours!'

"Indeed," continued Holmes, "Doll told the truth in saying that she knew where the jewels were hidden—because she had put them there herself!"

There was a sensation among the listeners.

Holmes went on. "Let us try to put ourselves in this woman's place. She had been in England for only a few days, and was still almost totally unfamiliar with the metropolis in which she found herself. When Kulakov, seeking vengeance, entered the room at the Angel Inn, she did not wish to oppose him directly in his murderous rage.

"Seeing that her patron and lover, Altamont, was doomed, Doll prudently gathered up the treasure that he had secreted in the next room and carried it to a certain place she had seen and remembered. It was a place from which she could easily retrieve the jewels, at any time between sunset and dawn, while they remained secure from accidental discovery by any of London's swarming, breathing folk.

"It was even possible to theorize that Kulakov in a daze might have put the treasure in that place himself, and then have forgotten the act. But if we accept the scene in the Angel Inn as factual, then the correct explanation must be something else.

"Let us consider carefully what the doomed woman actually said to Kulakov when she was pleading for his assistance. According to the recent testimony of Kulakov himself, while hypnotized, her words were these:

" 'The jewels are not here. But they are all safe in a place you know, where you can get them.'

"On hearing this, Kulakov, who was already convinced that Peter Altamont had the treasure, assumed that Doll meant the family estate in the country—Norberton House. But there are several reasons why that could not have been her meaning, assuming she spoke the truth.

"To begin with, Norberton House was hardly a place known to Kulakov—he had heard it mentioned, but that was all. Nor had Doll ever been there. Again, if Doll spoke the truth, all the pieces of treasure, her own bracelet included, must be together—but we know now that her bracelet had been on her arm, in London, only minutes before she began to plead with Kulakov for help.

"Norberton House is hours distant from London by modern train. Not even the speed of vampire flight would have allowed Doll to carry the jewels there and return to the Angel Inn in the time allowed.

"If any further proof is needed, consider: Had Peter Altamont ever come into possession of the jewels, he would certainly have kept them. A sudden increase in his family's wealth, dating from that time, would now be discoverable by a thorough search of the historical records—which it is not."

There was a murmur of agreement round our little circle.

Holmes went on. "We are faced with the inescapable conclusion that Peter Altamont never had the treasure; that Ambrose, who betrayed Kulakov, had given Doll one trinket and kept the others with him in London, until he was killed. And that immediately after his death, Doll, who must have discovered where the things were hidden, spirited them away to what she must have considered a safe hiding place, within a mile or so at most of the Angel Inn."

There was a murmur of comment around our circle.

Holmes resumed. "Remember, she told Kulakov: 'It is a place you know.' But at that time the Russian pirate had even less familiarity with England than she did. What places did she know in London, of which she could be certain that they were known to the Russian as well?"

"Execution Dock," I suggested.

"Bravo! That thought had crossed my mind. But the dock, and the ground in its vicinity, was daily washed by tides, and trampled by hundreds or thousands of people engaged in the common commerce of the waterfront. What other—"

To my surprise, it was Sarah Kirkaldy, fists clenched and eyes flashing, who interrupted sharply. "Newgate! By God, Newgate Prison!"

Holmes's eye twinkled. "Exactly! But then it seemed to me that we could probably be a little more precise. Doll's last rendezvous with Kulakov before his transformation took place, we are informed, was in one of the condemned cells. We have learned from other contemporary sources that some of the old prison's walls were actually crumbling at the time. None of the jeweled ornaments were large—they could be dropped into a hole or a crack too small to accommodate a man's arm.

"It requires no great stretch of the imagination to picture a crevice of convenient dimensions in the massive masonry—perhaps just outside the barred window through which Doll drifted on her visit—a recess large enough to hold the jewels, and practically inaccessible to breathing folk, but easy enough for any vampire to reach, particularly by night."

We all applauded Holmes's masterstroke of deduction, and he, pleased as a child, acknowledged our praise.

The treasure already having been retrieved by Mycroft from the ruins of the recently demolished prison, the question of who really owned it in 1903 remained to be discussed. The establishment of any genuinely just claim appeared to be impossible, and we agreed that if the matter were submitted to the courts, it might well enrich a generation of lawyers, but no other benefit was likely. In the circumstances, we chose unanimously to arrange for a quiet distribution of the value of the jewels among ourselves.

Martin Armstrong and Rebecca Altamont were married within the year. I have wondered, on the basis of no real evidence, whether the young American's fascination with the vampire Louisa ever caused him to experience a certain disappointment that his bride was not in that category.

Ambrose and Madeline Altamont, with their surviving daughter restored to them, enjoyed a gradual recovery from the fever and near-madness with which they had been afflicted—but neither was ever quite the same.

Since the war began, I have heard that Madeline at least, joining with a group of parents who have lost sons at the front, is still making plans for sittings with one or more of the new mediums, still convincing herself that they enjoy at least occasional success in their ongoing efforts to achieve contact with the departed daughter they so deeply love.

Thank you, Dr. Watson. Now I, Dracula, will have one more word . . .

Sarah Kirkaldy and I remained very good friends. I spent some time with her in Scotland. I really could not find it in my heart to condemn the lady too strongly for her career as a medium. By and large, her clients received in full measure what they paid for: feelings of excitement and contentment.

In fact, I even consented to help out my newly prosperous friend Sarah with a difficult client or two. There was in Edinburgh a certain psychic investigator, as he styled himself, a very determined skeptic who seemed really bent on giving the poor young woman a hard time . . . but that is another story altogether.

Probably I should also add that I planned and executed no revenge upon the peasant who had hypnotized me in St. Petersburg. In that case, life itself, as so often happens, exacted sufficient retribution.

In fact, there were witnesses who heard Mr. Prince, just before departing for Scotland, confide to his cousin Sherlock Holmes that he wanted nothing more to do in any way with Gregory Efimovitch Rasputin.